"Ethel Barker's novel is rich in the kind of detail that brings a past era to vivid life. Readers young and old will feel as though they are riding on that orphan train and braving the unknown in the wilds of Iowa! Best of all, Barker gives us three unforgettable young characters to root for."—Mary Helen Stefaniak, author, *The Cailiffs of Baghdad, Georgia: A Novel*

"Ethel Barker has clearly done her research, and *For the Love of Pete* puts an entirely human face on the dramatic history of Iowa's Orphan Train children."—Rebecca Johns, author, *The Countess: A Novel of Elizabeth Bathory*

"Barker weaves the compelling story of three wayward children named Iris, Rosie, and Pete—all of whom were gathered up from the streets of New York and sent aboard an orphan train bound for Iowa. Their trials and triumphs are undoubtedly representative of those experienced by the several hundred thousand children sent on America's orphan trains between 1854 and 1929. A must read!"—Clark Kidder, author, *Emily's Story—The Brave Journey of an Orphan Train Rider*

"Suspense crackles after little Rosie, plucky big sister Iris, and loyal pal Pete stumble off an orphan train in rural Iowa where unthinking adults callously force each of them to face harsh new conditions alone. Richly textured settings, engaging dialogue, and the children's increasingly dire circumstances make Ethel Barker's debut historical novel a fun read."—Cheryl Fusco Johnson, author and host of *Writers Voices*

D0877798

"Rich in detail, Ethel Barker has written the best kind of fiction—one that allows readers to peek through the windows of the orphan trains through the lives of three orphans while holding on to strength of the human spirit. Full of twists and turns, surprises and anguish, Barker unfolds the lives of three orphans in a memorable web of emotion filled with human dignity and courage. These unforgettable children of the train will remain with the reader long after the book is closed."—Renée Wendinger, author, *Extra! Extra! The Orphan Trains and Newsboys of New York*

"With her first novel, Ethel Barker takes us along on a lively, adventure-filled ride with the children of the Orphan Train. Her tale is richly woven, full of warmth, wit and surprise—and best of all, a cast of plucky characters who instantly drew me into this little-known chapter of American history."—Delia Ray, author, *Here Lies Linc*

"A moving, historically accurate account of the Orphan Train movement that will captivate the reader with the extraordinary trials of three young friends as they journey separately through the uncertain times that defined this period of American history. A great adventure with an unpredictable twist—engaging right through to the last page!"—Donna Aviles, author, *Peanut Butter For Cupcakes: A True Story From The Great Depression*

"Details of Iowa life illuminate the times and stories of three children who arrive on the orphan train. Ethel Barker presents a satisfying tale for young readers in *For the Love of Pete*."—Carol Gorman, author, *Games: A Tale of Two Bullies*

FOR THE LOVE OF PETE

AN ORPHAN TRAIN STORY

ETHEL BARKER

*To Sharon Kay
with thanks for our friendship.*

Ethel Barker

ICE CUBE PRESS, LLC
NORTH LIBERTY, IOWA

For The Love of Pete—
An Orphan Train Story

ISBN 9781888160659   1 3 5 7 9 8 6 4 2

Library of Congress Control Number: 2011943260

Ice Cube Press, LLC (Est. 1993)
205 N. Front Street
North Liberty, Ia 52317
www.icecubepress.com
steve@icecubepress.com

The paper used in this publication meets the minimum requirements of the American National Standard for Information Sciences—Permanence of Paper for Printed Library Materials, ANSI Z39.48-1992

Manufactured in the United States of America

Artwork and cover art © Susan Dresdale

Orphan photo used for *Afterword*: "Street Arabs at Night, Boys Sleeping in Quarters," ca. 1890, Museum of the City of New York, Jacob A. Riis Collection

ACKNOWLEDGEMENTS

Thanks to Margo Dill, author and teacher, an early reader of this manuscript who offered many helpful and valuable suggestions. Also, thanks to Susan Dresdale, my favorite illustrator, Anna Barker, Content Editor, Alice Miller, Page Editor, all of my friends at the Iowa City University Club Writing Group, and to Mary Humston and Karen Hughes for their constant encouragement. Thanks to Illia Thompson and her California Carmel Foundation writing class. Thanks to the many excellent writing instructors at the University of Iowa Summer Writing Festivals, to friends and family who read the manuscript: especially Sarah and Meg Richardson, Will, Nicholas, Thomas, and Emma Barker; Bob Ross, Mary Ross, and Roger Denk. Thanks to my sons, David and Jim Barker, both of whom helped enormously with technical and practical advice. Special thanks to publisher Steve Semken, Ice Cube Press, for his kind attention and perseverance.

An extra special thanks to Ed Barker, my loyal husband and partner, who patiently put up with the orphan train obsession. Iris, Pete, and Rosie became an important part of my life and still remain (in my mind) a delightful part of our family.

FOR THE LOVE OF PETE

CHAPTER 1

CONFESSIONS OF A STREET RAT
PETE

July, 1880, I was doing business at my usual work place, the corner of Anthony and Orange, New York City's toughest neighborhood. I'd about given up for the day, ready to give it one last whack. Mostly, I was just hanging around, staring at shadows that crept like dingy ghosts across the filthy street.

Two girls, with red eyes and sad faces, stood on the other side, the younger leaning against the older as they sang "Poor Drooping Maiden" and other songs that make ladies pull out their hankies and give 'er a good blow. I judged the little one to be seven or eight, the older one like me, about fourteen. It was plain as an empty belly those girls were down in the dumps, but odd as it may seem now, their voices chased away my blues. I'd been kind of low.

And I'd never laid eyes on such fine looking girls. The redhead forced a smile, and the little curly head held out a tin cup, but passers-by paid them no mind. They didn't even toss a penny or a glance.

I tried my best to stop eyeing them, to work my trade yelling the usual, "Extra extra, read all about it," but I was getting hoarse after hollering all day. The big girl stared across the street. Seemed like she was fixed on me, watching me jingle coins in my pocket. I figured she was sizing me up, wondering if I'd stored up a pocketful of cash.

Like most regulars in the neighborhood, I didn't think much about the other street rats. Not anymore. They hung around every corner, poking out cups or tin cans, all ragged, filthy, with blank stares. But these girls looked different. They weren't dirty, like the rest of us, and they wore real nice clothes. They weren't skin and bones either, and their clear eyes showed their brains weren't all mucked up like most of these poor slobs. I stopped yelling, crossed the street, and snuck in around behind them, like a mouse in a hole, listening.

The big girl was talking to the little one. "I know you're sad and scared and wondering what's to become of us," she said. "So am I! But I've been thinking about this mess we're in. We'll never give up like those kids. Look at her." She didn't point. The girl was up to snuff on manners and the ways of tony folks, but she nodded towards a grimy kid with matted hair. "Look how that one stares off into space," she said.

The little girl stroked a piece of her sister's skirt while the other one kept on talking. "Remember what Flora said about her folks? Her Ma and Pa?" The girl spoke in a real firm voice. "What was the word?"

"Pluck," said the young one.

The big girl squeezed her like girls do.

"Good!" Still holding the little girl's hand, the big one pointed at a patch of sky that showed up between buildings. "Look up there! Flora sees us. She's peeking down and smiling."

"I don't see her."

"On that puffy cloud?"

The little one stretched her neck. "Nope."

"She's there. You have to see her."

"I guess I do." A tear ran down the little one's cheek. She used her sleeve for a hankie.

I moved in closer, hands in my pockets, trying to look away, like I wasn't the least bit interested, but I couldn't wait to meet them. Funny how sometimes you're drawn to certain folks.

"Name's Pete," said I. "New here ain't you?"

"Why do you ask?"

I couldn't explain, so I didn't answer that one.

"How long you been here?"

"Three days."

"Then why ain't I seen you?"

She swallowed hard. "We're new on this corner. The last place didn't work out."

"How's business?"

"Awful."

It was later on, after I bought them some eats, that the big girl finally trusted me enough to tell their names. At first Iris was real suspicious. Her little sister's name turned out to be Rosie. Swell names, I thought, like real pretty flowers.

"Hungry?"

"Who isn't?" Iris snapped. Rosie twirled a lock of her curly hair.

"How come you're singing?"

"Far as I know there's no law against it."

"You ain't the type."

"We have to eat."

"Where's your Ma and Pa?"

"Where's yours?"

I busted out laughing. "Business sure is slow this time of day." I took a good look at Rosie's cup. She held it out and turned it upside down. Nothing fell out.

"Come on!" I waggled a finger and ran ahead, jingling the coins in my front pocket. It felt swell to have something to jingle. The girls scurried to keep up. I stopped them for a second or two and whispered, "If we're tailed, kick them in the shins, and if that don't work, we'll brain them."

Iris and Rosie eyed each other, then busted out in big grins when I told them, "I'm buying. What sounds good?"

"Beef dodgers," Iris said right off.

"Ice cream," squealed Rosie.

"Ladies, you shall have your hearts' desire." I was putting on like a dandy and feeling great. I couldn't help skipping down the street, peeking back once in a while to see if they were keeping up. We went splashing through piles of stinky muck, ducking between carts. I stepped up to a vendor's wagon and plopped down coins for beef dodgers. All three of us started gobbling, but soon Iris slowed down and ate like a lady. After that we moved on to another wagon where I ordered three bowls of fresh cranked ice cream.

"What do you think of this?" Iris said to Rosie. The little girl grinned. We all three licked our bowls clean and returned them to the peddler.

"Sure as angels got wings," I said, "you ladies bring sunshine to this dingy street, but you ain't safe without a protector." I made the kind of bow a gentleman might. I was pretty sure Iris was onto me, but she went along with the act.

"It's lucky you chose that particular corner," I said, "or you wouldn't have found me, and I'm your man. Most nights I catch my forty winks on the floor in Big Al's tobacco shop. It's warm and dry in there, and a good night's sleep's my pay for sweeping up. Tonight you're my guests." I bowed again. Even if I do say so myself, I done it swell.

Iris stopped. I cupped my ear and heard her say real soft to Rosie, "This is the kind of boy you don't find just any day of the week."

Man, did I puff out my chest. "Ever play mumbletypeg?"

"It's a boys' game," Iris said. "We play jacks."

I led them into a junk-filled alley. When we came to an open place, I dug in my pocket for my knife. "Lesson one." I wiped the blade on my pants. I'd been polishing it up in my spare time; so it sparkled, even in the shadows.

"No knives!" Rosie shouted.

"You got to focus,"

"We don't play with knives," Iris said.

"Everybody plays with knives."

"We don't," Iris insisted. "Flora never allowed it."

"Who's this Flora?"

"Our Ma—well, she was—" Iris looked around, biting her lip.

Rosie said, "We don't play with knives."

I stirred the dirt with my foot. "You ladies got to learn self-defense. I'll watch out for you, long as I'm here, but where'll you be if I get beaned?" Rosie leaned against Iris and rubbed a piece of her sister's skirt.

I drew a target in the dirt. "Watch close. There's a trick to it. First you flip like this." I flipped my knife, and it hit the bull's eye.

7

"Of course, you won't do that first off," I said. "Takes practice. Pat Finnegan and me used to play twice a day. He got almost good as me. Oh, we had us a high old time 'til he got sent up. Couldn't outrun the cops. He was thrashed twice that day. Last I heard, he's still in the pen." I just couldn't stop spouting off.

"Watch this!" I said, and then hit another bull's-eye. When I handed the knife to Iris, she gritted her teeth, and fixed her eyes on me. She handled that knife like it was a snake. Well, she threw like a girl. It flipped and landed some three feet from the target. Rosie ran to pick it up and tried a few flips of her own. Each time the knife landed in the dirt, farther and farther from the target.

"Too advanced for beginners." I myself had lots to learn on most everything but didn't know it yet. "Follow me for lesson two!"

The girls followed until I stopped, facing a high wooden wall. I carved a target, stepped back as far as I could, and positioned myself carefully. I closed one eye, lining up the knife, tossed it off, and hit the bull's-eye, sinking that knife deep in the wood. I was playing big shot.

It took some effort, but I yanked it out, then handed the weapon to Iris. I pushed her closer to the target. "Shut your left eye, and fix the right one on the bull's-eye. Push everything out of your head. The trick is to zoom in on that bull's-eye!" She tried her best, but it fell short.

"Rosie's turn," I said.

"Mumblety-peg, mumblety-peg, mumblety-peg," Rosie kept singing like that, skipping to pick up the knife. "Oh bother. I don't know which eye's which, but I'm going to get a bull's-eye." She hollered that way, flashing a big grin at me. Before I could lead her up close to the target, she'd sent the knife flying.

"Whoooa" boomed a thundering voice." We all three jumped, then stared up at a policeman, about as tall as a stepladder. He towered above us. Our eyes were fixed on his coat sleeve. It was plain as a pikestaff, the knife had ripped his sleeve, and more than likely split some skin.

"Beat it!" I yelled. Us kids tore off down the alley. I made like a monster was hot on my heels. That kind of thinking always helps me win a race.

I ain't proud of what I done next. I'd been bound and determined to save those nice girls from turning into street rats. But before I'd got a good start, I went racing off to save my own hide, kicking myself with every lousy step for being such a chicken livered louse.

On the one hand, I figured chances were pretty good the cop would find a soft spot in his heart for those girls. If the man had eyes, he'd know right off they were top-notchers and give them a break. On the other hand, I knew there wasn't one chance in a million for a street rat like me. So I did what came naturally—ran like a gang of crooks was after me, hot on my tail and fixed to rip me limb from limb.

CHAPTER 2

ROSIE, IRIS, AND FLORA
IRIS

The officer grabbed Rosie before she knew what happened. He captured me seconds later. In the little while we'd been with him, we had come to feel Pete was our ticket out, so I made up my mind to find him, but he'd disappeared like a puff of air.

I clutched Rosie's hand. "That boy was our best hope," I said. "We've got to find him." I gave a pleading look at the policeman, but his arm was cut and bleeding. Well, maybe not yet. We had to face facts.

That tall, stony-faced policeman stood over us like a mountaintop. He snatched Pete's knife from the ground, and spoke sternly in his deep, scary voice, "You bet your boots I'll find the little scamp, and when I do, I'll make good and sure you girls never do."

<hr />

Before Flora brought us to Five Points, Rosie and I always did whatever she asked without talking back. That's what she expected and what she demanded. We hated her gentleman friends, at least most of them, but she said we should be sweet, act nice, and pretend we liked them, make a game of it. That's what she did.

Just before we moved to Five Points, we rode around in a fine carriage with a snooty man that didn't like kids. Flora called him Mr. Moneybags, since she was sure he was really rich. Every time Rosie made a peep, he'd yell at Flora, "Children should be seen and not heard." That got Flora's dander up, so she made the sacrifice and sacked him. She said we had to be extra good now and make it up to her, since she gave up the good life for our sakes. It was our fault she wasn't living like a swell.

When we walked into our new neighborhood, the worst one in the city, we hadn't the least notion why things had taken such a bad turn, and Flora didn't explain.

She warned us when we were really little, "Don't ask questions, and don't call me Ma. Call me Flora, like we're sisters." She'd do most anything to hide her age.

So on that first day in Five Points, we huffed and puffed our way up three flights, following Flora on a narrow stairway that creaked and groaned with every step we took. We climbed one stair tread apart, Rosie's sweaty little hand gripped tightly in mine. It was muggy hot and smelled of the dust and dirt that clung to everything. She kept stealing scared little glances at me.

Flora wore a stylish silk dress fancied up with ruffles, ribbons, and an up-to-date bustle. She often got jobs as an actress, her curvy figure was perfect for a certain kind of part. Unfortunately, I don't take after Flora. Just my luck, I expect I never will. I don't have Flora's figure, her pretty heart shaped face, or her golden hair. She fixed it real nice, tucked up in back with a neat little twist, and topped off with the latest in hats, a crown of fluffy ostrich feathers.

Rosie and I wore long print dresses with white pinafores and bright plaid ribbons stuck in our hair. I was too old to dress like Rosie, but Flora made me do it. She always got what she wanted.

So, our Ma hurried ahead, ten steps above us, breathing hard. She had a hard time, wrestling two fat suitcases that bumped with each step against the wall and the banister. We held up our skirts, stepping over dried-up potato peels, rubbish, and broken glass. Rosie pinched her nose at the smell of sour cabbage.

On the top landing Flora dropped the bags with a bang and took a deep breath. She fanned away the nasty smells and waited for us to catch up. "Cheer up," she bossed as usual. "Of course you know I have a plan. Don't I always?" She spoke in that sharp voice she used with bill collectors, landlords, and tiresome gentlemen friends who were about to spoil things.

When we caught up, she kneeled down to Rosie, lifted her chin, spitting on her handkerchief to wipe away the tear stains. "Don't fret, my sweet. That chiseler had me fooled with his flashy trinkets and fine promises." She held out her manicured fingers for me to admire the fake diamond ring. It was just a huge hunk of glass she once thought was real. "Pretty as a picture; phony as paper flowers," she said.

We passed an enormous cobweb, where a giant spider sat, waiting for its next meal. Flora frowned but said nothing. She placed one hand on her hip, stroked her soft, highly rouged cheek, and struck a Sarah Bernhardt pose. "This time, my dears, I've set my sights on a man of means. This one's a Wall Street tycoon!" I nodded and smiled. It was expected. "He's got high-toned digs on Fifth Avenue!" She winked at Rosie. "Just you wait. I'll bag my new sweetie before you can say Jack Robinson."

"Jack Robinson," Rosie said.

"I'm going to tickle you," Flora teased.

On the third floor she searched out and found number 313, fished a key from her purse, and opened the squeaking door. I stared at the small, shabby room, furnished with a rickety kitchen set, cracked washstand, and narrow bed. The window was sealed shut. Nasty smells of mouse droppings, rubbish, and mold made me feel like throwing up.

When we tried to back out, Flora pushed us back in and slammed the door. "Look, you two. We'll clean it up!"

I kneeled down to hug Rosie. "It's a dump!" she wailed.

"Let this be a lesson, my princess," said Flora, stroking her hair, "For once you get a taste of how I once lived."

"Why do we have to? What good will it do?" I know my voice quavered. I tried to be brave, but tears ran down my cheeks.

Flora stood tall, like a queen. "It's time, my girls, for a history lesson. Sit!" Rosie flinched, but as usual, we did as we were told.

"When I was real little," she said. "I lived with my folks in Ireland. It's a pretty country, but poor as Job's turkey. It was Ma, Pa, and me with nothing but potatoes to eat, the only thing Pa could grow in that miserable, worn-out ground. The year I turned six, the whole field went bad. The blight turned every potato to mush. Our neighbors were all in the same fix. They were living scarecrows, eyes like chunks of coal, bodies skin and bones. Some folks boiled up grass. Some ate tree bark. One by one they dropped, some from disease. Most just starved to death.

"Ma and Pa sold all they had for a pittance. The three of us sailed in a filthy ship's hold, seasick, half dead, ending up in Five Points in a room full of rats—best they could afford. They made do without a fuss. Pluck's the word for them. Those brave folks were your grandpa and grandma. Say the word." She raised her voice and pointed at us. "Say it!"

"Pluck," I repeated as Flora jerked her head. "Pluck." Rosie stared at Flora as she said the word.

"They worked long hours, Pa in the iron foundry, Ma in a sweat shop, sewing men's shirts. There were all sorts of strange women speaking different tongues, like the Tower of Babel. Ma was a fine seamstress, a high-toned dressmaker, but she got paid like a rag-picker. While Ma and Pa worked and slaved, I roamed the streets and wandered about the tenement houses, food carts, and some very bad places, stumbling onto all sorts of low-down goings on. No little kid should live like that, but where could I go? What else could I do?"

She stared at me with fire in her eyes. Maybe she thought two spoiled girls like us could never understand what she'd been through. So then she shrugged her shoulders and said, "If you put this little inconvenience up against those days, it's nothing to even speak of. Besides, Five Points is a perfect hiding place. Archie's no good, and we're well rid of him, but he won't give up easy. He'll be out looking for me. He knows I hate it here, so it's the last place he'd look. Well, cheer up. We won't be here long. Oh, stop sniffling!"

"What if he does find us?" Rosie kept on sniffling.

Flora shrugged. "When he's fooled some new lady friend, which, knowing him, won't take long, I'll show up on my new sweetie's doorstep. This one's a pushover, fat and funny looking, but a Fifth Avenue swell. I met him at the Astor extravaganza, and guess what? He adores me. Well, if he doesn't now, he soon will." She laughed, showing her perfect white teeth.

Rosie clutched my skirt. Flora's eyes flashed about the room. She fixed her gaze on a corner heaped with trash and commanded, "Well, for goodness sake, let's make the dump livable. Down we go to fetch supplies. Snip snap!"

She emptied the basket, hooked it over one arm, and pushed us back into the hall. She gave me a little nudge towards the long, dark stairway, which led downstairs to the street below.

The outside air was thick with dust, the street clogged with horses, buggies, carts, and wagons. Everything was jammed so tightly, that we could only pass by darting through narrow spaces. Streets in Five Points were filthy. We had to wade through vegetable parings, horse droppings, even human waste. The smell was so nasty, I can't even describe it. The sight of the street children, rubbing their eyes as they woke up in shop doorways and alleys, was pitiful.

We walked holding hands, separating when necessary, past the mission where a collection of drunks and vagabonds lounged on the front steps. We passed lots of street vendors hawking things like firewood, fish, and newspapers. Flora bought cleaning supplies, bed linens, even some doilies.

A ragged girl stood on the corner of Mulberry and Orange, guarding a rusty pail filled with pink and purple phlox. Rosie and I buried our noses in the blossoms. "Enchanting," I said after smelling the flowers. I like pretty words. Little Rosie followed my lead. "Like a fairy's garden," she said, eyes closed, nose burrowed in. Flora fished out a nickel for an armful, handing them to me.

"We'll need to pump water from the well out back and fill our pail. That's how it's done here. Then it's back upstairs for a good scrub." Once inside our room, Flora arranged the flowers in a glass jar, drew in a deep breath, and then, unable to open the window, tossed a collection of rubbish down the stairs.

She poked the broom at me. "Corners first. Sweep dirt and trash into the hall and down the stairs. If we could open the window, we'd chuck it in the alley, but the fool thing won't budge." When the sweeping was done, Flora handed each of us a scrub brush and set us to work scouring the floor. She unpacked her basket and made up the bed, fluttering about the room, arranging our things, our few books, chalk, and slates.

"Now." She smiled. "We'll play pretend. This is our mansion; your Pa's filthy rich and off making deals. I'm the pretty governess." She fished a little bell from her purse and rang it. "Let the lesson begin."

We sat with our books propped up, enjoying the sweet scent of our pink and purple phlox. It was a cozy scene. I remember wriggling in our chairs, giggling at Rosie's incorrect spelling of "barberian" just before a rock smashed through our window. It crashed, splaying shards and splinters of glass across the room.

I winced, drew up in shock, as the object whizzed across the room. It landed with a thud, each tiny sliver of glass tinkling as it hit the floor. I felt a rush, a thrill of fear, and all three of us scrambled for safety.

Rosie screamed, clutching at Flora's silk skirt. Flora wrapped her arms around Rosie. Then she grabbed me too, like we were all three stuck together. When the first waves of shock wore off, we looked each other over. Not one of us even had a scratch.

"Close call." Rosie squeaked.

"How'd he do it?" I gasped. "And from where?"

"Third floor, across the alley." Flora pointed. "That window's wide open." She shoved us under the bed, lowering the blanket to give us cover. Rosie huddled close to me, waiting. We waited—and waited—and waited, but nothing happened.

"Maybe it wasn't Archie," Flora said. "It's just a bad neighborhood. You can come out now. We've got some cleaning up to do."

She hired a man to replace the glass, and we settled into life in Five Points. Flora organized drills—what to do if the former gentleman friend might ever pay us an unexpected visit.

One day, as we sat at our little table, playing at lessons, heavy footsteps came pounding up the stairs. "Hush," Flora whispered. I pulled Rosie close to me under the bed behind the blanket.

The steps thundered louder and louder; then came furious pounding on the door, a deafening roar. We covered our ears. Bits of hardware and wood splinters flew.

As we lay there, wrenched in like a nut and bolt, we heard Flora scream. A deep voice shouted some nasty words, and we heard scuffling sounds. Something heavy hit the bed and bounced on our heads. Then came another blow.

A wild scream was followed by a muffled cry, a choking sound, then the thump of feet galloping down the stairs, three flights to the street below, and all went silent. I held Rosie tightly. We huddled in our cramped space. I was too scared to say a word or even peek out.

I held my breath, growing red-faced and desperate, waiting for Flora's all clear, for the blanket to be raised, for her soft white fingers, her bright red nails and fake diamond to signal the storm had passed, but no signal came. Each time Rosie began to speak I pressed a finger to her lips, held her tightly to stop her shaking.

Finally, I summoned up courage to lift the blanket and peer at every corner of the room. I couldn't make out a man's feet, no clothes strewn across the floor, no human things. The small room was silent and scary.

I finally worked up the nerve to crawl out from our hiding place and help Rosie. Once she too was up and out, I stared in horror at the lifeless form lying cold and still on the bed. Rosie's scream broke the silence. I don't know how I found the strength, but I clamped a hand over her mouth, then pressed an arm around my terrified little sister. She clung to me like a tendril to the vine.

But after a while she pushed my hand away. "Flora's white as snow," she whispered. "Like a statue. Make her wake up! Iris! Please! We need our Ma! Make her!"

What could I say? What could I do? I felt a scream fill me up inside, but it did not come out. I wanted to tear out my hair, to shout out the window for help, to race out the door. But I just stood there with my mouth wide open, frozen like a lump of ice. How could this be? I had seen terrible things in the streets of Five Points, but never before had I seen the face of death. And this was our Ma. I stared down at little Rosie. Who would take care of the poor little orphan? I was not old enough to look out for myself, much less my little sister. Through all of this confusion something told me. *If not me, who?* I had all the responsibility of a grown woman now. I had no choice. I just had to calm down, to think things out, and to act quickly.

What I did next may seem strange, cold, and unnatural for a girl not yet fully grown. I can only explain that although I didn't much care for her way of living, I admired many things about my

Ma. She taught me to pitch in and do what has to be done, no matter how I felt inside, so that's what I did.

"We have to get out of here," I whispered.

"We can't leave her!"

"Hush! Staying won't help. We've got to help ourselves, get out now, while the getting's good. He'll be back. Criminals always come back."

"What happens if we stay?"

"We'll be statues too."

"No. Oh, no! A handsome prince will wake her with a kiss." Rosie's voice trembled as her hands fluttered nervously. Her eyes were pleading for me to confirm what she'd said, but I couldn't. I don't know how I did it, but I threw a little food in a sack, tossed underwear, an extra dress for Rosie and one for me in Flora's small satchel. Then, provisioned with these meager necessaries, I yanked Rosie out the door.

We ran down the stairs into the crowded street below. When I realized I should have taken Flora's purse, it was too late. I was sure it would be more dangerous to go back than to face the street armed only with our wits and our nerve.

We fairly staggered on to the street, not knowing what would happen next. How would I care for Rosie? What would we eat? Where would we sleep? A battered tin cup lay discarded in the gutter. It was dirty and bashed in, but I picked it up and tossed it in the sack. Who could know what the future would bring—what things we might need?

Chapter 3

THE ORPHANAGE
Iris

After Pete vanished, Rosie and I were nabbed by the cop.

"Where's your folks?" the officer growled.

"We don't have any," I said. "Not anymore." I didn't dare tell what had happened to Flora. For all I knew, he might be in cahoots with the murderer. Five Points is a terrible place. You don't know who to trust.

He grabbed our hands and kept us marching along. I was sure we'd end up in jail, and then what would become of us? It was bad enough for me, but Rosie was much too little. I couldn't think what to say or do. I couldn't even squeeze my poor little sister's hand. She was tripping along on the other side of the cop. I knew she'd be trembling, but I couldn't reach her. We didn't go far before he stopped in front of a tall, dingy building and yanked open a massive door. Once we went inside, it clanged shut behind us like a jailhouse gate. "You'll be safe in here," he said. "It's not home but better than the street. Behave yourselves. Do as you're told, and you'll come out all right."

A sour looking lady in a long black dress came toward us. "Where'd you find these stray cats?" she said. Her face looked hard as stone.

"They are children, not cats, Miss Harkin. Poor little orphans in need of a home."

It seemed like he was taking our part, but he didn't stay. Maybe he was scared of the old witch. As soon as he'd left, Miss Harkin started in on us. "I don't stand for rude words or bad behavior. Rules in this institution are strictly enforced. Children must work to earn their keep." She beckoned to a girl, not much older than I was, and ordered her to show us around. We went upstairs, where the girl showed us a dingy room with a low ceiling filled up with so many narrow beds, there was only a little crack between them. The room was dark and ugly, but, as the policeman said, it was better than the street.

We were given jobs, and before the day was over, we blended right in, just two more pathetic orphans. But at least we were together. I would guard my dear little sister, Rosie, with my life.

We were put to work cleaning rooms and hallways. Before and after mealtimes we were given kitchen chores. Even though our jobs were unpleasant, we both did our best, since we always worked under the stern eye of that ogress.

Every day was the same. The dining hall swarmed with kids, like chicks in a hen yard. I didn't know much about hens then, but I learned later. Some kids were short, some tall, all underweight. Most were wearing patched clothes that didn't fit. They hurried from table to table.

Our duties were outlined on that first day. Rosie must stack bowls on one of the long tables, placing spoons in a pail, toting all she could manage. She had to move really fast down a dark, narrow hallway. There she unloaded onto the long kitchen table, then raced back for more. The taller children wielded brooms and dishpans, piled high with cheap tableware.

One of my jobs was to mop the floor. I held on tight to the rough handle and stared at the floor to avoid Miss Harkin's mean little eyes. One day a strange feeling came over me. Something was going to change. I just knew it. Don't ask me why. That horrible woman sat on a raised platform, staring at all the goings on. In one hand she clutched a thin, pointed stick.

Sure enough, shattering the gloomy mood, a high-pitched yell came through from outside. This was followed by a series of whoops. We froze, scared like rabbits listening to a wolf howl. Kids sucked in their breath as the door flew open, and two fat policemen, flushed, huffing and puffing, hauled in a ragged, dirty boy. The boy thrashed and kicked against their well-padded hips while, from one kid to another, little whispers passed.

"Another street kid, just like us."

"No siree! I bet you my good agate, some preacher from the mission sprung this one from the pen."

A mid-sized boy, pointing his broom handle at the new boy, hollered, "By gum. I can tell by the look of him, this here's a thief—or else—a cutthroat!"

I tightened my grip on the mop. The policemen set the boy on his feet, grabbed him roughly by the collar, and dragged him, feet sliding all the way, to Miss Harkin's platform. "This here's a feisty one," said one officer with a grin. "All yours with our compliments, Miss Harkin."

"Courtesy of the good Reverend Peters," added the other with a chuckle.

"The good Reverend did he say?" one of the taller boys called out.

The new boy was tossed like a bean bag onto the platform next to Miss Harkin. "So long, kid," said one of the policemen, taking off his hat. "Sorry about all this."

"Good luck to you," called the other, and as they strolled out the door, one smiled at the boy while the other winked.

I winced as Miss Harkin whacked her stick against the reading stand. Most kids lowered their eyes and went back to what they'd been doing. I couldn't help myself. I peeked from the corner of one eye as Miss Harkin stepped quick as a wink from her platform. She was clutching the new boy's skinny arm. His dirty cheeks were tear-stained. He went along with an angry face as she placed him on a high stool, where he stayed, arms folded, eyes on the floor.

Miss Harkin made a speech about good children and bad and what happens to both kinds. "You will all face the grim reaper sooner or later. Most likely sooner," she said, "but good children fly right on up to Heaven. On the other hand, bad ones slide down a dark, smelly coal chute to a very nasty place, where I wouldn't care to tell you what becomes of them. But let me make one thing clear. It is horrible." She shook all over at the thought. Then she ordered Tony Crumble, one of the older boys, to take charge while she left the room. He was to report all misbehavior.

Every child kept eyes peeled on the door, the one where the scary witch just disappeared. After a while Rosie tiptoed to the door, peeked down the hall, and whispered in my ear, "He looks a fright, all banged up and filthy, but I'm sure that new kid is Pete.

We're in luck!" Of course, I'd already figured it out. I couldn't stop smiling.

⁙

"The coast is clear," Rosie whispered, just loud enough so I could hear. I passed the word on down the line. At once dishpans were dumped, brooms and rags tossed. Rosie skipped to Pete's perch. Tony stood guard at the door.

"Is it really you? Pete?" Rosie peered up into his eyes. "Remember me?" She tapped her chest. "I'm Rosie! You were good to Iris and me, and now we'll take and do for you." She stretched her little hand to give his foot a friendly pat, but he stomped on it.

"Ouch! That wasn't very friendly," Rosie said. "We thought you were nice. C'mon, tell the kids your name. Show them what you're really like."

Pete's lips tightened.

"Nobody's going to bite you," Rosie said. "Tell them your name."

"Don't get so close," I warned her. "I don't like the look in his eyes."

He stared at the floor as he mumbled his name.

"When you get to know him, you'll like him." Rosie nodded, addressing the other kids.

She turned back to Pete. "Watch out for Miss Harkin. She's a tiger!"

He didn't answer.

"He's a good kid," I tried to reassure the other children as I squeezed Rosie's hand. I knew she was disappointed.

"We know him. He's a good kid," Rosie repeated as her audience watched and chuckled.

"Them sisters would stick up for the Devil his own self," one cross looking boy said, approaching Pete. Of course, that wasn't true. Most of Flora's gentlemen friends gave me the creeps. With one exception, I wouldn't lift a finger for any of them.

"Ain't I seen you someplace?" The cross boy stared at Pete, looked him over, head to toe, then started rattling on like some street rats will do.

"Yup! I knew it. You're the kid with the big mouth." The boy stood tall, like somebody making a speech on a street corner.

"This here Pete and me was hawking papers at Five Points, me working the corner of Bayard, him on Mulberry. Tough spot, though once in a while fancy folks stroll by. This one big swell sauntered up, all decked out; black suit, silk tie, top hat, shiny shoes, new leather brief case. I was hollering the usual, 'Extra, extra, read all about it! Big fire on Canal Street.' A few folks come by, tossing me pennies. Then this high-toned feller come strolling along. Pete here hollered, top of his lungs, 'Big time evangelist caught in love nest with scarlet woman. Burnt to a crisp!' The swell stiffed me, crossed catty-corner, grabbed one from Pete's stack, and plunked down a big shiny coin. Pete flipped it so high, it sparkled. I'd swear to God it was a gold piece. Pete sold out in ten minutes. I sweated out the rest of that scorcher for next to nothing."

"It's called salesmanship," Pete said, puffing up his chest.

"Flimflam!" shouted the boy.

Pete drew back a fist.

The other boy stuck out his tongue and thumbed his nose. Pete leapt down, drew back his fighting arm, and the excited children surrounded them. Most everyone was thrilled, hoping to watch a big fight.

Just that minute Tony Crumble waved his arms and raced to grab a broom. All the kids snatched up piles of plates and whatever else they had tossed. Everybody changed their grins to hopeless expressions for Miss Harkin's benefit. As soon as she came through the door, she demanded a report.

"All's well, Miss Harkin," said Tony Crumble. "They done their jobs." Tony pointed at Pete. "You can rest easy about the new kid, Ma'am. He ain't gonna give you no trouble a-tall."

Miss Harkin's snake eyes swept the room. "Line up!" she shouted. "March! Single file!"

One morning in August a serious looking gentleman, wearing a preacher's collar under his black Prince Albert coat, came in tapping a black walking stick. He marched on through our stuffy dining room with its low ceilings, dirty walls, and small sealed windows.

Rosie and I were playing hangman. Whenever grownups came near, we sat on the paper and pencil stubs Rosie had managed to swipe from Miss Harkin's desk. That gentleman stood right up next to Miss Harkin and announced in his deep preacher voice that a special train would arrive in the city the next morning. It would carry orphan children west, away from the city, to be "placed out" on farms or in small towns.

"We have thirty spaces yet to be filled." He spread his arms like he was giving us a blessing.

"Our purpose is to find good homes for you who have no homes, a golden opportunity to develop acceptable work habits and grow into fine, law abiding citizens." That's what he said.

He marched up and down the aisles, pointing his walking stick at one table after another. I squeezed Rosie's hand under the table as he came near.

Quick as a summer storm comes on, he stood in front of us, lifting his stick. First he pointed at Rosie, then at me, like he was aiming two shots. When his stick smacked the floor, he checked his papers. I dabbed at my eyes. Rosie wiped her nose on her sleeve. The Reverend counted names on the list, scowled, and began counting again. "I can take one more," he said. He clapped a firm hand on Pete's shoulder and raised his voice. "Young man, this is your lucky day."

Miss Harkin gasped, "Oh no! Not that boy."

"Not that boy?"

The minister breathed deeply. He spoke so softly, I bent my ear to listen. "A troublemaker?"

She gave a sharp, snappy nod. He polished his glasses, set them firmly on his nose, and matched a piercing look against Miss Harkin's scowl.

"Manual labor on a wholesome western farm is the very thing to turn a hoodlum into a Christian, Miss." He said the next part in a soft, almost gentle voice. "Surely you know, our Lord came to save sinners."

Miss Harkin didn't say one word after that.

The Reverend faced all of us kids and preached a short sermon about how children are loved and cared for in God's kingdom. When he'd given us all he had to say, he cleared out fast, and that was that.

"Hurry up, children!" Miss Harkin snapped at those picked. "Upstairs for a good scrub. The Reverend has generously supplied new clothing and a little suitcase for every child. The way you look, nobody on God's earth would take a one of you."

I hardly dared look up, but I peeked as she aimed her usual crabby look at Pete. He kept quiet and well-behaved until he'd rounded the corner where she couldn't see him anymore. Then he kicked the shins of every boy who tried to haul him upstairs for a bath.

But when Tony Crumble took after him, Pete threw up his hands like a crook surrendering. "So, it's you, Tony Crumble! Well, I owe you one." He tossed an arm around Tony's shoulders and trotted up the stairs, a well-behaved boy if I ever saw one. That was amazing!

As I scrubbed Rosie's elbows and knees, we talked things over. "I was beginning to think we wouldn't see Pete ever again. He's rougher, tougher, and lots dirtier."

Rosie curled her hands around her mouth to cover a giggle. "He looks like he had a ride through Miss Harkin's coal chute. The one that dumps bad kids you know where."

"Where do you think they'll take us?" I couldn't help but wonder.

Rosie shrugged. "Why did the Reverend pick us?"

"Who knows?"

"Well, at least we'll ditch the old witch. It can't be worse than staying here." I couldn't believe Rosie had said that.

I stroked her soft little cheek. Up close she smelled pure and clean, like a baby. "Have you already forgotten how it was on the street? We were that close to turning into hungry, filthy street rats." She wouldn't answer, just stared at the ceiling.

They woke us in the dark. After breakfast, morning prayers, and the usual scary lectures, we were sent with a new set of clothes. Each girl got two everyday dresses, one for Sundays, three sets of underwear, three pairs of socks, and one pair of shoes. We carried the clothes we didn't wear in cheap suitcases the Reverend gave us for free. I also stuffed in the few things we'd brought when we rushed off from the tenement house. We'd packed so fast, our suitcases were a mess. Some kids even had socks and sleeves hanging out. It all happened so quickly, I had no time to think, but my heart was racing. Could I still look after Rosie? Would it be all right?

When we reached the station, we stood in the middle of a crowd, waiting for the train. Rosie wouldn't stop jabbering. She jumped from one foot to the other and couldn't seem to stand still. I tried to answer her questions, but I didn't know the answers. We were going out west, hoping to get a new home. That was all. What kind of home? What kind of people?

As these questions bounced around in my head, I noticed a boy who looked a little like Pete. The trouble was, all clean and dressed up, I couldn't be sure. He was having a long talk with a ragged looking man, a derelict, like those we saw every day in Five Points. Pretty soon I watched the bum lean down, hand something to the boy, and squeeze his hand. The raggedy man blew his nose, and then disappeared into the crowd. I tried, without letting go of Rosie's hand, to inch towards the boy, but the crowd pressed in. Try as I might, I couldn't push through.

As we boarded the train, everyone talked at once. We hadn't the least notion where we were going, except we were headed west. And, of course, I wondered if we'd be all right. Could it be worse than the streets of New York? I couldn't imagine such a place.

We hadn't the least notion where we were going, except we were
headed west.

Rosie and I found seats side by side. I felt a poke in my back, and when I turned around, there was that clean, well-dressed boy I'd seen in the crowd. He was sporting a dapper cap and matching tweed jacket. He pointed the eraser end of a pencil at my heart. "Hey there, Iris!" he said. "It's me! Pete! Tell Rosie, um—tell her— aw shucks—just go ahead and tell her—I'm sorry."

Rosie turned around to look. She giggled. "It's Pete!" She pointed. "Look Iris. Who'd ever guess? All gussied up."

"Ain't I a swell?"

"Swell headed's more like it." Rosie was quick with smart remarks.

"Aw shucks, I should've stomped harder." Pete grumbled.

After Rosie and Pete exchanged a few more insults, she noticed something.

"Oh no! My new dress is dirty. I wanted to make a good impression. Now they'll take me for a street rat."

"You've got three spares in the suitcase," I said, hoping to calm her down.

"Stand up and shake off the dirt," Pete said. "It's just a little soot." She shook it off. Except for a few streaks, the black dust fell to the floor.

"That black stuff is dust from coal they burn to heat water to make steam that makes the train go," Pete said.

"How'd you get so smart?" Rosie said, her mouth all screwed up.

"Comes natural." He winked and then started whistling a peppy little tune.

Rosie and I tapped our toes and got almost kind of jolly, but you can't keep that up forever.

We made up jokes about Miss Harkin, and Pete told so many stories about bad kids at the orphanage, I forgot to ask about the ragged fellow at the station.

In time, even Pete got tired of talking. The noise of the whistle, the belching steam, and the clanking wheels made it hard to hear unless we hollered. Rosie curled up beside me. Sometimes we'd hold hands. Sometimes she'd sleep in my lap. Pete read from *Boy's Own Magazine*. "I can read anything I want," he said. "While the peddler's back is turned, I just swipe one from the newsstand. Easy as pie." He sure seemed proud of himself.

It's hard to believe I was even able to sleep, I was so nervous, but at the same time, I was worn out. Once, when I woke up with a jerk, I looked out the window at a field of tall corn, a red barn, and a large, freshly painted farmhouse. Children were tumbling in green grass, thick as a magic carpet. One little girl was pumping a rope swing that hung from a huge spreading oak tree.

"Look!" I shook Rosie 'til she woke up too. "Did you ever see anything so nice?" We both stared backwards, mouths open. Finally, that lovely picture slipped away. Something was going on in front of the car.

"Food!" I told the other kids. "We're going to eat."

Sandwiches were passed and tin cups of milk. Rosie made a face at two slices of dry, crumbly bread. An ugly yellow mess was spread in between.

"I'm not hungry," she said, clamping both hands over her mouth.

"You've got to eat. I mean it." I scolded. "If you find something moldy, just pick it off. Shut your eyes, bite, chew, and gulp. If you throw up, you've got to clean up your own mess."

"Not so fast," Pete said. "Hand it over. That's just mustard in the middle. It ain't rotten. Won't make you puke. Don't ever throw food away. I'll eat anything."

Rosie handed it around sideways behind the seat, but I slapped her hand and told her, in my bossiest voice, to eat. I hated acting that way, but the poor girl didn't have a Ma. Somebody had to take charge. Just like Pete and me, she ate her mustard sandwich.

It was like a riddle, not knowing the answer, what would come next. After life on the street, I should have been used to the guessing game, but does anybody ever get used to feeling unsafe? We were puppets, with strangers yanking the strings, grownups who didn't know a single thing about me or my little sister, what we'd been through, how scared we felt inside, and even if they found out, they'd soon forget and wouldn't care at all. Why should they? The one good thing was that Rosie and I were together. I knew her needs; she knew mine. It would be like that forever. I had to make sure.

We watched the sun go down in the western sky, and before long everything went dark. Rosie snuggled up in my lap. I stroked her hair and her smooth, sweet skin. I made up a little story in my head, just to make me feel better. I was the mother sheep, and she was my little lamb. I wished we were in a nice green pasture.

In the morning Pete lay stretched out on the floor under our seat. I touched him, nudged, waited. I wanted him to get up, so I tapped him with my foot 'til he groaned, opened one eye, smoothed both hands over the floor, twitching around, acting kind of nutty.

"Lose something?" I asked. He seemed really worried.

He checked his pockets, his face turned pink, and then red as beet juice. "Did you girls see a little slip of paper?" We shook our heads.

When the agent walked by, Pete tugged at her skirt. "A little piece of paper was in my pocket. Now it's gone!" He was like a puppy down on the floor, staring up with pleading eyes.

"Somebody swiped it," he finally said when he got no reply. Now there was a bitter tinge to his voice.

"You'll have no use for that," the woman snapped, staring far off, as if something more important was happening at the end of the car. Quickly, she walked away.

"What's this all about?" I asked.

"My pop," Pete said, his voice all choked up. "He went on a toot and was gone for weeks. Showed up at the station a couple minutes before we got on the train. He slipped me an address to write to, and I was supposed to let him know how I'm doing when we get there, where we end up, all that. I got a feeling I ain't going to see the old geezer again. Not soon. Not ever."

I gave Pete my hankie.

His eyes squeezed up into thin little slits. "I kept holding onto that little slip of paper," he said, "slept on it, and then—that old woman—that witch—by gum, she lifted it."

I could feel my eyes blazing. Popping from my seat I shouted, "I'll give the old biddy what for!"

"Iris," Pete got up, touched my arm, and spoke softly. "Iris, we'll pick our fights, and this ain't one of them."

<hr>

As our train rumbled across the land, all the kids got cranky. First one would pull a trick on another one, and that kid would do the same to the next, all the way down the narrow aisle. They were bouncing on the hard wooden benches like loose rubber balls, kicking, crying, wailing. That went on for three long, miserable nights. The train clickety-clacked westward out of the city and then through deep woods. What a surprise we got when we reached wide-open country. Those flat farm fields looked different from anything we'd seen in our lives. They seemed to go on forever without end.

"Ain't nothing here but cornfields," groaned one sleepy-eyed girl.

"Don't blink. You'll miss another one-horse town," grumbled her seatmate.

We all sat up and listened when the conductor shouted, "Mississippi River. Keep your eyes peeled, kids. Don't miss the mighty Mississipp.' And here she comes." We rumbled across a long, rickety bridge. The train's sounds changed and seemed to sing a different tune. The kids piled on top of each other to look down at the dark brown river, so wide, we all hooted and hollered.

We didn't know how much longer the ride would last. Each stop meant just one more letdown for those of us who didn't get picked. But we were used to it. Hard luck was stuck to every kid. We'd been passed over in Elmira, and Mansfield, and Union, and Peoria. After we crossed the Mississippi, we stopped at Burlington. Then, an hour or two past the big bridge, the train slowed, jerked, and groaned. Metal rubbed on metal, making a high, squealing sound. The conductor shouted, "Hartfield, Iowa. Collect your belongings! It's Hartfield, Iowa."

The windows had been slammed shut by the agent when some of the wild and crazy boys reached out to catch passing tree limbs.

It was just a game, but one kid almost fell out, so we all had to suffer. We tried to see through those sealed up windows. The toughest kids pushed others away to get a look outside. They pressed their noses against the hot, steamed up glass and tried wiping off the fog, but it just misted up again like a steam bath. Sweltering. Things reflected in the windows looked bent out of shape, like carnival mirrors. Kids acted silly one minute, cranky the next, fidgety, worn out, and wondering where in the world we were, and what would happen next. This was a huge improvement over Five Points, for sure, but nobody was shouting, "Whoopee."

I kept thinking about how we got here. Everything that led up to this place and this minute was depressing, so I forced myself to change the subject inside my head. Still, I couldn't help noticing how just a handful of kids were let off at each stop. Nobody knew a thing. I looked around and saw I wasn't the only one wondering if this spot, this little dot in the middle of a cornfield, would be our new home, and if we had to stay would it be for good? It was like watching a play, only we were in it, crossing our fingers, hoping for a happy ending, but pretty sure, from what happened so far, the end would be worse than the beginning.

Finally the agent, a big, clumsy looking woman with a wide pimply nose, ugly men's shoes, and voice like a street hawker, shouted out names. She yelled each name three times, then checked the list, then checked once more, and then picked out a wiggly kid to stare at, just to show who was boss.

I sat there chewing my knuckles. Rosie twisted her hair. The real little kids kept sucking their thumbs. I'd hoped and prayed to hear our names called, but felt in my bones this would be like all the other places. Kids were complaining, some with angry looks, some with little cries. Rosie let out a wail.

I watched Pete turn purple, holding his breath. I could almost read his mind, knowing he hated getting his hopes smashed—again. Before we left the orphanage, Miss Harkin scolded him, shaking one finger. "One more misstep, young man, will send you spinning, back to the orphanage. Back to the street. Back to the jail. The felon-filled jail." That's how she talked to everybody, but she picked on Pete more than most.

These thoughts and worries ended with a bang. I almost jumped out of my skin when three names were announced in a loud, bossy voice three times: "Iris O'Leary, Rose O'Leary," and after a long, scary pause—"Peter Freeman."

Pete let out a deep breath and mopped his brow with my handkerchief. All three of us jumped up like popping kernels of corn and started moving forward with the other lucky kids, smiling our way down the aisle past the sad kids left behind.

Then poor Pete tripped over a shoelace he'd forgotten to tie and fell on the hard, wooden floor. It looked like it hurt, but he didn't say a word. His feelings showed on his face, though. That sweet round face lit up like a ripe strawberry.

"Hey Pete. You okay?" I couldn't keep the worry from my voice as I bent over to help him. Rosie held out her hand, trying to do what I did. She wasn't much help, but he grabbed both our hands anyway and held on.

I felt sorry for him. The kid always managed to hide his feelings, but this time he couldn't. Something huge was going to happen, something that would change our lives for good and all.

Pete's one eyelid started winking and blinking. He scrunched his mouth around in a funny, twitchy way, but what he did next was the biggest surprise of all. He gave Rosie a big squeeze and then did me the same way. His voice was hoarse. "Thanks girls," he croaked. "You stuck up for me when you didn't have to." He stopped and said the next part fast, like it might stick in his throat if he didn't get it over with. "You're my best pals. I won't forget."

CHAPTER 4

WE ARRIVE

IRIS

As we stood there, feeling all happy inside that Pete really did like us, the steam was wiped off the window, and we took our first look at the town bigwigs, marching two by two through a crowd of people. They pushed their way right up to the train and forced others to back up. "Inside folks! You'll all get your chance!" Somehow, our tired little troop of kids stumbled off the train.

A man in a gaudy plaid coat hollered through a homemade megaphone. It was really just a rolled up poster. I couldn't read all the words on it, but I could make out bits of an elephant's trunk and letters that might have spelled *Barnum and Bailey*. In the orphanage we'd heard about the circus. Of course, we never got to go, but one kid had been there and told about how he'd sneaked in under a tent and didn't even get caught. I poked Rosie and whispered. We giggled, thinking and hoping we might at least get a peek.

"Wait'll you're inside," the man hollered. "This here pushing and shoving gets you nowhere fast. Now, if you'll just hold your horses 'til we get everybody inside, you'll be free to look 'em over like picking out a registered purebred down to the sale barn, only these little fellers won't cost you a plugged nickel. We'll put 'em up on stage, and you'll get your turn to size 'em up, top to toe."

Folks outside were pushing and shoving. It was hot. My dress stuck to my skin. As soon as we stepped down from the train, we were pressed forward through a path, sliced through the middle of the crowd by the bigwigs, and pushed towards a building they called the opera house. It was three stories high, very nice, with big fancy letters above the entrance that said, *Hartfield Opera House.*

The man with the megaphone shouted, "I expect you can guess who built it." He pointed to a man in the crowd. "You got it right. Donated by Mr. Jefferson Hartfield. The man paid a princely sum for this fine palace of entertainment."

Inside, we stared up, down, and all around, mouths wide open. For such a little town, the place was amazing. There were three tiers of seats: main floor, first and second balcony, and a stage. And it was nice and cool in there. After the heat outside, it was a real treat. The walls were two feet thick and the floor seemed to cough up cool air.

The man wouldn't stop hollering. "Most of you know me, but if you don't, you can call me Jackson—George Jackson." His chest puffed out, and he stuffed his hands in his back pockets.

I edged up to him, pulling Rosie along. "Is the circus coming to town?" I wasn't scared of him.

"Nope. I went to Turner Falls to see it. They don't come to little burgs like this one."

I whispered to Rosie, "Don't you fret. There'll be other fun things to do."

"What I'm saying now is for you kids," Jackson went on. "Everybody else in town seems to be busy, so I'm standing in for the preacher, since the man's laid up with the flu and can't get out of bed, but he left you in good hands. Mine. Now, I'll give you a tour of the place, before we get down to brass tacks. We're mighty proud of our opera house." He looked down at his notes, then waved his hand, making a wide sweep of the room. "Them fancy columns up front are called–um—Doric I do believe. And up top of that fancy arch with the lady's name in big, fancy letters—let's see my paper here. Oh, um. That there's some gal called Minerva. Nice name, don't you think?"

We had big, swell theatres in New York. This was smaller, but it had the same rich feel to it. The walls were papered with prints that looked like silk, and upholstered seats stuck out from the side walls. I got so taken up with the place, I forgot about the circus.

"On special occasions the bigwigs sit up there." He pointed to the box seats and grinned, showing dark, stained teeth. We were herded towards the stage like calves to the slaughterhouse.

"Nice place, but we've been tricked," Rosie said, biting her lips. "Please, Iris, don't let go my hand."

In the orphanage we'd been taught to kneel beside our beds and pray at bedtime. I never paid much mind to it, but Rosie took it to heart, so now she crossed fingers on both hands, squeezed her eyes shut and said the only prayer she knew.

> Please make my life a little light
> Within the world to glow.
> A little flame that burneth bright,
> Wherever I may go.

As we marched to the stage, I put her ahead of me in line. We were told where to stand. The people in the crowd below elbowed their way to get a good look.

I held onto Rosie and edged up front. "We're a pair!" I called out, squeezing Rosie's hand. The folks down below laughed. They laughed!

One by one, names were called, and when a kid's turn came up, that one was ordered to stand for inspection. The older boys were most in demand. Tall ones with strong backs were chosen first. A few people wanted girls for housework. Rosie and I stood together, faking smiles. She wanted to link arms but was too short, so I squeezed her hand really tight.

Mr. Jackson stood with one hand on me, the other on Rosie, hollering, "I don't expect anyone would care to take on two sisters, a big one and a little one."

Somebody yelled, "What about the rule?"

"That's right." Jackson said. "You hit the nail on the head. The rule is, kids from the same family can't be placed out together." He turned to the man beside him and talked kind of low, but I heard. "I came up with that rule for a mighty good reason. Blame it! Then I almost went and forgot."

The man whispered something back, right into Mr. Jackson's ear.

I hugged Rosie, tight as the peel hugs an apple. She hung onto me the same way. I could feel her trembling hands. Mine were shaking too. Nobody spoke up, but whispers flew. George Jackson stood back and took a long, hard look at Rosie. Then, without so much as how-de-do, he yanked us apart, and shoved me in with the big kids.

I faced the crowd, eyes narrowed, fists tight, feet planted. "We're a pair!" I shouted over and over 'til my head felt like a split watermelon.

Mr. Jackson pinched my shoulder. "Pipe down, girlie. Your little sister's already spoke for. If you don't mind your P's and Q's you'll be back on the next train for New York."

I couldn't think what to do next. I'd tried so hard, and nothing seemed to work. I just stood there, tears streaming, staring at the floor.

A thin woman in a faded, wrinkled dress said, "The Lord ain't seen fit to give Albert and me a child." She directed her sad eyes upward towards Albert.

"I've kind of taken a fancy to that little one." She pointed at Rosie, who stood with a sad face, her head tilted to one side, a perfect imitation of the poor orphan on the fliers folks were carrying.

"My, what a pretty child," another woman cried out. Lots of hands shot up. I bit my knuckles 'til blood started spilling out. I had to lick it up and wrap the finger in my skirt.

Mr. Jackson shouted, "Order! Come to order! We won't have no tug-of-war over the little dumpling." He grinned again, and that same mouthful of stained, ugly teeth showed. He chucked Rosie under the chin, then raised his voice so loud, it was scary. "I almost forgot. This little dolly's already spoke for, and a lucky little miss she'll be."

A young man, dressed in city clothes, a strange sight in this country town, stepped forward. People poked each other, whispered, and chuckled.

"I represent Mr. Jefferson Hartfield," he announced in a loud, clear voice.

The gossip and chatter in the hall suddenly got quiet, as if the President of the United States had just popped in. "No need to say so," said Jackson. "I had you pegged right off." He looked down at the folks below, the way preachers reading scripture on street corners do. "My decision is firm as the US Constitution, since what I got in mind is the little dearie's welfare." He stopped to tickle Rosie under the chin. "Lucky little muffin. Cute as a bug's ear, ain't she? I hereby award this child, this adorable little missy, to Hartfield's founder, foremost citizen, and Iowa big shot, Mr. Jefferson Hartfield, and the missus."

Complaints came from below. George Jackson pounded his wooden hammer on the speaker's table. "Quiet! There's plenty of these orphans to go around. Aw, pipe down!"

"She was pick of the litter," one farmer grumbled.

Another farmer, the one who had just whispered in Mr. Jackson's ear, stepped forward. He was all shaved up and wearing clean, ironed clothes. Stuffing hands in his pockets and swelling out his chest, he addressed the crowd. "Now folks. Most all of us owe whatever good fortune we've got to Mr. Jefferson Hartfield. That child" (he pointed at Rosie) "pretty though she be, wasn't born with no silver spoon in her mouth, but sure as the sun comes up of a morning, she'll have one now. So tell me, who'd begrudge the poor tyke? If somebody's got a bone to pick, speak now or forever hold your peace." Dead silence followed that. The man stepped down from the stage, smiling.

After long minutes a high-pitched, whiny voice cut through the silence. "That's all well and good," the woman said, "but we was set to take the little missy to fill in for the one we never did get. Now I suspect we'll wind up with a homely one." Three women standing nearby poked her. Their fingers shook in her face. Warnings seemed to be whispered.

"But then, to look on the bright side," added the woman, "I suspect a plain one might do for a hired girl." She laughed in a way that seemed more like a snort. When my name was called, it was that woman and her husband that took me.

"Ain't pretty like the little sister," complained the farmer, "and she's still a kid. Ain't trained up enough to do us much good, but seeing how the land lays, I suspect the wife could try her hand at it. Hey, girlie, what's your name?"

"State your name," ordered Mr. Jackson, tapping me on the shoulder.

I was so scared, I could barely whisper, "Iris."

"Kind of skittish, but I suspect I can fix that." The farmer laughed like he'd come out with a good one. "Once I brung home a high-strung filly from the sale barn. Got her broke in no time flat, and after a spell she turned out a fair to middling workhorse. Come on, Minnie," he elbowed his wife. "Let's take the kid and go."

"No!" I screamed, stomping my foot, but after Mr. Jackson gave me a terrible stare down, in a miserable, shaky voice, I said, "Not 'til I say goodbye to my little sister."

"Make it snappy. We got to get home for the milking," Albert said.

Rosie and I hugged and kissed, clinging to each other. "Don't cry, Sweetheart," I whispered. "And don't ever give up. Somehow, someway, no matter how long it takes, I'll come for you." I placed a finger on my lips. Rosie did the same, and with tears streaming down both our faces, we gave each other one last big hug. Remembering that moment still brings tears to my eyes.

The farmer and his wife filled out papers at a table up front. Then they each grabbed one of my arms and yanked me towards the door. I guess they thought they'd got a stubborn mule that wouldn't move. The farmer had a strange limp when he walked, but he was strong, with a grip that didn't let go.

I peeked back over my shoulder. Remembering that last glimpse of Rosie still makes me cringe, even today. She stood there, like a rag doll with worn-out stuffing, crimson cheeked, and wailing. Mr. Hartfield's driver had a pretty good grip on her shoulder. Both of her hands were busy, the left one moving restlessly, as if searching for my skirt. The right one twirled a clump of her own sweet, curly hair. How helpless I felt. The poor child was scared half out of her wits, and I couldn't do one thing about it. It was the worst moment of my life.

CHAPTER 5

THE UNFORTUNATES
PETE

I stood on that stage, all in a stew, wondering what would come next. My fists were clenched, like I was fixing for a fight. I was furious, grinding my teeth, especially when Iris and Rosie got yanked out like weeds.

Mr. Jackson ordered us, in his loud, street vendor voice, to "Come on down from that stage, you leftover kids, and mingle." So we did. Pretty soon a farmer sallied up behind me. The old coot wore dirty overalls that looked like he'd worn them night and day for a year. On top of that, he smelled of old sweat and barnyard stink. His bony elbows poked out from raggedy sleeves. That miserable critter poked me in the ribs and growled, "Step forward, young feller. Let's have a look at them muscles."

"Go buy yourself an ox!" I snapped at the old buzzard. He grunted, lost interest in me, and didn't take more than a finger snap to pick out a pale, pitiful boy. The kid was shaking in his boots. Scared of his own shadow. That one wouldn't talk back.

One by one, kids were claimed. The crowd thinned out, but it was plain as hard tack and ship biscuit there wouldn't be enough kids to go around. Not the kind these folks wanted.

Still, four kids were left, besides me. One girl had a limp that made her hop like a rabbit. She said she'd broke her leg on an ice patch when she was little. In Five Points, true to form, nobody bothered to fix it.

A skinny boy, with his nose in the wrong place, said he'd worked in a rich man's livery stable. The guy's favorite horse was wild and skittish. When the kid sneaked up from behind, the beast kicked him in the kisser and squashed his face like a ripe tomato.

Another boy talked in a high, squeaky voice. Folks steered clear of him. I expect they thought he was coo-coo.

There was a girl who would have been all right, except she couldn't look at you straight on. Her eyes went both ways at once. Folks didn't want her either.

I caught on, way too late in the game, my carryings on did me in. Nobody had any use for me. It seemed perfectly reasonable at the time, to act the way I did, but it soon became clear, the cards were stacked against me. So, dumbbell that I am, I started acting even worse. My dander was up and spilling over, like kerosene on a fire. I just stomped around, trying to cool off. Another farmer, who smelled like moldy cheese, took some pokes at me and gave me the willies. I thumbed my nose and stuck out my tongue. Not a good idea.

Jackson thumped me on the head. "Straighten up, blockhead!" He growled.

The five of us were paraded around the room like hogs at the sale barn. Folks reached out to touch us, feel our muscles, ask if we knew how to work. Everybody said the same thing. Would we try to be good children? Would we give them more trouble than we were worth? That kind of fiddle-faddle went on the best part of the day.

Finally, the other four got dragged off, even the cuckoo. So there I stood in the middle of the mob, my eyes drilling through the floor like a jailbird waiting for the hangman.

A filthy old farmer snuck up from behind, spun me around, pried open my mouth, and poked a dirty finger inside. "Let's have a look at them back teeth," he ordered. I bit him, and the old geezer jumped from one foot to the other, howling like a dog with his tail caught in a trap.

Mr. Jackson grabbed me by the ear and whispered, "If you don't straighten up, Kid, I'll toss you back on that train faster than greased lightening. We might could ship you farther west, but I've a notion to send you back to the orphanage." His eyes got up so close, they almost drilled into mine. "That orphanage ain't got room for incorrigibles, which means the clink, last stop for scallywags and troublemakers this side of the gallows." I didn't know what to do, so I scuffed my shoe against the floor, watching the mark it made.

A stern, barrel-chested man poked his wife with an elbow. The grooves between his eyebrows seemed to grow deeper as the two of them got their heads together, whispering. Then, pulling a straw from his mouth, he stepped forward, ruffled my hair, and aimed his words, in a loud, take charge voice, at Mr. Jackson. "We already got us two young whippersnappers but might could take on one more. Of course, we won't put up with no monkeyshines, but I suspect this one ain't as tough as he puts on. We got no end of donkey work out home. That's about the size of it. So maybe we could use one more donkey." He poked his wife but did not smile. Neither did she.

I stared at those birds. Was it them or the gallows? Seemed like it. I was pretty sure I had things sized up right. I'd have to go along, but I'd light out when the getting was good. If I made a squawk here and now, I'd get sent someplace worse. After the geezer had signed some papers, he wheeled around, glared at me, and waggled a crooked finger, like I was some kind of critter that couldn't talk. I guess I acted like one, because I followed, and off we went to the slaughterhouse.

His wife climbed up first. The geezer shoved me in the buggy. After we'd all sat down, he slapped the horses with his whip. "Folks call me Old Man Olson—among other things," he said. "You got spunk, but that was the dumbest act I've seen yet. You might wonder why I'd take on such an ornery brat, when it's plain as a pikestaff nobody else would."

I stared at the cornfields.

"Kid's deef and dumb, Mabel," Old Man Olson shouted. "Looks like we backed the wrong horse."

"Horse?" Mabel said.

"One thing's sure," he said. "We ain't got time or inclination for mind reading. Out where you're going, it's backbreaking grind, sunrise to sundown. Next week threshers come, so after dark you'll lift the lantern and sweat and slave some more. Now, here's a tip, free for nothing. No more smart aleck tricks, see? Straighten up. When it comes to taking on hands, my specialty is young hooligans. Strictly business. Give me a hard-nosed, ornery tough; I'll have him broke inside a week. Mabel and me ain't in the good deed game. Strictly business. Got it?"

"Strictly business," Mabel repeated his words exactly, staring at me with her black, beady eyes. She reminded me of an old crow.

"And one more thing," shouted Old Man Olson over the squeaking wheels, the clip clop of the horses' hooves and the flying clods of dirt, "You can thank your lucky stars you didn't get picked by one of them pinheads back there."

"Pinheads," Mabel muttered.

"You won't be wasting time in no brain factory with a bunch of nincompoops neither."

Mabel laughed, slapping her knee.

"When I was a whippersnapper, about your size," said Old Man Olson, "I snuck out the back door of that little jailhouse they call school before teach' knew I'd give her the slip and never did go back."

I raised my voice. "The Reverend promised I'd be sent to school."

Old Man Olson nudged his wife. "Ain't deef after all, but looks like we got us a dummy. Ain't never seen inside a school. Can't read nor write."

"I can too!" I felt more frustrated and angry than ever. "But there's more to learn than just reading and writing. All placed out kids must go to school at least through eighth grade, or as long as the state requires. Reverend Brace said so."

"How'd you get so smart if you ain't never been to school?" Old Man Olson growled.

"My Ma taught me."

Old Man Olson scratched his head. He only had two or three hairs on it. "I thought you was an orphan," he said.

What was the point of answering. I just glared at rocks bouncing off the buggy wheels and flying in the road.

"The kid's all played out," Mabel said.

"My Ma taught me, before she passed on." I had to make that clear. Seemed like it was good enough, but of course, it wasn't. Old Man Olson stood up, gripped the reigns with one hand and whipped the horses into a gallop. He was raising a thick cloud of dust, which followed us, as the horses raced down the road. I went bouncing against the hard seat, my head knocking against the buggy.

Looking out, I got a glimpse of some sturdy barns, simple wooden farmhouses, dogs rushing out to chase us as we passed. One farm looked about like another until we came to a huge red barn, healthy fat cattle in the pasture, big strong draft horses, and a large, nice looking farmhouse with wide front porch. Could this be the place? Maybe it wouldn't be so bad after all.

But we passed on by without slowing down. Farther on down the road the horse pulled into a long, dusty lane, then continued along a bumpy path through a field and stopped with a jerk before an unpainted barn that leaned sadly to one side.

Mabel hopped out and tramped through a tangle of weeds towards a tumbledown shack. Old Man Olson grabbed my arm and yanked me towards the barn.

"I boarded up this end to make sleeping quarters for the help. I'll take that satchel," he snapped.

"It's mine," I said, pulling back.

"Ain't no more," said Old Man Olson. He snatched it in one swift stroke, like catching a bug, then tossed it in the weeds, blocking my attempt to retrieve my property. He shoved me into the sleeping room. "Now, take off them fancy duds and hand them over."

From a nail on the wall Old Man Olson pulled down a ragged pair of pants and tattered shirt, waved them at me, and growled, "Don't just stand there like a dummy. Put them on and make it snappy, before I get my dander up."

What good would it do to argue? I did what he said.

"You'll be three to a bed. Butch and Joe are in with the cows, so you'd just as leave go see how it's done. Ever tend cows?"

"Ain't seen too many cows in New York City," I said, maybe a little too quick.

"I don't stand for smart mouths," growled Old Man Olson, cuffing my ear.

The horrible thought hit me like a load of rocks falling on my head. What about Iris and Rosie? Were they in for it like me? I'd have to do something about that, but I couldn't figure out what. Olson didn't give me time to work my brain.

⁘

I pinched my nose when the first whiff of manure hit it. Old Man Olson gave me a shove. Before I knew what was happening, I stumbled into the room where two boys sat on milking stools. The older boy had a thick mop of straight brown hair and a long, worried face. Big freckles, even more than I had, covered the fair skin of the redhead. He looked to be about my age. Both boys wore torn, dirty overalls and were grubby, head to toe.

The older boy glanced up, then stared back into his pail. The other didn't look up at all. They sat, heads against their cows, squeezing, like keeping time to music, as milk splashed with pulsing beats into the pails.

"This here's Pete, the new hand," said farmer Olson. "He's a greenhorn, so it's up to you boys to break him in. I got too many irons in the fire, so it's up to you, Joe, to be straw boss. Make sure you keep a tight reign on him. If you need to, use an iron fist, same as I'd do. Got that?"

"Yes sir," Joe said.

Only after farmer Olson left, and long, silent moments passed, did we even try to talk.

The redhead squirted milk at one of the barn cats, then laughed as its mouth opened to catch it. "I'm Butch," he said. "We sneak in a couple laughs—when we dare. Can't be too careful though."

"I'm Joe," said the tall boy without a smile. "Welcome to purgatory."

"Feels like a furnace in here," I said, mopping my forehead with a sleeve.

"Wait 'til threshing day, and you'll find out what hot is," Joe said.

"This is closest I ever got to a cow," I said, fanning myself. "Sure a mess of flies in here."

"We got to break you in," Joe said. "We're just about done with these two, then we'll toss you a pail and learn you the basics. Come on over, but take her easy. Bossy goes nuts if you rush her."

"You can forget about that," I said. "This ain't my style. I'll stay the night and hit the road in the cool of the morning. Thanks anyhow."

Joe glanced at Butch. "This kid's green as grass," he whispered. "Still wet behind the ears."

"Just as fool headed as we was," Butch said.

When the last drop had been squeezed from both cows, those boys set their pails aside, and Joe motioned Butch and me towards the open door. Joe peeked out.

"All clear," he whispered, then squatted on his haunches, motioning for us to do the same. "Hadn't ought to keep the girls waiting."

At first I didn't get it. Then I caught on. The girls were cows.

"The old buzzard threw my satchel in the weeds," I said. "I'd best go out and fetch it."

"Don't bother," Butch said. "Your duds are gone for good. He done us the same way. More than likely, he's already sold them."

I hadn't expected a dirty rotten crook out here in the boonies, but, not knowing yet if I could trust these two, I tried to act like nothing. "How long you fellows been doing this?"

"A year."

"Almost to the day."

"You stuck it out a whole year?"

They both stared at the cows.

"What's holding you?"

Butch and Joe rolled their eyes but remained with tight lips.

"Is the old guy as mean as he puts on?"

"Ten times worse," Joe said.

"Then why don't you clear out? Give the old hayseed the slip."

They stared at the floor.

"You don't know beans," Butch grumbled.

"Go easy, Pal," Joe said. "He can't help it. City slickers don't know chalk from cheese."

"We was city boys once. Now we're just plain old farmer boys," Butch said. He acted cocky about the country boy act he'd picked up in the past year, like I did showing off my street savvy skills.

That Butch kid's main feature was a show-offy smirk. Watching him was kind of like looking in a mirror.

"How'd you wind up here?"

"Same as you. Come by train. They hauled out a bunch of us last year, just like you."

"I thought the New York folks sent out inspectors once a year to make sure things were on the up and up." I said that like I believed it.

"I guess they lost track of us," Butch said. "We got moved so many times, I expect they were just glad to see the last of us."

Joe said, "Enough talk. He'll catch us sure, and then you'll find out what you're up against."

So they went back to their milking, and I watched.

Joe walked over to the door and looked around, then came back in, looking just a little less nervous.

The next time Joe stuck his head out the barn door, Mabel, in her Mother Hubbard apron, stood on the front porch, feet wide apart, swinging the dinner bell.

"Time to put on the feedbag." Joe said. "Then it's chores and hit the hay. Not much night life hereabouts.

"Supper's usually over and done with before we do the evening milking, but tonight, since you and that doggoned train of yours messed up the show, we're going at it backwards, which won't improve the boss's temper. If you ain't come up against it yet, you soon will. The man's got a mean streak wider than the Mississippi! That's a fact."

CHAPTER 6

FARM LIFE
PETE

The screen door squeaked, and a swarm of flies buzzed in as we swung open the back screen door. A flypaper strip, hanging inside, caught what seemed like hundreds of those pesky little critters. Others darted towards the food. We placed our milk pails on the floor by the dry sink and stood, side by side, arms crossed, waiting for orders.

Farmer Olson was already seated at the kitchen table, face tight, like carved stone. "What are you waiting on?" he growled.

"I smell eats," I said, trying hard to put on a winning smile. "What's for supper?"

"Just like bedbugs and head lice," Butch said, "you can count on pork, spuds, and corn bread. Three times a day, every day of the week."

"None of your lip," Old Man Olson growled.

"He didn't mean nothing," Joe said.

"Who asked your opinion?" said Olson.

"I—I didn't mean nothing," Butch began wiping sweat from his brow. He forced a smile and said friendly like, "Good old pork, spuds, and corn bread."

Old Man Olson fixed his eyes on me.

"Won't take much grub to fill up this stray pup. I hear where you come from they eat hog slop from the gutter."

"Hog slop from the gutter!" Mabel chirped.

"Well, don't just stand there like half-wits!" shouted Olson. "Set yourselves down, and stuff it in. Time's money, and we wasted way too much of it going after this little bone picker." His piercing eyes sized me up, like arrows taking aim at a target.

Mabel, stumbling from stove to table, upset a cardboard box. Corncobs went flying all over the place, and a family of cockroaches scampered higgledy-piggledy from their hiding place. Joe nudged me, and all three of us stomped on the bugs. Then we tossed the cobs back in their box and sat down to eat. I'll bet my eyebrows shot up a mile watching Butch and Joe. They went after that food like starved dogs.

"Won't be more than a blink of an eye 'til dark of evening comes on," said Olson, "and you boys still got chorin' to do. Just one more week to get them oats cut and slammed into shocks. Then comes threshing day. You'll need to be up crack of dawn, dig in your heels and get ready for the biggest blowout of the season. Don't look for no fun and games. You'll be needing to work hard and quick as the snap of a horsewhip."

Butch and Joe kept their faces blank, almost like they were dead and didn't feel a thing, while the old man kept shooting off his mouth.

"Neighbor Goodman's always the early-bird. He'll be here before sunup, hustling to mess with them newfangled contraptions," Olson said. "He'll have his pots of grease and oil and belts all lined up just so, checking this and that, clutch, flywheel, and what not. More finicky fuss than you can shake a stick at."

He slapped his knee so loud and hard it made me jump. Butch poked me from behind.

"Old Genevieve done the job with considerable less commotion," Olson said.

"Genevieve's his horse," Butch whispered.

"I hate the very thought of threshing day." Mabel sighed.

"You'll have all the help you need," Olson said in an odd (for him) and gentle tone.

"That don't make it to my liking," Mabel said in a whiney voice. "Goodman will show up when I'm not yet half out of bed, and, before I can throw on my dress, that passel of female busybodies will come swarming in, thick as flies on a dung hill. My stars, wears me out just thinking on it."

"Well now, Mabel," said Olson, "You know good as I do you ain't up to feeding that oversized crew by your own self. Sure, them womenfolk talk their heads off. They're stuck-up and show-offish, but they get the job done, and it's a big one." He patted his belly. "I tell you, boys, them womenfolk serve up the best victuals you ever socked a tooth in: fried chicken, roasting ears, mashed potatoes, pie. Hey!"

He shook a warning finger at us. "You've been at the feed trough plenty long enough." He glanced up at the kitchen clock and snapped his fingers. "Two minutes more. That's it! Wolf it down and get to work!"

We stuffed our mouths, wiping our plates clean with cornbread, swallowed in deep gulps; then scrammed out that squeaking door and jumped off the back porch.

"Ugh!" I moaned. "When it comes to lousy eats, I've had more than my share, but the garbage she served up is the worst so-called food I've tasted yet," Butch laughed. "Old Mabel fries a slab of pork 'til it chews like rubber and tastes like it too. Then she burns the 'taters, and makes sure the corn bread's stale and smelly as second-hand shoes. Count on it, she'll dish up the same slop every meal."

"Watch your mouth," Joe barked at Butch. "Didn't you see the old man's eyes flashing like lightning bugs? One more crack out of you, and we'd all three been splayed out on the woodpile."

"Then you'll hear Elvira sing," Butch said.

"Who's Elvira?" That was a name I hadn't heard before.

"Who do you think?"

"If I knew, would I ask?"

"She's Old Man Olson's girlfriend."

"And he's madly in love with her."

"Elvira's kiss is worse than snakebite."

"You don't want a smooch from her."

Butch made a loud smacking sound.

"But he's married to Mabel!"

Butch and Joe laughed. "We're pulling your leg," Joe said. "Elvira's his razor strap. Get it?" They stopped laughing and got serious.

"The old buzzard will sit there of an evening, giving us the evil eye, stroking that kid-whacker like she was a soft little kitten."

"We can't let down our guard. Always got an eye out. If the old geezer comes roaring across the fields on the reaper, we're obliged to race after him. If we slip up, we get whacked so hard, we're knocked halfway to kingdom come. So we rake up oats, set up shocks, and get the fields set for the big day. The threshers show up bright and early to start loading shocks, ready to get tossed into the big machine."

"You got to jump like a grasshopper," said Butch, "One bad throw might do you in. Not while the crew's here though. That comes later, when nobody sees."

Joe tossed an arm over my shoulder. "The place will turn into a swarming beehive, blistering hot with the sun burning our backs and Farmer Goodman's machines clanging away like thunder."

"Joe and me are old hands," Butch said with a grin. "Tell him about it, Joe."

"Last year, about the time we got here, they'd just got the new threshing machines."

"Modern, up-to-date contraptions!"

"Farmer Goodman put together twelve farmers in a threshing ring. Butch and me worked every last one of them farms."

"Too bad you ain't experienced like me and Joe." Butch swaggered around with a smug expression.

"What kind of experience?"

"We got superior jobs." Joe grinned. "Butch is water boy, and me, well, I'm a bundle pitcher."

"You don't need to be so stuck-up about it," Butch said.

"It's the honest truth."

"Next year I'll be bundle pitcher too." Butch narrowed his eyes.

"Can you ride a horse?" Joe aimed this one at me.

"Never had call to."

Butch laughed. "Well, if you ever could learn to ride a horse good as me, you might get lucky and turn into a water boy, but for now, you ain't good for nothing else but—"

"You'll start out like we did," Joe said. "Straw boy."

"A moron could be straw boy," said Butch.

"Lay off, Pip-squeak," Joe tossed an arm over my shoulder. "Last year Butch was straw boy. He's stepped up in the world, and the promotion's gone to his head."

"Look here, Pete," Butch said. "You'll be standing there where the straw comes flying out the spout, and you'll have to keep on raking 'til you got a pile like a mountain. Straw sticks to your skin and flies in under your shirt, pants, and socks, but you daren't scratch an itch, or take a drink of water, even if you're bone dry like a desperate man in the desert."

⁓

When we reached the barn, we stopped talking and got to work, pitching manure through the open barn door into the pile outside. We filled the feed troughs with hay, and fed the pigs. When we got back to the house, we hauled the strained milk into the root cellar. Then, at last, sick of drudgery, we trudged back to our sleeping quarters.

Once inside Joe spoke up. "O.k.," he said with a sigh. "It's safe to talk now. The old geezer goes to bed right after supper."

"Well, how come you're orphans? What happened to your folks?" I said it first thing. I was that curious. "Are your folks dead?"

"Not mine," Joe said. "Not so far as I know."

"What's your story then?"

"Too many mouths to feed."

"How many's that?"

"Sixteen, plus Ma and Pa."

"So?"

"So it was earn my keep or do without."

"I never did have folks," Butch said. "A crazy old lady took me in. She said I got dropped on her doorstep. I don't recollect. She kept a roof over my head 'til I was eight and then bit the dust. I knew I'd get kicked out when the landlord showed up, so I took to the street."

"Butch and me got together one day, fighting off a gang," Joe said. "We teamed up after that. Been thick as thieves ever since, though we've tamed down some."

"We were street toughs, ornery as mules," Butch said.

"Planned our maneuvers and got right handy at swiping food from stalls, picking pockets, things like that," said Joe.

"Once we'd showed what we were made of, we got called on to join up with a gang," Butch said. "Seemed the thing to do."

"We strutted around twirling key chains we'd swiped. Real big shots."

"But the cops were onto the bums in our gang, long before we joined up."

"Didn't take a week. All of us, the whole kit and caboodle, got tossed in the jug."

"After a month or two, a preacher sprung us. I expect he thought he was doing something fine when he put us in that orphanage, but it sure did cramp our style. I expect you know all about that. We planned to bust out, but before we got around to it, they herded us, like hogs set for market, onto a train and dropped us off in Hartfield. First time we ever knew there was such a place. But we're still here, stuck in the sticks."

"They took us to the opera house, pushed us up on stage, and looked us over head to toe, like livestock at the county fair.

Somebody gave us a tip, so we played the game and put on like fine, upstanding boys who'd never gripe no matter how they used us. The kind they could take home for a pet, you know. By George, it worked. We flexed our muscles and showed our strong backs and got picked right off."

"We fooled them good," Joe said, "but didn't take long before we got in Dutch. We struck out three times."

Butch slapped his knee and laughed. "We was always dreaming up high jinks, skylarks, and such. First place we caught us a mess of frogs, filled up the beds, and tucked them in under the covers. The little buggers wouldn't stay put, and got to jumping from pillar to post and back again."

"You'll find, Pete," Joe said, clapping a manly grip on my shoulder, "as you go along in life, some folks just don't know how to have a good time."

"Second place," Butch continued, "just to pass the time, when we weren't on the job, we caught and tamed us a big old bull snake."

"We named the critter George and got him so civilized he come to think he was part of the family and took up residence in the parlor."

"They'd built onto the old house, which was no more than a log cabin with open beams. But they kept the parlor in the old-timey part." Butch rocked back and forth, laughing. "That pet snake curled up nice and cozy on a crossbeam."

"Worse luck, good old George lost his balance and fell off."

We all three jerked around when a loud beller came out of Bossy and another one from Cora. Butch stopped to think, but then went on. "Maybe old George jumped. Who knows what really got into him."

"But he landed in Aunt Molly's lap."

"She was sitting there in a rocking chair, wearing her Sunday go to meeting black dress, sipping sassafras tea."

"Can't you just picture it?" Butch snickered.

"Those folks kicked us out faster than you could skin a cat."

"Third place we got on fine, though."

"But Sundays were dull as prayer meeting," Joe said.

"Thinking just to liven things up, we tossed a bit of birch fungus in the drinking water, stirred it up, and waited for results."

"We'd read up on its finer points in *Home Library of Useful Knowledge*." Butch laughed 'til he turned red, and big tears welled up in his eyes. "Birch fungus is absolutely guaranteed one hundred percent to bring on the trots."

Butch and Joe slapped their knees and gave out loud belly laughs. Wiping his eyes, Butch gasped, "We sent Grandpa, Grandma, Ma, Pa, the whole kit and caboodle hotfooting it to the two holer."

"They did not take kindly to our enterprising ways," Joe said.

"So then we packed up, set to move on yet again."

"But, being upstanding, churchgoing folk, after careful consideration, they turned the whole thing upside down and allowed as how we could stay."

"Dragged us along to prayer meeting though and then made us stand up front and own up to our evil ways."

Joe bit his lip, got up and peeked out the door, then came back, giving a nod to Butch. "All clear," he said. "The old buzzard's likely sawing wood."

"All them good folks fell down on their knees singing Hallelujah and prayed 'til they were about blue in the face," Butch said. "After all the commotion, they announced they weren't about to give up on us."

"The good Lord must have whispered in somebody's ear, they had a mission in life, and it was us."

"Next thing you know, they got all fired up to turn us into Sunday School boys."

"We tried our level best to help them out."

"But we just weren't cut out for it."

Joe pulled out a bandana, mopped his forehead, checked the door again, and continued talking. "One fine Sunday, while they were reading their Bibles, we snuck out the back door for a breath of fresh air and happened on a pile of corn silk, all dried out and perfect for a little experiment."

"Scraps of paper were easy to filch," Butch said.

"Same thing with the hooch and matches."

"Kitchen matches hung in their holder by the cookstove, and hooch was nice and handy in the medicine cupboard. All this while they were reading scripture in the parlor."

"A singing preacher couldn't pass up them opportunities."

Joe drummed his fingers, eyeing the door. I could tell he was scared the old man might fool us and show up, but he finished the story anyway. He sure did like spinning a yarn.

"We got all cozy in a pile of straw out in the barn and got drunk as fiddlers."

"Smoked 'til we went green in the face."

"Never could remember just how it all came to be."

"But next thing you know, as folks said later, flames came shooting out the haymow."

"They even began to think, with all that thick smoke pouring out, the world was coming to an end, and judgement day was begun."

"All the neighbors came, tossing pails of water. As they tell it, each pailful hissed for a second or two, and then the fire blazed up worse than ever."

"Horses whinnied, cows bellered, dogs yelped, but the neighbors got them all out. Hauled us out too, but the shame of it was, the barn went up in smoke. Burnt to a crisp. Nothing left but cinders."

"So now they were bound and determined to lock us up for good and all."

"But before you could sneeze, Old Man Olson showed up. We didn't know him from a bale of hay back then, so at first glance, we thought God sent him down from Heaven, not knowing he came straight from the other place."

"Standing there in the black remains, he stood head to head with Sheriff McCarthy." Joe got up and took another peek out the door, then hurried back. "We watched them squinty eyes look us up and down, inspecting our every wart and pimple, head to foot, and then we heard him swear he could reform the evilest, most depraved criminal types."

"The man can talk the bark off a tree."

"Sheriff McCarthy sidled over to have a private talk with us. Said we might could get one last chance, if we'd turn over a new leaf."

"We'd go along with most anything," Butch said, "being up a creek without a paddle, as the saying goes."

"Sheriff told Old Man Olson he was free to take us, and good luck."

"We figured it beat reform school."

"Were we ever wrong. Dead wrong," said Joe.

"Well, why in tarnation don't you just run away?"

Butch and Joe eyed each other. "Take a peek under these shirts," Joe said, making a motion with his head, "but use the soft touch." I tiptoed behind them and lifted up first Joe's shirt, then Butch's, sucking in my breath, as I looked at the deep purple scars across both backs.

Pretty soon Joe broke the silence. "After the first larruping, we slunk off like whipped pups, bawling our heads off, but then, since all we wanted was to get shut of this cussed place, we put our heads together and cooked up the perfect hideaway."

"The big haystack," Butch interrupted. "We hollowed out a cubbyhole with little cracks for air, so we'd be able to take in a breath or two."

"Had it all planned out just perfect,"

"Hide in the hole; sneak off after dark."

"But once he saw we were missing, he sicked those infernal dogs on us. They smelled us out in less time than it takes a cat to kill a rat. Must've thought we were chopped liver."

"Old Man Olson snapped his razor strap and one by one gave us each another walloping, worse than the first."

"Next time he swore he'd chop us up in little pieces, dig us down deep in the dirt, and tell the sheriff we'd run off."

"He'd do it too," Butch said. "There ain't no doubt about that."

After all that talk we were good and ready to hit the hay. "The bed ain't made for three," Joe said, but Butch and me are used to a tight squeeze. Back in the city, when we got lucky enough to find a place

Butch and me'll stick to the outsides going this way. You plop down in the middle going the other way.

that somebody'd let us sleep in, we'd cram in four or five. The way we'll do it now, Butch and me'll stick to the outsides going this way. You plop down in the middle going the other way. We won't aim to trouble you none, but don't get all put out if somebody's big toe pokes you in the eye."

Butch rubbed his eyes. Nothing mattered but a chance to lie down and rest. We hung our clothes on nails in the wall and plopped down on the bare mattress.

"Too blamed hot to mess with covers," Joe said, tossing the dirty blanket on the floor. "Well—good night."

We crammed ourselves in and kept quiet, listening to the cicadas, while mosquitoes buzzed around our heads and feet. Butch turned over. I tried but couldn't do it, squirmed miserably, then tried again. Joe said, "How's a fella' supposed to get any shut-eye?"

"I can't sleep," Butch said.

"Me neither," I said.

"Too blamed hot."

"Too many bugs." All three of us sat up, and Joe lit the lantern. Tiny gnats hovered around the light as kerosene stink spread through the air. Then, with a thoughtful look on his face, he doused the thing. Even in the dark I could see those boys' shapes in the dim light of the moon. "We'd best not shine a light," Joe said. "The old coot measures how much kerosene we use. And if he wakes up and sees even a glimmer, he'll jump on us like a vampire, fixing to suck up our blood."

Joe poked me. "We told you our stories," he said. "Now it's your turn. How'd you come to be an orphan?"

"I'm not," I said. "Not exactly."

"You came on the orphan train."

"Well, they call us orphans, but in my case it doesn't fit. Pop's still this side of the grave—just can't hold a job."

"Well then, where's your Ma?"

I didn't want to talk about it, but they kept needling me. "She took sick," I finally said. "So bad she shook like a leaf in a windstorm, head to foot, with fever and chills. One day she started acting up, addle-brained, talking to ghosts, reaching up, smiling, laughing, shaking hands, like she was meeting up with President Hayes himself, only looked to me like she was grabbing onto thin air. I got the cold shivers.

"Pa was passed out cold, and I hadn't the least notion what to do, so I ran out in the street looking for somebody, anybody, to help out. I didn't know what else to do, but nobody gave a rip. When I'd start in telling my story, they'd wheel around and go the other way, so I tore back in to do for her best I could, but she'd already took her last breath."

Butch and Joe didn't say anything. I figured they were paying their respects.

I drew in a few deep breaths, ashamed to tell the rest, but I did. "Pop's been a hopeless drunk, long as I can recollect."

"Did he sober up when your Ma passed on?"

"When he came to, he went nuts. Even worse than usual. Smashed plates, smacked holes in the walls, pitched whatever he could lay hands on out the windows."

"So what did you do?"

"The landlord kicked us out, Pop ran off, and I took up a trade."

"Joined a gang?"

71

"Nope. Honest work. Peddling papers. Well, of course, I picked a few pockets just to make ends meet."

"Where'd you sleep?"

"In the alley—with the street rats. That's what they call us, you know."

"We're familiar with the term," Joe said. "We were street rats too."

"It was late February," I went on, "bone chilling cold. No blankets. No warm coats. We snuggled up together in a heap, best we could."

Butch and Joe nodded.

"Every day a bruiser, Big Al, came strolling by. Never missed a day. Always whistling Yankee Doodle. He'd toss me two cents and rip a paper off my pile. One day he stopped and bent down right next to me. I was pretty short back then. He aimed to chew the fat. Seemed he took a fancy to me. Kidded around some, spinning yarns, poking fun. Well, that day we made a deal. I'd sweep out his tobacco shop; he'd let me sleep on the floor. Inside. No more dirt and rain. No more freezing half to death. I'd reached paradise."

"You got snookered," Butch said with a snort.

"Hey! Big Al saved my life." I wasn't going to let Butch or anybody else throw mud at Big Al. "That same frosty morning, before Big Al came by, I woke up in the usual heap, chilled to the bone. There wasn't a breath of heat coming from the kid next to me. When I put my ear up to his mouth, listening, and then felt for a heartbeat, it was plain as a nail in your shoe, the kid was a chunk of ice. At least he was out of his misery."

I could hear Joe scratching his head, "How'd you end up here?"

"I did some bad things and got sent up."

"Sent up you say?"

"You mean state pen?"

"Worse. Ever hear of *The Tombs?*"

"You were in *The Tombs?* Holy smoke! That's where they put the hard cases."

"It's the worst hole in Five Points," said Joe, "and that's saying something. Everybody knows Five Points is the lousiest slum in the city, and *The Tombs* is filthy, full of rats, varmints, busting at the seams with crooks and lawbreakers."

"You've got that right. It was so chuck-full, they couldn't find a spot for a kid, so they tossed me in with a safe-cracker, the most respectable of the lot."

"No lie!" I wished I could've seen Butch a little better. By the sound of his voice, I'll bet his eyes lit up like June bugs.

"Did he teach you how?" Joe asked. "Can you crack a safe?"

"Sorry, boys. He aimed to, and we were just getting to the good part, when a preacher showed up. The man was bound and determined to straighten me out, make my Ma up in heaven ever so proud, if I'd change my ways and walk the straight and narrow. He was dead sure the orphanage would do the job."

"Might've been the same preacher that sprung us," Butch said.

"Ten minutes later," I went on, "two cops showed up to haul me off. I wasn't in the orphanage a week before they shoved me on a train with a carload of kids—all down and outers like me—and I wound up here. Who knows why? Folks do the dad-blamdest things."

"We know all about it, little buddy," Joe tapped my shoulder like a real pa would. "Here's a word to the wise—straight talk from me to you." I heard him slap his chest and then poke at me. "I'm telling you as a pal—a partner in this fix we're in. It'll serve you best to take it right. Stay on your toes, eyes peeled, ears wide open. Keep your nose to the wind. If Old Man Olson catches you, even once, loafing, talking back, even dawdling, Elvira, will make your back a perfect match to ours. Got that?"

"Yes sir," I said.

"Sure wish we had a light," Joe said. I could hear him yawn kind of loud, so I took the hint, and I guess Butch did too. We got ourselves arranged in bed once more, like pieces in a jigsaw puzzle, and the talk stopped. But long after the other two lay still, mouths open, softly breathing in and out, I sat up in bed, scratching bug bites, wondering what new torments tomorrow would bring—unless—I could manage to escape.

CHAPTER 7

MY NEW HOME

IRIS

I'd been pulled out like a bad tooth, and it hurt even worse when they dragged me from my little sister. Next thing I knew I was bouncing around with each bump in the road against a hard wooden platform. My legs hung down from the back end of the buckboard. I tried to keep my mind busy, so I wouldn't go crazy, tried to think of a way to rescue Rosie, but I couldn't do a thing about what had happened until I figured out where I was going. Maybe I shouldn't even try. After all, it seemed like she got a good home. But how would I know for sure? Just because they're rich doesn't mean they're nice.

I was determined to find Rosie. I knew she'd really miss me, and I'd made a promise I had to keep. I felt like a steamed up tea-kettle, trying to whistle, but right now it didn't seem a whistle or a scream would help. I'd been tossed in back of their wagon. Maybe they thought I was a dog or a sack of flour. Road dust was flying through my hair. When I turned around to look, there sat farmer Albert and his wife, Minnie, riding comfortably up front like the king and queen of the prairie.

That blast furnace July sun blazed down on me. The wind, breathing fire, messed up my already tangled hair while the wagon rumbled down the dirt road. I craned my neck to get a good look at Albert and Minnie, squinted my eyes and glared at them, but they faced the other way and didn't see. Then I muttered under my breath, "Dirty rats! Dirty rats!" I said it soft so they couldn't hear. I had to say something to make myself feel better. It did seem to help a little bit. What would become of me with those two in charge? How could I get away?

Flora was dead, and the only person that mattered was Rosie. If and when I found out where she was, I had to find a way to set her free, to get us both out of this mess. If I'd realized what we were stepping into, I would have grabbed her hand and bolted before we got herded onto that train. We could have run for it—but where would we have gone? What could we do?

For as long as I could remember, even with Flora in charge, I'd felt like running away, but I never tried it. Rosie needed me, and I loved her like she was my own child. What we had, even when it was bad, seemed safer, a better choice, than running off on our own with no money and no way of getting food or anything.

In the city, folks smiled and made a fuss over Rosie. She's little and cute. Folks liked to look at Flora too, but all I had to show was a plain face, big feet, and wild red hair. I sat there thinking of all the strange things that had already happened, that crazy, mixed up life with Flora, our fun loving, beautiful Ma. Even in that last, cramped room in Five Points she had tried to keep us clean, dressed in nice clothes, with the promise of better days "just around the corner." The way it ended was horrible, but there was no changing things now. It seemed my only chance was to keep my mouth shut, stay out of trouble, at least for a while, and then somehow, some way, I'd find a way to save my little sister.

Albert steered the buckboard into a farmyard. It looked like others we had passed along the way, except this barn needed paint. So did the clapboard house. The tall, rusty windmill towered over a big water trough for the horses. A skinny, spotted dog came running, wagging his tail as he barked.

Minnie said, "Don't let the mutt worry you none. He don't bite unless you come at him fast. That's sure to scare him. Don't mean no harm. Just kind of skittish."

"He will bite, though," said Albert, "if he don't know you, so don't go at him too fast. Walk slow and kind of look the other way. You got to make friends easy, careful, like walking on ice." I tiptoed as far from the dog as I could, while he kept his evil eyes glued on me and growled.

Minnie opened the squeaking screen door, waving her liver spotted hands to keep the flies out, and we entered a smelly kitchen piled high with dirty dishes and garbage.

"Ain't much, but it's home," Minnie said with a laugh. "I ain't been up to snuff lately. Not much pep and go, so it'll help out if you sort of tidy up the place. Now, if you don't mind, I'm going upstairs and kind of take 'er easy. Make yourself to home, and if you feel like it, you might just clear up a space to stir up a bite of supper."

After Minnie left the room, I found a chipped dishpan and soap. Albert came in, walking fast, but in a peculiar way, like one leg was shorter than the other. He started a fire in the cookstove, set the teakettle on to heat, then clomped back out the same way, without a word. I wiped my sweaty forehead. The food I was supposed to fix wouldn't be the only thing cooking, but I set my jaw firmly. I figured I'd already suffered through some things most folks couldn't even imagine. I guessed I could stand most anything.

From the window I watched Albert cross the dusty driveway, heading for the barn, where sounds of mooing and horses' neighs got all mixed up together. I had a big job to do and didn't know how to do it. And how would I rescue Rosie? What I'd worried over, on the ride out, kept nagging at me. Would it even be the right thing to do? If I stayed and learned to handle this job, awful as it might be, maybe Rosie would have a wonderful life, with a rich, loving family. Was it selfish to try to rescue her?

As I scrubbed caked on plates and greasy kettles, I mulled over my predicament. At least these folks hadn't yelled at me. I'd be stuck out here in the country with piles of disagreeable work, but it was possible, once I got organized, learned the routine, I could at least stand it.

First thing, I hauled out the garbage and threw it behind the barn. Albert would have to deal with it. The place smelled better when I came back in. As the dishes soaked and came clean, and one spot after another in Minnie's messy kitchen improved, I felt pretty good about myself. I thought about Flora, and how pleased she'd be to see her oldest daughter being a real grownup in this new, strange situation.

Finally, feeling kind of proud of myself, I stood, chin cupped in both hands, surveying that shabby kitchen. There just didn't seem anything in the room to work with. Minnie expected me to make supper, but how and from what? At the orphanage, since I was one of the older kids, I'd helped out in the kitchen, even learned to bake a cake, but I'd never planned a whole meal. And I'd sure never cooked one, not even a side dish, without a cranky grown-up telling me what to do next.

Minnie's kitchen didn't have a pantry or a single cupboard. It had no workbench or dry sink either. A homemade table was stuck in one corner. I figured I could peel and chop on that. On one wall, two rough, cobbled together wooden shelves were stacked up. Some cracked dishes and cheap, rusty utensils were piled on the bottom shelf. The top shelf was untidy. It was cluttered with flour (some of it spilled) corn meal, sugar, and a few other things to cook with.

Opposite the stove, a small table with two chairs was shoved against the wall, so there was just enough room to move through that little room. I sat down and looked at the table cover. You couldn't call it a tablecloth. It was just a worn-out oilcloth with a few patches of color stuck on. It looked like once there had been pictures of drakes, peacocks, and roosters, but only bits and pieces of these pretty things still clung to the brown backing.

I tried to picture how it might have looked when everything was new. Albert and Minnie must have been young once, but that was a real long time ago. Hard to imagine, although I know for a fact that nobody starts out old.

It would have helped if Minnie had bothered to tell me what to fix and where to find things. Under the window I found a cracked old crock filled with dirty potatoes, a sad looking onion, and a bunch of withered carrots.

I sat myself down on a wobbly chair and started brushing clumps of dirt from the potatoes. Soon Albert came clomping in, moving in that strange, bumpy way he had. He must have been hurt in a farm accident. Maybe broke a leg or a foot. He didn't say.

"I expect she didn't give no directions," he said. "Poor soul ain't much for kitchen doings. Never did get the hang of it, and on top of that, she's been poorly of late."

"Sorry to hear it," I said, my head down, so I wouldn't have to look at him.

"You got the makings here," Albert said. "Before I took up with Minnie, see, I bached it a good number of years, so I got a few tricks up my sleeve. Now, you take a pot like this here." He tapped a fingernail on a kettle. "You toss in some 'taters, carrots, onions, whatever you can lay hands on, and boil them up, soft as mush. I'll dump out the boiling water when you get to that part, so you don't get yourself burnt to smithereens. Then you mash up the whole mess with a splash of milk and a hunk of butter, and you'll have good old 'tater soup, and if I know my onions, it'll hit the spot."

With Albert watching every move I made, I peeled the vegetables. As I chopped, he warned me, "Watch out for them pretty little fingers of your'n. It won't do to lop one off."

I could feel my eyes smart. Pretty soon tears were rolling down.

"Them cussed onions can make a grown man cry," Albert said.

I dabbed at my eyes with the hem of my apron. When the vegetable broth started bubbling, Albert said, "A notion just popped into my fool head. I got a corker of a sweet tooth, but my poor Minnie don't know how on God's green earth to do one thing to calm it down, so I was just a-thinking. Little Lady, can you bake up a cake?"

"Hmm. That's the one thing I do know how to do." I stood there and didn't say any more for a minute, thinking hard. "Besides the things on the shelf, I'll need some butter, eggs, and, if you have any—sour milk will do." I said all that quickly, like I knew what I was doing.

"Let me see what I can rustle up," Albert said. "Them kind of fixings are down in the cave. And while'st I'm there, I might just hack off a hunk of side meat. Don't you worry none. I can fry it up my own self." In just a few minutes he was back with all the things I'd asked for and then some.

Albert poured some grease from an old tin can into the frying pan and watched the side meat sizzle, while I set to work putting my cake together. Here was a way I could show I was worth something.

I mixed flour, baking soda, and a few shakes from the saltcellar into one bowl, then creamed the butter and sugar, stirred in an egg and some sour milk. I added a heap of dry fixings, then the runny ones, and back and forth like that, trying to smile at Albert once in a while. I poured the whole mess into a greased baking pan, stuck it in the oven, and after that kept poking the vegetables with a fork until they felt soft as mush.

Minnie showed up when the house filled up with mouth-watering smells. She plunked herself down at the table, tin bowl at the ready, rusty fork and spoon spiked, one in each hand. Albert did all the helpful tasks he'd said he'd do, then cut up the fried meat into little bits and dumped them in the soup.

I hadn't set a place for myself, but Albert fetched a stool, and plopped the soup pot on the table. Then he tossed on an extra bowl and spoon, and said in that rusty gate voice of his, "Set yourself down, Girlie, and have at it."

I was that surprised! Once, a long time ago, Flora came home late at night and woke us up to tell what she'd been up to. She'd gone to a fancy party with a rich gentleman friend. It sounded like a fairy tale, how the servants stood behind folks' chairs and watched them gobble up their dinners. Everybody acted like the servants weren't even there, until they ran out of something. Then they acted like kings and queens, bossing them around right and left.

With that in mind, I figured Albert and Minnie would expect me, the kitchen maid, to stand behind on tippy toes, peeking over their shoulders, so I could jump when they took a notion to act bossy, but they didn't.

Albert thumped the chair, meaning I should sit down, so I did. "Thanks," I said.

"Go ahead. Help yourself," Albert let me fill my bowl first.

Minnie slurped a spoonful right from the pot and said, "This ain't bad soup."

Albert did the same. "Tasty!" he said, smacking his lips. "And something even better's coming, Lady of Mine. This little girlie here baked us up a fine, mouth-watering cake."

I popped up to remove the cake from the oven. I'd almost forgot about it. I was not pleased with its dull color and spotted, crusty top, but taste was, after all, what mattered. When we'd all three finished our soup, although my cake was still warm and unfrosted, falling down some when I cut three slices, I dished it onto plates, and served Albert and Minnie with an anxious smile.

Albert lit into his with a big grin on his face. It was clear he was pleased he'd ordered something nice for Minnie, but in less than a minute, after the thing hit his taste buds, he spat with such force and such an explosion of nasty words, I just about jumped out of my skin.

"I had the recipe in my head. I did everything same as always," I squeaked in a high, nervous voice.

After I tasted a forkful myself, I felt like my eyes would pop out. I clamped both hands over my mouth and raced outside to the pump for water. Albert and Minnie came chasing close behind. Albert worked the pump handle like a big, strapping man, which he was not, and all three of us drank and spat and drank lots more.

"Why?" I sobbed. "Why does it taste so—salty?" Albert and Minnie laughed so hard they had to wipe away tears with their sleeves. Albert slapped his thigh. "It ain't your fault. Fact is, Minnie keeps salt in the sugar can, which just plain slipped my mind. Sorry, Girlie, I plumb forgot."

"My, oh my." Minnie got that out, through spasms of giggles. "We can't feed it to the chickens. Not even the hogs. When it comes to vittles, them critters ain't particular, but sure as salt ain't sugar and sugar ain't salt, they'd slurp it up and drop down dead as doorknobs."

<hr/>

"Bedtime!" Minnie beckoned, leading our little band of three upstairs. Then she pointed her crooked finger towards a door that stood open, and she blew out the lantern. I stumbled through the dark, my hands groping for something solid. I felt like a blind person, trying to touch things and guessing at what they might be. I needed something to hold onto. I grabbed at the wall, then felt around 'til I touched something with the shape of a narrow bed.

<hr/>

I woke next morning to a rooster's crow. The summer sun almost burned through the open window. I reached out for Rosie and then remembered the awful truth. We'd been ripped apart. She was somewhere else, somewhere safe and nice, "Oh please God," I begged.

I could hear cows bellering in the barn. It seemed real close by. The dog yapped so loud, I leaned out the window to scold him. But before I got started, I remembered my place and kept quiet. That nasty pig smell hit my nose. It was mixed with the mildewed smell of decay that reeked all over the place.

Gruff voices rumbled from the next room, but I couldn't make out the words. I'd just tried to sleep through what turned out to be an anxious, restless night. I pulled back the blanket and took a good look at my narrow cot, a rope bed topped by a tightly packed canvas bed tick with a few samples of the stuffing, dried corn husks, poking out from a corner. I felt all itchy, and when I took off my nightgown, I found red spots—bedbug bites. Wouldn't you know.

A pitcher of water inside a large bowl sat on top of a worn-out dresser. That pitiful stick of so-called furniture stood on three wiggly legs with a block of wood where the fourth should have been. I didn't see one pretty thing in the room, just stained floor, cracked walls, and most everything turned the color of dried tobacco.

The portrait of a scowling old crone, framed by a wreath of human hair, hung on the wall, adding a fitting touch to the gloom. If you want to know the truth, the whole place gave me the heebie-jeebies. The picture hung crooked, so I made it straight, but then flying dust blew into my nose and got me sneezing. I shot that old hag a dirty look, and she shot one right back. Those cranky sounds from the next room kept getting louder.

But then I heard something sweet through my open window. A bluebird was perched on the tree branch just outside. It seemed like he knew how I felt and was trying to cheer me up. I leaned on the windowsill, smiled, and said "Hello."

The bird cocked his head and smiled back. Well, not really, but he did look at me. I started thinking, maybe I could change things. Maybe there was a little bit of hope.

My favorite dress was blue gingham with tiny yellow flowers, high in the neck, puffed in the sleeves, and decorated with rickrack around the neck and hem. It flowed down to the floor and had white petticoats underneath. Flora gave it to me one time when she'd left us alone all night. I knew she was trying to make up to me, since she could tell I was really mad. All the same, it was a nice dress, the one I grabbed when we left our tenement room in such a hurry.

I washed and dressed. Brushing my wild red hair didn't do much good, but I did try. Then I put on the same apron I'd used the night before. I was so anxious to beat Albert and Minnie to the kitchen, I raced down the hall towards the stairs. Halfway, I bumped into Albert.

"I've got a hankering for fried eggs, fat back, fried 'taters, and strong black coffee." He barked those orders like a general. "Make them eggs runny." His voice had the ring of a buzz saw, and his eyes popped out like big round buttons.

"Don't get spooked," Minnie yelled from her bedroom. "Albert just got up on the wrong side of the bed."

Once we got downstairs, Albert built a fire in the cookstove, placing straw, kindling, then dried corncobs, striking a match on the side of his overalls and starting a blaze. I paid close attention to every step of it. If I could learn to fire up the stove and manage whatever chores they'd need to have done, I might win them over. Then maybe, just maybe, they might help me find Rosie.

Albert gave me a little nudge and tossed his head, his signal to follow him outdoors. When we got there, he threw open the big cellar door. I peeked in. It was black and scary, like a deep, dark cave. The stairs squeaked with every spooky step going down. When we hit bottom, he whispered in that gravelly voice, "Kind of like a burial pit, ain't it?" He filled a basket and my apron with all the things we'd need for breakfast.

Back in the kitchen I looked things over, first the work table, then the hot stove, then the food. I couldn't figure out what to do next. Albert grumbled, "I expect it's up to me to break you in." He plopped a cast-iron frying pan on the stove, poured in grease from a tin can, and said, "Toss in them 'taters like last night, shove them around 'til they're brown and crispy, and while you're at it, throw some fatback in that pan over there. You got to watch like a hawk. When that's done, throw some eggs in the grease, and don't forget, I like mine runny." Soon the meat was sizzling, eggs were popping, and potatoes sputtering in the smelly grease.

Albert sat down at the table, and I served up his breakfast. He poked at his egg like it was made out of tin. It was sort of scrambled and cooked hard as a plate, but he didn't complain. Then Minnie showed up in her nightdress, long straggly hair uncombed and sticking out all over. Her face was wrinkled, white, and swollen with sleep.

"Something's burnt," she squawked. "A whiff of that'll wake the dead."

"Aw shucks, for a little heifer, she could've done worse," Albert said. "Come on, Girlie." He patted the stool. "Park yourself."

Soon the meat was sizzling, eggs were popping, and potatoes sputtering in the smelly grease.

I filled my plate and asked, "What's a heifer?"

"My stars, the girl's a puddin'head," Minnie said with a great big sigh.

"Pipe down," Albert snapped. Then, like some kind of miracle, he turned to me. "Eat up, Girlie. You'll need all the get up and go you can muster."

Even that awful breakfast tasted pretty good to me. After Albert limped off towards the barn and Minnie tripped upstairs, I set a kettle of water to heat for dishwashing.

It was stuffy in the kitchen with the stove belching heat. I fiddled with the dirty window, but it would only open a little bit. I looked out at the windmill, the water trough, where the horses drank, and then at the crooked barn, badly in need of paint. That awful pig smell again. I washed dishes, cleaned the window inside, and holding my breath as long as I could, I ran out the backdoor to quickly wash the outside as well. My bluebird friend was perched on the clothesline, singing its cheery little song, and I remembered to try looking on the bright side.

Even after all my scrubbing, the kitchen was still pretty greasy, and in the sunlight, streaks showed up on the window, but all the same, I felt I'd done pretty well. Minnie came back down in the same rumpled housedress she'd worn the day before. She'd topped it off with a stained cover-up apron and had her hair pulled back in a bun. Stray hairs went flying every which way.

"Come on, Pun'kin," she piped up. "Bring that pan of scalding water along. Let's go bushwhack a chicken and send her up to glory."

Minnie chased the whole flock, waving an axe. She grabbed one by the feet, slammed it on a tree stump, and whopped off its head.

I couldn't believe what I'd seen. Then she jumped back to watch the poor headless creature hop about in a crazy dance. The scene was getting worse by the minute. Blood spurted from its neck. I grabbed my mouth with one hand, my stomach with the other.

Minnie hung the poor limp thing upside down from the clothesline. When all the blood had come out and the dripping stopped, she dunked it in the hot water. Then she started yanking out feathers by the fistful. "Stuff them in this here," she said, poking a gunnysack at me. "When it's full, hang them on the clothesline to dry. You'll need to fluff them out once in a while, but they'll do for pillows." How could she talk like nothing unusual had happened after what she'd done?

Once, when I looked up and across the lane, Albert stood leaning against the barn door, watching my every move. His straw hat was tilted at a sporty angle on his funny little head. He'd curled his thumbs under his suspenders. My stomach was churning.

While I plucked a few stray feathers, Minnie started bossing. "Now you go fetch some sticks, grab a kitchen match, and start up a nice little bonfire, so we can singe them pinfeathers." I was shaking all over, but I did what she said. When I'd finished, she stuffed one wrinkled hand inside the chicken and yanked out the bloody guts. A strange, disgusting smell filled the air like a poison cloud. "I always aim to save the gizzard," Minnie said, holding the bloody thing next to my nose. I hid behind some bushes and lost my breakfast.

Minnie was giggling, waving at Albert when I came back. "Next time you get to deal with the innards," she cackled. "Now go fetch some clean water. I expect you can work the pump. If you don't know how, you'd best figure it out."

I struggled with the pump. How had Albert done it? I raised the handle. It creaked and groaned. I used all my strength to push it down, then up, then down, and kept it up with all my might until a stream of water gushed into my pail. Even shaking all over, and with my weak stomach, how good it felt to know I'd taught myself a brand new trick.

When I came back after running, water sloshing all the way, Minnie plopped that pitiful bird into its bath. She scrubbed it inside and out, while I watched without saying a word. At last, Minnie held up a carving knife and slapped it around on a whetstone. It made a ringing sound that set my nerves even more on edge.

She must have had a long list of things for me to do. Well, she didn't waste time. Right off she announced, "All right, Pun'kin, I got a job for you. Might help turn a city gal into a fair to middling hired girl. Here's what you do. Chop off two legs, two wings, two thighs, a big fat breast, and whatever's left over goes in the stewpot. Slice them out, neat as a pin, and make double sure—make that triple sure—you don't spoil the wishbone."

CHAPTER 8

HIGH POINT
ROSIE

I sat way up high in a fancy coach, stiff as a board, staring down at the street but not seeing one thing, just remembering all the terrible things that happened that morning. When I thought about how Mr. Jackson yanked me away from Iris, I just cried and cried. I felt like a one-legged girl without her crutch. Once I saw a girl like that in Five Points. I felt like somebody swiped my crutch and left me helpless so that those mean, snoopy folks could peck at and paw over me, and I couldn't do a thing about it.

Then a tall stranger, all dressed up in a fancy suit, showed up. He stood in front of me and tipped his high silk hat, like he'd do for a fine lady. Why did he do that? In that crowd he sure did stick out. The other men wore dirty overalls, and the ladies' dresses were frumpy. Since then I've seen the same prints on flour sacks. I barely got a chance to say goodbye to Iris, and then he whisked me away.

Soon I was sitting up high in a fine carriage, right next to him. He called his buggy a barouche. In New York you only see that kind with bankers and big shots in them. Come to think of it, his fancy rig reminded me of a buggy ride I once took with Iris and

Flora on a sunny afternoon in the city, before everything blew up. Well, it wasn't quite up to this one, but at the time, we thought it was swell. One of Flora's Gentleman friends took the three of us for a ride along Fifth Avenue.

This time I hadn't the least notion where I'd end up. The driver seemed to know how scared I was. He flashed a big grin and said, "Nothing but the best for Mr. Jefferson Hartfeld and friends." He patted the soft leather upholstery. "You're one lucky little girl!

"I've got the best job in Hartfield," he said, "and if you play your cards right, things could turn out very rosy for you."

"I don't need to play cards, Mister," I said. "That's my name. Rosie!"

He laughed. "Yes indeed, Rosie, and there's a good chance in the future you will be known as Miss Rose Hartfield, the heiress."

"Fiddlesticks!" I said. "That's a word I learned from the street rats." I said it, because I didn't have any idea what he was talking about.

He grinned and winked. "I thought you ought to know and appreciate what's happened, because you just hit the jackpot!"

I was about to ask what "jackpot" meant, but just then a small wagon, pulled by a mule, passed by. A girl wearing a yellow sunbonnet was driving. I couldn't help thinking of Iris, and I got all hot and sweaty.

If only I had stomped and screamed, maybe I'd still have my Iris, but everything happened so fast. I'd had no time to figure out what came next. I just did whatever they made me do.

Well, I did try to change things, but it didn't do any good. At the opera house, when we found out they wouldn't let us stay together, I made a horrible face, trying my best to spook that stupid farmer, so he wouldn't mess with either of us. I twisted my mouth like a tiger who'd tear him to bits, but it didn't work. He kept saying mean things about Iris, talking like she'd be just another workhorse.

And then there was that skinny wife of his, with manners like an organ grinder's monkey. Some nerve! She was set on making Iris her servant—her hired girl! A big fat lump swelled up in my throat.

Riding along in that fancy buggy we bumped along the dusty street. I tried to think up ways to get even, but I couldn't come up with anything bad or mean enough. *Now I know how a fly feels,* I thought, *with a swatter slamming down hard, hitting him like a blue streak and squashing the stuffing out of him.*

"Cheer up, kid," Clarence said with a grin. "You're in for the surprise of a lifetime."

———

The ride was over so fast, that before I could think up a way to rescue Iris, the driver shouted, "Whoa," the horses slowed and came to a stop before a great big brick mansion. Clarence named some of the fancy things about the house, the bay windows, pillars, and widow's walk. "I declare!" I said, even though I could hardly get my breath. "We must be riding around in a story book, and this is Cinderella's castle."

Clarence hopped down and lifted me to the ground. "Come along, young miss." He took my hand and spoke in a gentle way that was brand new to me. "I'll see you to the door. Then I'll take my leave, and the maid will let you in."

I gripped his hand, the way Rapunzel in her tower must have grabbed onto the window sill, so she could look down at the prince.

When I was little, Iris used to read me that story. I made her read it over and over. She must have read it at least a hundred times. It was so good. Of course, Iris is a great storyteller. She makes it seem real.

Clarence and I meandered up a winding stone walkway. His big hand felt warm and comforting. The path was lined on both sides with colorful blossoms. "What pretty flowers. Do they have names?" I couldn't think of much else to say, but I was real glad I asked, since he was good at answering questions.

He pointed at each kind, one by one. "Foxgloves, four-o'clocks, snap dragons. There's more, but you won't remember if I give you too many at once. Now for trees, there's oak, elm, maple, and plenty of shade on a sunny day so you can sashay around on this nice green lawn."

Sashay. Nice word. He must have noticed I was fidgety as a squirrel. I've never been one to sit and twiddle my thumbs.

"Oh yes, and you'll like Homer, the gardener," he said. "Splendid fellow. Last summer he put up this trellis." That thing he called a trellis was covered with beautiful climbing roses. He pulled down a flower and stuck it in my hair. "Homer does have a green thumb."

"Look!" I shouted. I know I was all eyes and ears. "There's another path just beyond the trellis. More flower beds and stepping stones. I just love stepping stones!" I was holding onto the rose in my hair and jumping up and down. I hate to admit it, but for just a little while I forgot all about Iris.

We climbed the steps to an enormous front porch that looked like the deck of a great ship. I'd seen some in New York harbor. This place was that big and that grand. Just as we reached the top, the huge front doors flew open. There stood a maid in a white apron and a stiff looking headpiece. She was bigger, taller, and wider, than Miss Harkin, and not near as old, but she reminded me of the old witch, because she wouldn't smile. I didn't get a little hug. Not even a warm touch of the hand. The woman was cold as ice in January.

Clarence tipped his hat, said goodbye, snuck in a little wink, and left me with my new keeper. As soon as the door shut behind us, Agnes showed what she was made of. It wasn't sugar and spice and everything nice.

"So, you got here, did you?" She curtsied, but her face looked like she'd swallowed a sour pickle, and it didn't go down right. I smiled and tried the curtsy thing, but I got all hot and sweaty. My face felt on fire, and I hadn't the least notion how to pull off that bothersome trick.

"Call me Agnes," the woman said in her prickly voice. "Mrs. Hartfield gave strict orders. First I have to clean you up. We allow no filthy street urchins in this fine house. After your bath you're going to your room straightaway. No wandering about. No lollygagging. Come along then."

She dragged me to the kitchen and yanked off my clothes, then practically threw me in a tub of cold water. It was supposed to be warm, but she was in a big hurry and didn't wait for the boiler to heat up. I shivered as she scrubbed and wished she'd hurry up and get me out of there. When I was finally clean enough to satisfy her, she dried me off with a scratchy towel and dressed me in a long nightgown. I was still shivering.

As we started the long walk up the grand staircase, Agnes sniffed, "Pretty fancy, huh? You never saw the like. I can see that." A nasty smirk settled on her mean mouth. "Your eyes are round as silver dollars. These are the kind of things only the well-heeled can afford." She gave a little harrumph and started in again. "The Hartfields ain't just rich. They're blue bloods." She stopped and thought for a minute. "Well, for sure, the mister is."

If that didn't take the cake, I don't know what would. She'd told a whopper! Even two and three year olds know everybody's blood is red, but I let it go. My eyes were just about popping out, watching all the things we passed on the way. Looking up, I saw a sparkling chandelier, huge and dripping with dozens and dozens of sparkling little thingamajigs, and just as many candles stuck out the top to make everything bright and cheery.

All the way up those stairs our feet found a soft path on carpet that felt like velvet. The wallpaper had pictures of pretty, lazy ladies wearing dresses that blew out like sails on a ship. They were pumping high on swings that hung from big leafy trees, and smiley cupids flew around like hummingbirds. All the way up the stairs, new, magical things popped out and more and more and more, like a stairway up to Heaven.

If I'd been my own boss, I'd have stopped to have a good look at those paintings. Big, beautiful ones hung on every wall, but Agnes kept yanking my arm, like she'd do to a dog or a monkey. If only I could spend some time with at least one painting, pretend I walked right in. That would be like visiting storybook land, but Agnes kept poking, pushing, and pulling.

"All right then. Here's your room," Agnes sniffed as she yanked open a heavy door that creaked and groaned, like it really didn't care to be bothered.

"Oh!" My hands flew to my face, as I saw for the first time a room filled with more amazing things than I'd seen in my whole entire life.

"That's a princess bed," Agnes said, "and that fancy thing on top is a canopy. You never heard of such things before, did you?" The huge room was filled with the finest furniture and toys. My eyes flew right to the bookshelves, cram-full of beautiful children's books, and then to the dressing table with three mirrors stuck together so you could see yourself, front and sides all at the same time. There were bottles of wonderful smelling things. When I picked up a blue bottle and started squeezing its little ball, the smelly juice inside squirted all over the place. Agnes ripped the thing from my hand and said, "Look but don't touch!"

Oh, what's the difference, I thought. Try as she might, Agnes couldn't spoil my fun. I just wandered around the room, thinking I must be in a dream. I sat down at a little desk, just my size, all fitted out with papers, pen, and pencils. I'd never seen the like. Flora couldn't afford any of those things. With her we used chalk and a slate. I moved to a short table, with an embroidered cloth and a blue and white tea set, all ready for a party. There was a dolly corner with a small wooden rocker, a wicker doll buggy, a pretty doll with a porcelain head, real hair, and lots more.

Before I opened the twin doors to the wooden cabinet, I stopped and gave Agnes a polite look. I was sure, if I knew what was good for me, I'd better ask permission.

"I wondered when you'd get around to that one," she said. "It's a French armoire, very fine and very expensive. I know just what you're thinking. You're a poor little orphan, and you never heard of such things." She didn't say I couldn't, so I opened the doors,

I just wandered around the room, thinking I must be in a dream.

slowly, just in case I'd get yelled at, but she didn't yell, just kept her eyes stuck on me, like a bird eyeing a worm. Inside was a whole row of dresses, fit for a princess—silk and satin with ribbons, ruffles, and flounces.

"Okay, now I understand," I said. "This is their little girl's room, and I shouldn't be in here at all."

"There has never been a child in this house," Agnes answered right back. "Not 'til now." Her black eyes were flashing.

Another thought popped into my head. Now I was pretty sure I'd figured it out, but it was so sad. I looked at the floor, the way I'd expect folks would at a funeral. "When did the poor girl die?" There, I'd said it.

"They never did have one, silly. Not together, and not in this house, anyway."

"Well then, why are all these pretty things here? Do they belong to Cinderella?" *Oh, the whoppers that woman could tell.* That's what I was thinking.

"You say the oddest things, child," Agnes said. "The fact of the matter is, Mr. Hartfield drew up a list of everything a girl your age could possibly want or even dream of wanting. Then he talked some high-priced shopkeeper in Chicago to ship a wagonload all the way to Hartfield. Cost no object. I heard it from Miss Grandquist, the old maid next door. She's a great one to poke into other folks' business. My stars! She was more than glad to come over and arrange everything once it got here. Well, it's beyond me why Mr. Hartfield would go to such trouble and expense for a charity case, but the man does the most peculiar things. Don't ask me why?"

"Why?" I said, hoping to get her goat. I did.

"That will be about enough out of you," Agnes said, shaking a finger in my face.

Iris and I had grown so used to Miss Harkin at the orphanage that this crab apple didn't scare me one bit. I grinned, thinking how the two of them would squabble if they ever got together. Then I slapped both hands over my mouth, so Agnes couldn't read my mind.

"You'll soon figure out, the missus ain't one bit like the mister," Agnes said. "They're night and day, but don't get me started. Now, you're to stay up here and mind your own business. Is that clear?" She kind of squinted, with one finger pointed at my nose.

"Yes Ma'am." I was about to try the curtsy thing again but thought better of it.

The fun I had with that first little peek at the paintings and fine furnishings had made me want more. I decided that tomorrow I'd ditch Agnes and see the rest of the mansion all by myself. Her orders to stay put in my room and not lollygag about were just a way to show she was boss. Well, she wasn't. Not of me.

I knew, deep down, I'd better get to business soon and go looking for Iris, but first I'd have myself a lark, a sightseeing trip through this fairy tale palace. Once I found Iris, maybe we could sneak in the back way so she could see it too. I could hardly wait to show it to her. And what fun we'd have reading books and playing with new toys in my brand new room—a room fit for a princess. For now, all I had to do was get Agnes out of my way. Then—whoopee!

Next morning, as sunshine poured in through the lace curtains, clumsy Agnes banged her way in, toting a tray full of fancy covered dishes. I stretched and yawned as she slammed down the tray on the little table. "Now, Miss, you're to sit here and eat breakfast with your new dolly. Mr. Hartfield's off on a business trip. Mind you, be careful of that doll. Her head's made of porcelain." Agnes clucked and shook her head. "I don't know what the man could've been thinking."

The oatmeal reminded me of the cold, thin gruel at the orphanage. We called it muddy water, but only when Miss Harkin couldn't hear. This was thick and warm, but it was still porridge, not what I'd hoped for. On the other hand, it was sprinkled with sugar, and drowned in cream, a big improvement.

When the last bite had disappeared, Agnes washed and dressed me in a fresh new frock. Then she sat me down at the vanity table to brush and comb my curls. I kept staring from one mirror to the next. It was fun to see myself from all sides.

"You hit the jackpot," Agnes said. "I hope you're properly thankful."

"Oh yes Ma'am." I said. There was that jackpot word again.

"Well then, hurry up. Miss Henderson's waiting in the library, and she won't stand for a tardy pupil."

"Miss Henderson? Who's that?"

"You'll find out soon enough." Agnes rubbed my face with a soft, white napkin, then rushed me down the hall. She signaled to hush, as she pulled open the heavy, creaking door. A frowning woman with spectacles and hair pulled straight back in a bun sat at the head of a long table. Wow, I'd never seen anything like it before. Piles of leather-bound books were neatly stacked next to a jar of sharp pencils. Instead of chalk and slates there was a stack of shiny new paper that didn't even have scribbles on it.

She cleared her throat. "You shall address me as Miss Henderson. I shall call you Miss Rose."

"Good morning, Miss Henderson!" I laid it on thick, pasting on a cardboard smile. I knew, at least for now, I'd better act like a nice girl, even if I didn't feel like one.

"I have been employed by Mrs. Hartfield as your governess." She kept talking, not once moving those bulldog eyes from me. "In the state of Iowa, few people are fortunate enough to have a private governess. Your privileged situation is highly unusual."

I almost said, I hope so. I was starting to wonder if Mr. and Mrs. Hartfield were part of a story like "Hansel and Gretel" or "Cinderella," but I bit my tongue and let her rattle on.

"The Hartfields are exceptional people," she said. "They descend from distinguished English families. Mr. Hartfield is the most important gentleman west of the Mississippi River, and he insists your education be of the highest caliber."

"I bet I know more than most kids my age," I said, "thanks to Iris." I was kind of proud of myself, I'd finally thought up something smart to say. "Ever since we were little, Iris played school with me. Sometimes Flora played too, and that's how I learned to read and cipher like a big kid."

"Pay attention! Remember everything I am about to say," said Miss Henderson.

I straightened up and put on a stony face like hers. I thought that might make her laugh, but the poor lady was born without a funny bone.

"I have instituted what I call the four P's. In your pursuit of knowledge you must be painstaking, precise, punctual, and most of all, you must persevere!"

"Bet I can read as good as you," I said.

"As well as you!" she snapped, "and I don't think much of children who tell lies." Her frown made her look a lot like Miss Harkin.

"I don't either," I said, all nice and polite.

"Have you ever attended school—anywhere?"

"My sister Iris taught me at home. Flora helped some." I wanted to say more—to tell how much I loved Iris, and how fun it was, playing school, but I could see she didn't want long answers.

"And who is this Flora?"

"My Ma," I said. "She used to be."

"Then refer to her as Mother."

"Nope," I said. "We called her Flora. Better for business."

Miss Henderson's face turned red as a brick, like she'd looked down and found her dress unbuttoned.

"Flora bought us a book about princesses and queens and frogs turned to princes. All kinds of magic. I think the world is kind of magic. Don't you?"

"Of course not," said Miss Henderson.

I twirled around the room and had a good laugh as my skirt flew out, big and wide. "This is my castle." I sure was enjoying putting on a little show. "I'm Cinderella, and I'm magic!"

"Sit down and stop that." Miss Henderson pursed her lips.

I knew she meant business, so I sat down while she kept up the lecture.

"You have become the beneficiary of great good fortune. There is not another home in Iowa with wealth and luxury to compare with this one."

"Magic." I whispered it, but Miss Henderson heard and didn't appreciate it one bit.

"Remember your place and be suitably grateful." She sure had a mean look on her face.

"Oh, I sure am grateful," I said, "except for the one thing that's all wrong, and that's about Iris and me. We tried to tell them down at the opera house, but they wouldn't listen. It's no good splitting us up. We're a pair! I need her, and she needs me!"

Miss Henderson frowned and tapped her pencil. "Mr. Hartfield requested one child. One seven year old girl. Do you understand? One."

"My bed's plenty big enough for the both of us," My voice turned squeaky. "We always slept together. That's not a problem, and Iris doesn't eat very much." My brave self had run out of steam, and I'd turned back into a poor orphan, holding out the tin cup and getting nothing.

"Let me make one thing perfectly clear." Her voice was sharp and cruel. "You must forget about Iris. She has a good placement. She will get along just fine."

"No, she won't! She wants me! I need her!" I even stomped my foot. A lot of good that did.

Miss Henderson started in, like she hadn't heard a word I'd said. "Time for today's lesson." She raised her chin, screwed up her mouth, and drummed her fingers. "I have been employed by the Hartfields to begin your instruction with the basics: reading, writing, and arithmetic." Seemed like she was practicing for a declamatory contest. I almost asked, but thought better of it. Miss Henderson pulled a large book from the shelf, one with tiny print, lots of words to a page, and not a single picture.

"You say you are a reader, Miss Rose?" She poked the book in my face. Her mouth twisted up, like she was trying to smile, but her face would crack if she did. "Outside voice, please."

"*Ivanhoe*, chapter one," I read:

> "'In that pleasant district of merry England which is watered by the river Don, there extended in ancient times a large forest, covering the greater part of the beautiful hills and valleys which lie between Sheffield and the pleasant town of Doncaster.'"

I kept reading fast. I don't mean to brag, but I went twenty-five pages without a single mistake, well, maybe one or two, but hardly even stopping to breathe.

"That will do," Miss Henderson made me stop. She didn't say one thing about how good I did, just poked a piece of paper at me and told me to write down answers to her questions. "I am quite sure you did not understand a word of what you read." She used that snappy voice that sounds like a scolding. Her eyes got all squeezed up into little slits. It was fun having real paper and a pencil. I wrote the answers lickety split and handed my paper back with all the answers. I knew they were right, and I couldn't help laughing, but Miss Henderson didn't like the joke.

"Here!" she slapped another piece of paper, pencil, and an arithmetic book in front of me. The book's cover, in small print, said, "For Advanced Pupils." I knew what she was up to.

"Page forty-three," she gave out orders. "Write your answers quickly. Your work will be timed. When the little bell rings, stop. Immediately!" I worked those problems almost as fast as my pencil would fly and finished before the little bell rang. Boy, did I want to laugh, but I thought better of it.

I guess she got tired of the game, because she tapped her pencil and announced, sort of like Mr. Jackson down at the opera house, "I shall suspend lessons for today, but report tomorrow at the same hour and in the same place. Do not forget the four P's. Repeat after me. I must be painstaking, precise, punctual, and I shall persevere!"

I said the four P's. Maybe I sounded a little sassy. I wanted to do my magic dance. Iris would have liked that, but Miss Henderson didn't look like she was in the mood, so when she turned away, I slipped out the door and hurried off to explore the house.

When I got far enough from the schoolroom, so I wouldn't get caught, I wandered from room to room, looking over the fancy furniture, bouncing on sofas, fingering the gorgeous curtains and drapes. I even took off my shoes and stockings. It felt so good with my bare feet on those carpets. Most of all, I took my time looking at the beautiful paintings and played my favorite game, pretending I could walk right in and live inside the picture.

When I reached the attic and looked down through the little window, it seemed like the highest point in the world, like the top of Jack's beanstalk. Below were little houses on tree lined streets. Everything looked like toys. I kept wondering which toy house had Iris in it and if she'd shrunk to doll size.

Like Jack, I somehow had to get rid of the giant. In my case, I had two giants. I'd have to get rid of Agnes and Miss Henderson. Jack killed his giant. I wouldn't go that far, but I could give them the slip. I'd climb down my beanpole and find Iris. There had to be a way. I'd turn detective.

But I still hadn't seen the dining room, so I slipped down the servant's staircase and was about to peek into the kitchen when I thought about Agnes. What if she was in there? I spun around, lickety-split, and ducked through a back door. There I was, magically surrounded by beautiful gardens.

After being cooped up with Miss Henderson all morning, the bright August sunshine pumped me full of happy thoughts. I wandered from one pretty flower-bed to the next and soon bumped into a little white-haired, bent over man. He was wearing stained bib overalls and carried a spade and watering can. I knew right off he was the gardener.

"Well, if it ain't the new little Miss," he said. "My name is Homer, and I'm pleased to meet you. But why ain't you in the schoolroom?"

"I needed some fresh air," I said.

"Agnes figured that old maid schoolmarm would put you through the paces," he said.

"I cast a spell on her."

"So you came outside to play, did you?"

"Can I please work for you?"

He just smiled, didn't say I could or couldn't, either one.

"I love pretty flowers," I said, twirling about so my new dress would flutter like flower petals. I'd never had a dress that would do it quite so well, and I felt like a ballerina.

"I'm doing some weeding today," he said. "They seem to grow a foot a day this time of year. Tell you what. I pull; you toss. Here's the wheel barrow." Pretty soon I had a big pile of weeds. My pretty dress got dirty, but it's kind of strange, I didn't even care. I told Homer all the funny stories I could think of. He seemed to like them, since he didn't know much about New York.

"You're a very nice man, Homer," I said. "You make these flowers happy. That's why they're so pretty. The pink ones are my favorites." I pointed to a bed filled with beautiful pink blossoms. Their stems were staked to stand up straight. "They're lined up like sisters." I kept going with my fairy tale. "Princesses decked out in their best gowns. Why, they're dancing all the way to the ball. Each blossom is a fine lady."

"'My dress is prettier than yours!' That first flower is using my voice," I said.

"Mine is."

"No mine."

"'We need a prince to settle this. Come here Mr. Snapdragon!'"

"'How do you do, ladies.'" Mr. Snapdragon made a deep bow.

"Whoa! Look there!" Homer interrupted, pointing to the circle drive. A carriage was coming up to the grand entrance. "Here comes Mr. Hartfield's finest, the George IV Phaeton. Only one like it, this side of the Mississippi. Did you ever see such a rig? Cost a bundle! So did them horses!"

We watched the coachman jump down and help the lady out. It was Clarence, the nice man who'd brought me to High Point, still dressed up all fine and fancy.

"That's the missus!" Homer whispered. "Ain't she a queen?" I watched everything about her: perfect face, blond curls shining in the sunlight, fashionable silk dress.

"We're in luck!" Homer whispered. "She's coming this way. She don't pay me no mind, except what to plant and such, but I suspect she's headed here to meet up with you, little miss."

The fine lady came toward us, her parasol clutched tightly, stylish boots clicking along the wide brick walkway. I took a deep breath. This queen from a storybook was to be my new mother. I felt light as a sunbeam, ready to jump into her arms. I'd be pressed against her warm loveliness, and as the princess flowers would dance their way to the ball, I'd go with this beauty and dance to the kitchen. We'd celebrate with milk and gingersnaps. I closed my eyes and breathed in the flowers' delightful smell as the glorious being came near.

Step by step, I heard her rustling skirts. I sighed, opened my eyes, entranced like girls in stories, by the fairy creature who was going to be my new mother. Mrs. Hartfield was so close that I could smell her perfume. She lifted her skirts, just enough to show the fine pointed toe of her handsome leather boot, and gave a little kick. Her toe hit one of the princess flowers. "Pink gladiolus?" She gave a little sniff and pointed a finger, sparkling with its shiny ring, at Homer. "I told you to plant yellow." Her silk skirts rustled past us without looking back.

I watched her go, watched her lively walk and swinging skirts. I didn't want to cry, but I couldn't help it. When she was out of sight, I sat down in the dirt, muddy tears splashing on my dress. More than ever, I just had to find Iris. Somehow, in some magical way, we had to get together and be happy ever after. That's how things turn out in fairy tales, but this wasn't one. Not anymore. I was shaking all over. This was a nasty story with a very bad ending.

CHAPTER 9
COUSIN LAVINIA
ROSIE

I hurried back to my room before Agnes found out I'd escaped. If she brought my meal to an empty room, I'd catch it for sure. I got bread and honey and a big glass of milk. The best part about that was when that old crab left and slammed the door behind.

In the afternoon, when Agnes opened the kitchen door to sweep out a pile of crumbs for the birds, she let out a yelp. She found me sitting on the stoop below. When I picked that place to sit down, I didn't know it was the kitchen door. It was just a nice spot to relax and enjoy the garden. I stood up and shook the crumbs from my skirt.

"So, you thought you'd get away with it. Thought I'd be upstairs," Agnes scolded. "Well, I fooled you. It's cook's day off. Haven't I told you time and time again not to set foot out of your room?"

I didn't talk back.

Agnes kept on with hands clamped to her hips. "It's not like I've locked you in a dungeon. Any other child, especially one fresh from the slums, would thank her lucky stars and never want to leave such a fine room."

I stood still as the stone steps.

"When I was a little girl, I had to work. I certainly had no chance to sit wasting time. Do you think I got paid a single penny for my efforts?" She answered her own question before I could nod either way. "But you, Young Lady, are treated like a princess, given a swell room full of high-priced toys, free for nothing, just because you're—well, sort of—cute." She said that last word like it almost stuck in her throat. Agnes was never much to look at, but right then her face looked like a dried-up apple.

"It seems the cat's got your tongue, and you don't know how to mind, so you'd better come in the kitchen, sit down and try to behave. It ain't in your nature, but do your very best at least to act like a good girl." For once, at least, she didn't send me upstairs.

I tiptoed in. I could smell the cinnamon sweet odor of baking. It was pretty hot in there with the oven going, but I didn't dare say a word about it. I noticed a lady in the big rocking chair, moving slowly like a ticking clock. I guessed she'd moved far from the cookstove to get a cooler spot. She was holding a baby in her lap.

"This is Cousin Lavinia, from South Dakota," Agnes said, pointing at the lady.

"Hello." Lavinia looked me over and smiled.

"Cousin Lavinia's been visiting on the farm, but today she's come to take afternoon coffee with me. I've baked my prize recipe, 'World's Best Coffee Cake.' It's just about to pop from the oven."

"Hmm." That's what I always say when I can't think up something interesting.

"Baby's name is Effie," Agnes said. "Say hello, Effie."

"Hello, Effie," I said. "Can Effie talk?"

"Of course not," Agnes snapped, grabbing a hot pad. She pulled her pan from the oven. "That child's way too little. My, don't this look scrumptious?"

"Googoo," I said to Effie.

"She don't talk baby talk either," Agnes said.

Cousin Lavinia didn't look a bit like Agnes. Lavinia was pretty and wore a stylish dress. She reminded me of ladies in Flora's fashion magazines with her creamy white skin; rosy cheeks; and round, curvy figure. Her curly brown hair was swept into a neat bun, but little curls swirled around her face. I thought she looked like Snow White. We used to have a storybook with a picture like that. I couldn't take my eyes off her and the plump baby in her lap.

"I'll bet you're that orphan girl from New York City."

I tried to think of something smart to say, but nothing came out. I really was scared of both of them.

"She's a very pretty child," Lavinia said to Agnes, while she kept smiling at me. After that I was only scared of Agnes.

"Nothing but trouble—stubborn and disobedient." Agnes turned to pour the coffee, and, while her back was turned, Lavinia winked at me.

They gossiped about the neighbors and drank coffee, nibbling on bits of the newly baked sweets. Agnes poked a glass of milk at me, and a plate with a piece of coffeecake. I let the first bite roll around in my mouth, thought about it, then decided not to say so, but Agnes was wrong. It was not the world's best coffeecake. I'd tasted some that Iris made at the orphanage, and hers was better.

The baby began to squeal and kick its fat little legs. Cousin Lavinia unbuttoned her crisp, white blouse and offered a big fat breast. Effie sucked noisily. I watched. After all, I'd never before seen how babies do it.

Agnes eyed me like a snake ready to bite. "I bet you never saw doings like that before," she said with kind of a mean laugh.

"Sure I did, lots of times." I hoped it was just a harmless fib. Flora would whack us if we lied. I kept on watching. Cousin Lavinia nursed that baby, first on one side, then the other. After a while, holding onto the sleeping baby, she buttoned up.

I watched Cousin Lavinia and her baby all afternoon. Soon after Agnes started making supper, Lavinia's husband tapped on the kitchen door. Agnes signaled through the window, and he came clomping in with his work boots making noise like sledge hammers. "I come to pick up my family," he said, and I watched Lavinia wrap up her baby and wave goodbye.

After the door closed behind them, Agnes told me to go upstairs at once.

"This time stay put," she grumbled. "You got yourself an eyeful."

In my room, with the door closed tight, I unbuttoned my dress, held onto my porcelain headed doll, and pressed its mouth to my own flat chest. "I'm your Ma," I told the doll. "Look how beautiful I am. My name's Lavinia. You're Effie, and I'm going to stuff you with milk 'til you get so sleepy you can't keep your eyes open. That's how we do with babies when they get noisy and act cuckoo."

When Agnes came banging in with a supper tray, she scared me so, I jumped like a frog.

"Caught red-handed!" she yelled. I dropped Effie and winced as I heard her head crack. She'd landed hard on the wooden floor.

"Now you've gone and done it!" Agnes scolded. "What will Mr. and Mrs. Hartfield say? You've gone and broke the very best of your expensive toys. Oh, they'll send you packing. It's back to the orphanage for you, and that's just what you deserve!" I started shaking all over. If she sent me back, I'd never see Iris again.

I clamped my eyes tight as they'd go. I didn't want to see Agnes' face, but I saw it anyway, with that magic eye that sees in the dark. She'd changed from a dried apple to a beast with teeth sharp as carving knives, mouth wide-open and ready to take a bite out of me. I couldn't say one word and wouldn't, even if I could. I wanted Iris. Now!

It was a Wednesday afternoon when Clarence brought me to High Point. That business with Mrs. Hartfield happened on Thursday. I didn't see her again or Mr. Hartfield either. Where was he? Was he real? They were supposed to be my new mother and father. Besides Clarence I'd come to know Homer, the gardener; Agnes, the maid; and Miss Henderson, the governess. Maybe a governess was supposed to be cranky. Maybe the woman was just doing her job. Best to humor her. Better not complain. I'd be sent back to New York anyway. That's what happened to bad girls, and they all knew I was really bad. But while I was still here, I was going to get some answers. Rosie the detective. That's me.

After supper Agnes put me into a steaming bath. It felt lots better than the cold one when I first arrived at High Point. That time she must have been in such a hurry to clean me up, she didn't have time to heat the water. After the warm bath, when I was all scrubbed, she let me put on a pretty nightgown I'd found in the armoire. When she'd got me all set for bed, she said in a snappy voice, "Stay in your room. Don't set one foot outside that door," and more of that kind of talk.

After a while she must have got tired of yelling. "I'm all done in." She yawned. "I've put in a long, hard day. Now, with this pretty room and all the toys and books, you should have plenty to keep you busy 'til bedtime. You're a lucky but undeserving orphan." She made a clucking sound like a chicken setting on a nest full of eggs.

Once Flora told us that before they left Ireland, her Ma kept chickens in the yard near the house. Flora could cluck like that. She'd do it just to make us laugh, so I couldn't help laughing at Agnes. That made her so mad, she stormed out.

Well, it was the grandest room I'd seen in my entire life, all filled with toys and books and pretty clothes, but where were the folks who were supposed to be my parents? I felt like a crumb under the table. Nobody cared about me—nobody but Iris, and I hadn't yet discovered a way to find her. I hadn't even laid eyes on Mr. Hartfield, if there was a Mr. Hartfield, and I'd learned, right off, the missus wasn't half so pretty inside as she was outside.

At eight o'clock sharp, Agnes came to hear my evening prayers. Then she tucked me in. "Remember, the chamber pot's under your bed," she said. "Go right to sleep. I mean it. I'll bring breakfast in the morning. Good night."

"Will I meet them tomorrow?" I took a deep breath and let it out slowly, hoping she would finally realize how important this was. "Will I have breakfast with them?"

"Go to sleep," Agnes said. "It don't pay to fish in troubled waters." Now what did that mean?

At what seemed like midnight, I woke up and looked around for the window. I wanted to see the moon and stars, but it was pitch dark. No moon at all. I'd been dreaming. My dream began in such a nice way, a series of picture postcards, shuffled like cards you play games with, so the characters moved gracefully. I was with Iris and Pete. We were holding hands in a circle, dancing in a field of pink gladiolus. The smell was sweet. Flowers had turned into princesses, with dainty feet flying, light as dandelion puffs. Iris led the dance. Pete gathered bouquets and bowed, like he did the day we met him. Then he ran to us, filling our arms with blossoms. They smelled like the phlox Flora bought for our room in Five Points, but a black cloud showed up in the perfect blue sky and grew bigger and bigger. A witch popped out and lowered herself on a rope. We watched her fancy leather boots with their sharp, pointed toes kicking and jerking all the way down. Her head was full of springy curls, and her skirts rustled like bird's wings. The head thrashed about horribly as she grabbed our flowers and ripped out all the petals. Then she climbed back up the rope, flailing and thrashing the whole way up. Back in the cloud she popped and was no more, like bubbles when water sets to boiling on the stove. I stared at the sky, shaking my fists, but there was nothing and no one left to fight. I just stood there, stuck, like a carrot, in the hard ground.

I woke up, crying in the dark, curled up in a bed with clean, ironed sheets, but one that seemed too new and strange. Rosie, the detective, had a mystery to solve. I found the chamber pot, then got up, felt my way to the wall, then the door, opening to the sound of a long drawn out, spooky squeak. I couldn't see much of anything, so I stumbled into what felt like a narrow, carpeted hallway. Then my bare feet felt the soft rug.

"Iris?" I kept my voice low, so I wouldn't wake anybody.

My arms were stretched out in front, searching the darkness. "Iris? Iris?" I called softly.

Everything was black. I thought I'd died and become a ghost. That must be it. Nobody could see or hear me. I'd read stories about ghosts. Funny, I hadn't noticed the change, but how would a person know? I found a railing, something solid to hold onto. Mixed up as I was, I stumbled and fell down the stairs, crashing with a bump as my head hit the wall on the first landing. Now, for sure, I was dead, like Flora. I'd seen what that looked like. I stretched out like a statue, waiting. *The angels will come for me, if they aren't too busy. They must have lots to do. Plenty folks to watch out for. I kind of hope I don't meet Flora. I'd rather be with Iris.* That's what I thought.

I heard feet racing down the stairs. "What in Heaven's name?" Agnes scolded in a muffled, cranky voice. She was wearing a long, white gown with a white cap on her head. She carried a candle. The flame made flickering shadows on the wall.

"Back to bed! Naughty girl!" She put down her candle, picked me up, like she would a bad puppy, balanced the candle with three fingers, and hauled me off to bed. I remember the smell of hot candle wax.

"I don't know what gets into you," she scolded. "How many times have I told you not to leave your room? You'd better hope Mrs. Hartfield didn't hear. If she finds out you're this much trouble, she'll send you packing, and I won't blame her one little bit!"

"Iris!" I wailed.

"I've had just about enough of that," Agnes said. "Miss Henderson told you, and I'll say it once again. It won't do no good to keep blubbering. Now behave yourself and go back to sleep. If you stay in bed and don't make another peep, I won't tell on you. But if there's so much as one tiny squeak out of you—"

My hands were clamped over my ears, so I wouldn't have to listen. It seemed like my bed was shaking, but it was just me. My eyes were open wide. Try as I might, I couldn't get back to sleep, so I stayed there all curled up, feeling like a mouse in a dark hole, only I was trapped in a fancy bed through that long, dark night.

CHAPTER 10

FARMING, OLSON STYLE
PETE

The way folks talk out here in the sticks don't even come close to how we put things in Five Points, but I've been around long enough now to get the hang of it. I just mention the fact, since my lingo might be taking on the ring of a country boy.

It was just coming light as I opened my eyes and took a peek outside. Skinny beams of sunlight squeaked through the one dinky, dirty window. I could finally get a good look at our gloomy room. It was what folks in these parts call a lean-to, slapped onto one end of a falling apart wreck of a barn.

The stink of wet cow pies seeped in through cracks in the thin wall that separated us from the animals. The smell of musty hay blew down with wisps of whatever was in the loft above the main part. The floor was just packed down dirt. A rusty, potbellied stove, with a chimney pipe stuck through the outside wall, sat in one corner. We didn't need a stove that day.

Yellowed old pictures of farm tools, horse troughs, and windmills, ripped from the Montgomery Ward catalogue, were fastened with tacks onto the wall. A homemade washstand, some wobbly shelves, and a lumpy bed were the furnishings. That was it. Not very homey, if you get my drift.

Gentle lowing came from the stalls, but it gradually got louder, until all the cows were bawling and bellering like a circus gone wild. Butch and Joe woke up, but it was no use trying to talk. The cows drowned out everything else.

Joe clapped his hands over his ears before getting out of bed, spitting on the floor, wiping his mouth on his sleeve, and yelling in my ear, "Look you! Ain't no two ways about it. Those gals ain't about to wait."

Butch groaned and hollered, "We've got to get to work. Can't you hear them? It's Bossie, Sally, and Cora raising a ruckus."

Joe got his mouth right up to my ear, "Butch and me have got to teach you how, before boss comes sneaking up. The geezer's like a weasel on a chicken. It's the beatenest thing, how he can show up out of nowhere and spring on a fellow."

We dressed fast and moved to the next room. Butch tossed me a pail, and Joe said, "Come on, Greenhorn. It'll take some doing to get the hang of this, so there ain't time to dawdle." I plopped myself on the milk stool and watched Joe in action. When he turned it over to me, I tried to do it his way, make him think I was a crackerjack, but only a trickle came out.

"Come on, Boy! Give her all you got," Joe shouted. "Squeeze like the very devil."

I squeezed, but it didn't get better.

"Do like a calf does," Joe yelled. "When the milk don't come, he'll bang the udder with his head, like it was a punching bag."

"Does the trick every time," Butch added.

I squeezed, but it didn't get better.

Joe kept on yelling. "Work upwards with your thumbs, and use your paws like they was famished little calves, tying into their Ma, just as tight and firm as harness hitches."

Butch shook his head and rolled his eyes. "Pitiful," he snorted. "Just what I'd expect from a city slicker."

"You was a city slicker not all that long ago," Joe snapped, "and I seem to recollect your first go round."

Butch lowered his eyes. "You would bring that up."

Joe laughed as he turned to me. "First time out, Butch here missed the pail, and when he finally got the angle right, he stepped smack-dab in a cow pie. He kicked to shake the danged thing off, and spilled the whole kit and caboodle. Old Man Olson was already done with the first milking. I tell you, the geezer was so put out, he packed Butch off to the house, where Mabel could teach him to clean lamp chimneys, but she soon sent him back. Said he was a stinkin' mucker."

Butch stomped a foot and turned his back.

"Give him time to think it over," Joe said with a wink. "Now, about you. I never did hear of man or boy who got it right the first time. Folks ain't born with super strength in the forearm, but you'll find, just like Butch and me, you'll work yourself up 'til you've got the iron grip, squeezing and squirting like you was born to be a farmer boy. So keep on working Bossie. I'll go ahead and take care of Sally, and Butch will do Cora."

Butch moved towards his cow. Milk splashes soon pounded against the tin pails like drumbeats. I watched from the corner of one eye as foam began rising on Butch and Joe's. Nothing happened on mine. In less than fifteen minutes, when Joe had milked his cow dry, he rose and ambled back to supervise me. I squeezed my eyes shut, all set for a scolding. My level best didn't cut the mustard, and I knew it.

Joe shoved me off the stool and finished the job himself. When all the cows were milked and calmed down, Joe and Butch released each one from its stanchion, threw open the barn door and let them out to pasture. "Now," Joe said, "we haul these pails to the house for Mabel to strain out the flies and whatever else got in. We'll have to go back after a spell and set them down in the root cellar to cool.

"For now, we got to hightail it to the field, so we can cut and shock oats. All that's got to be done before the big day."

"What big day?" I hoped it meant a circus or a county fair.

"Threshing day," Joe said with a grin. "That's one you won't forget."

We worked all day under the blistering sun with only short times out for food and water. All I could think of was threshing day, the big one, hoping it wouldn't be the least bit like today.

CHAPTER 11

PAPA
ROSIE

Sleep wouldn't come. I felt jumpy inside. But then, whatever was troubling me shook loose. All my worries flew away 'til morning when I woke up, so scared that goose pimples started popping out all over me.

Who could explain these people? Were they even real? Was I going to be in this family or not? What would Iris do? I stayed in my bed, propped up on one elbow, thinking the whole thing over.

Iris would stand up straight, spit it right out. "What's going on here?" she'd say. "Why don't you pay attention to me?" She'd demand to see Mr. and Mrs. Hartfield. Insist on explanations. She'd put her foot down, slam a fist on one of those nice tables, demand somebody pay attention—or else! I scratched my head. Or else what? I couldn't think of what.

I sat up, stared out the window at the beautiful gardens, remembering Homer, how nice he'd been, and tried to think what to do, but Agnes' nasty words from last night came back. "If they find out you're this much trouble, they'll send you packing!" To top it all off, I kept picturing Mrs. Hartfield's fancy boot and how she kicked those pretty pink gladiolus.

Then, all of a sudden, a new idea popped into my head. I jumped out of bed, grabbed the little suitcase from the *Children's Aid Society*, threw in an extra dress, an extra set of underwear and socks, and slammed the satchel shut. I dragged it to the door and stopped to think. Why leave those nice dresses just hanging there? I could squeeze in at least a couple. And all those wonderful books on the shelves. Two or three wouldn't be missed.

I dropped the satchel, sat down at the tea table, squeezed my head 'til ideas drifted in and out like clouds. I even said the prayer I'd learned at the orphanage:

"Please make my life a little light
Within the world to glow.
A little flame that burneth bright
Wherever I may go."

I made up my mind to take only what I'd brought with me. When I'd packed my own few things I slammed it shut, gripped the handles and did not look back. I might turn into a pillar of salt. I tiptoed out the door.

As the hinges squeaked and whined, I froze in my tracks, waiting for the worst. But nothing happened. The house was dead quiet while I inched ever so slowly down the hall. I couldn't help but sniff as I tiptoed past the door to Mrs. Hartfields' room. Whiffs of perfume oozed out and hit my nose like the tail of a fox.

As I stepped carefully down the stairs, my feet sinking into the thick carpet, a different, delicious smell made my mouth water. I stopped. It was sizzling bacon, all mixed up with the sweet, yeasty odor of cinnamon rolls baking.

In New York, Iris and I never got to taste the kind of food these fine folks feast on every single day. Flora hated kitchens. Her gentlemen callers brought candy and pastries, but I'd only once tasted crispy bits of bacon. One of her gentleman friends treated us to breakfast in a restaurant on a very special day that I'll never forget. I chewed slowly, closing my eyes, licking my lips, enjoying every delicious bite.

But none of the others treated us like that. Those gentleman friends usually shooed us out the door and laughed as we raced down the hall to Mrs. Fletcher's room. I think Flora kind of liked us, but most of the time we were in the way, so that's where we had to go. We didn't much care for Mrs. Fletcher either. She was grumpy.

Anyhow, that nice man gave us each a nickel and played with us like a real daddy might. We kept looking for him, hoping he'd come back, but he never showed up after that one special day. Flora must have sent him packing. She always did. When we asked for him, she got cranky, so we let it drop. Mostly, Flora knew how to have fun, but if we asked too many questions she'd slap our faces and say, "Mind your own business."

So, as I was saying, I was running away, and when I reached the main floor, tiptoeing past the kitchen, what did I hear but the spatter of frying eggs? That made me remember the day when I stood, watching through window glass at a New York diner while the cook flipped fried eggs, catching them in his frying pan.

For sure I was going to run away—but maybe—maybe not right that minute. What could it hurt to wait 'til after breakfast?

I tiptoed up the back stairs and got to my room without getting caught. I tucked my satchel under the bed just in time, and as I sat down, Agnes banged through the door with my breakfast tray. While she slowly lifted the silver cover from the plate, I watched, hoping for something really good. Guess what! Instead of the delicious breakfast I'd been smelling, I found another bowl of porridge.

"Always something wrong," Agnes grumbled. I guess she was still mad that I'd been a ghost in the night. I tried to act like nothing. Just lifted my spoon and shoveled it in thinking, with every slurp, what I should do next.

I would not go back to the orphanage, not back on the train. I would find Iris. It seemed that bacon and eggs, cinnamon rolls, all the good things went to the wicked witch. And where was Mr. Hartfield, the man who was supposed to be my daddy, the man who never did show up?

Well, I didn't care. I'd made my plans. Too bad I got fooled, but there'd be another chance to run away. Then I'd clear out of this house. Fine and fancy wasn't all it was cracked up to be. I'd live by my wits. I'd find Iris, the one and only person in the world who cared a row of pins. When my bowl was empty, I felt a tear trickle down. I turned my head fast to wipe with my sleeve. I'd never let Agnes see such a thing.

Another boring day with Miss Henderson. Late in the afternoon she finally let me go. I found Homer and asked to help with the weeding, but he shook his head, meaning, "No." He talked about plants and bugs and weeds and rain and most anything else he could think of, but I knew there was something on his mind, so I wheeled 'til it came out.

"The missus will fire me if you get another dirty dress. Agnes says she's all put out."

"Oh, dear, I got you in trouble, Homer. I'm sorry."

"You can stay and visit," Homer said, "but leave the dirty work to me."

"I haven't even seen Mr. Hartfield," I couldn't keep from complaining. It was easy to tell Homer. He didn't get mad. "The only time I saw the lady—well, you know about that. Why did they pretend they wanted me when they didn't? What's wrong? How come they hate me?"

"The mister wants you. He'll treat you nice. Too bad your first days were such a muddle, but he got called off on business. He's an important man, he is. That's why Clarence came for you. When the boss comes home, things will be different.

"I begged to go with Iris. Nobody would listen."

"Rules are rules," Homer said, but the way he said it, I could tell he didn't like those rules any better than I did.

"Homer, please, will you help me find Iris?" I was begging, and I didn't want to stoop so low, but what else could I do?

"Give me something to go on," Homer said.

"Well, she got picked by some crabby folks who live on a farm."

He scratched his head. "That covers most everybody around here."

"They're old. He tries to walk fast, but kind of limps, like one leg's shorter than the other. She talks high and whiney. First they wanted me, but Mr. Jackson said I was spoken for. Then Clarence came for me, and the old woman talked mean and terrible, like she didn't want Iris, but guessed she'd have to take her if that was the best she could do. I got really mad, but it didn't help."

"I still can't think who they are," Homer said.

"Albert and Minnie!" I shouted, when their names finally popped in my head. "Mr. Jackson said their names. Now I remember. They hauled Iris away in an old cart, pulled by a sick looking horse. Iris had to sit on the floor with her legs hanging loose off the back end, like sleeves hanging out of a suitcase. We passed them as they went by the barbershop towards the meat market. They turned the other way, and that was the last I saw of Iris." I cried hard when I said that. Just couldn't help it. Homer looked like he didn't know what to do with me, so I tried to calm down.

"Must be Albert and Minnie Knudtsen," Homer said, wiping my teary face with his shirttail. "You're lucky you didn't have to go with them."

"How bad are they?" I was huffing and puffing. That's what happens after a good cry.

"Well now, They ain't all bad." I could tell he was sorry he'd got me riled up.

"Where? Oh, where do they live?" I couldn't wait to find out.

"North of town."

"Which way is that?"

Homer pointed. "Past the barbershop, past Nielsen's meat market and Hattie's dressmaking shop."

"Then where?" I could barely catch my breath.

"First place, right side of the road. House and barn sit back a ways. There's a long bumpy lane."

"Thanks, Homer! Thanks a million!" I hugged him as tight as I could squeeze. "You're my best friend after Iris—and Pete." I'd almost forgot about Pete.

"It don't surprise me none, Albert and Minnie would need a hired girl," Homer said. "They ain't real ambitious, and they're getting up in years."

I would have told him I was planning to run away, but just then Clarence came around the circle drive in that fancy buggy. When it stopped, a gray-haired gentleman in a fine black suit, top hat, and walking stick jumped down and walked towards us. He was going at a pretty good clip.

"Who's your little helper?" His question was for Homer, but he smiled at me.

"Mr. Hartfield, Sir, may I present Miss Rosie O'Leary." Homer said it like I was a princess or something, so I curtsied. This time I got it right. I'd practiced by the mirror, hoping something like this would happen.

Mr. Hartfield flashed a big smile, opened his arms, and gave me a great big hug. He breathed a long, happy sigh and still smiling asked, "Have you and Mrs. Hartfield enjoyed your time together—just the two of you?"

I looked at Homer.

"They haven't made acquaintance yet, Sir," Homer said. "I expect the missus thought she'd wait 'til you got home."

Mr. Hartfield got a funny look on his face, but he quickly said, "Well then, there is no time to waste. Come along, dear child!"

He laughed and moved so fast, he almost danced. That made me think things might turn out right after all. I skipped along, trying to keep up. He saw it was hard for me, so he slowed down.

We held hands and went inside. I'd never been treated like that, except by Iris. It was swell.

"Her name is Venetia," he said, "but I hope you will call her Mother. As for me, I'd prefer to be called Papa."

"Papa," I said, trying hard to please.

The house smelled of coffee and pastries. Clarence bumped through the front door, hauling Mr. Hartfield's high-priced luggage into the mansion. It was plain from sights and smells, they'd been getting ready for his return, making coffee, cookies, and pastries. Earlier, I'd watched Agnes carry a big box of cigars to the smoking room.

Venetia came slowly down the curved staircase, all dressed in blue silk with lots of lace, tucks, and ruffles. She didn't smile, but she looked like one of those fancy ladies in the Montgomery Wards Catalog.

"I am so pleased to welcome you home, Jefferson," she said, poking out her hand. He kissed it long and slow. That was something to see. She looked too young to be his wife. More like his daughter.

"My dear," he said, bowing his head politely, "May I present Miss Rose Hartfield."

The lady turned her head.

I curtsied. If I do say so myself, it turned out pretty good, but she didn't seem to think so. Her face changed. She reminded me of the witch in my dream.

"I saw you in the garden." I knew when I said it, I shouldn't, but I couldn't help it. Sometimes I'm like that. It's a problem.

She stared at the floor.

"When I got dirty that day, well, it was all my fault, not Homer's. He's so nice, and I like helping him. It's fun pulling weeds and planting flowers. I just love pink gladiolus. Why don't you like them?" Now I'd put my foot in it.

She looked at me like I was a warty frog. Her smooth white hand, with its sparkly ring, grabbed Papa's arm.

"Jefferson!" the word came out high and shrill, like a lady singing higher than she ought to. She called for Agnes, who came running, wiping red, wet hands on a kitchen towel. The fine lady pushed me at Agnes and then linked arms with Papa. He followed like a limp noodle as she yanked him through the parlor door.

Agnes dragged me upstairs. Fine as it was, full of wonderful things, right then, my room felt like a prison. Poor Papa. I was scared of what she'd do to him.

CHAPTER 12

HARTFIELD
ROSIE

I hoped reading would make me feel better, so I reached for a book. I thought any book would do. How funny it was that *Alice in Wonderland* fell into my hands. Its beautiful pictures made the strange characters seem alive. On any other day I would keep reading 'til I fell asleep. But now, trying to get my mind off what was happening downstairs, I stared at the pages thinking of other things.

I poked it back on the shelf, tried playing with my broken doll, tried playing tea party, tried looking out the window. Nothing helped. All I could think of was that beautiful, scary witch downstairs. To me High Point was like Alice's world, all mixed up.

In my mind, as in a dream, I saw Mrs. Hartfield turned into a big bird, her fancy, ring- spangled fingers swooping down on Papa, like an owl might poke its claws at a mouse. She'd make him get rid of me. She'd say orphan train kids are liars and cheats. She'd say I'm a bad girl, a street rat. She'd have me sent to Mr. Jackson, who'd send me back to New York on the train, this time alone.

I knew I'd better get out fast, find Iris while I still could, or I'd be sent back to the orphanage, and Iris would have to stay on as a prisoner with Albert and Minnie. I'd been dumb. Why didn't I run away when I had the chance? I pulled out my satchel. It was now or never.

I heard a knock on the door and froze. It might be Agnes coming to give me the news, but she wouldn't knock. Could it be the witch with a poisoned apple? I shoved the satchel under the bed. My hands were shaking. I opened the door just a crack, and there stood Papa. Behind his wrinkles and gray mustache he looked sad and sorry.

"I hope you know, dear child, what you saw downstairs is not—well, it's not like her. Once you get to know Venetia, she's a nice—a very—nice—lady."

I gave him a funny look. He knew I didn't believe a word of what he'd said.

"You must understand, dear child. She sometimes gets—spells."

"Don't worry about it. It's okay, Mister," I said.

He drew back, like I'd socked him in the belly. "Won't you call me Papa?"

"She's a pretty lady, Papa." I said it trying to act like nothing had changed, but it had.

"She reminds me of the queen," I said.

"The queen?"

"You know, in Snow White. The wicked stepmother."

He rubbed his forehead and groaned.

"She'll probably send the poisoned apple on my supper tray."

"My dear child, Venetia would never hurt you."

"If you'll just help me find Albert and Minnie, I'll get out of here and never trouble either of you again. I have to find Iris."

"Who is Iris?"

"My sister!"

"Your sister?" He raised his eyebrows, like he'd never heard of such a thing as a sister.

"They didn't tell you about Iris?" I was getting really steamed up. "They split us up at the opera house. We begged Mr. Jackson not to, but he sent her off with two crazy old people who were not a bit nice to her, and then Clarence brought me here, and I —"

"Who took your sister?"

"Albert and Minnie!" I almost shouted. Didn't he know anything?

He looked out the window, like he was trying to find one special cloud in the sky. After a long time he spoke, "Things are moving too fast. There is much to be considered. Please be patient, Rosie, dear. I must deal with my problems one by one."

So he had problems too. Well, that was just too bad. I had to have an answer.

"What problems do you have?" I said, trying to sound nice, when I didn't feel a bit nice.

He winced, then started pacing around the room, talking while he walked. "While I was away, my wife received a letter from England." Again he went to the window.

"Where's that?"

"Far across the sea."

"Once, long ago, Flora lived somewhere far across the sea." I didn't know a thing about far away places, but I told him she came from Ireland.

"Who, may I ask, is Flora?"

"She was my Ma. I guess I can call her that now, since she's dead. Iris says she's sitting on a cloud, watching what goes on down here, so she can help us out when we're in trouble. That seems to be most all the time, and I'm sorry to say she's not doing a very good job, but then she never did, so it's nothing new."

He gave me a warm hug. When he let go, he took off his glasses and wiped his eyes.

I didn't cry. I was already used to having her up there. I couldn't bring her down, and besides, I'd rather have Iris. "Well, what about the letter?" I'm sorry to say, I said that in a pretty snippy way.

"It takes a long time to receive a letter from England. It is a great distance, you know."

"Flora never got letters. At least, I never saw one, but then you never could tell about Flora. She had lots of secrets."

"My wife must leave for England," he said, mopping his brow. "She must go at once, since her brother passed on unexpectedly, and she must attend to family business.

"That wife of yours hates me," I said. "She wants to send me back to the orphanage."

"My dear child, how could anyone feel anything for you but kindness and love?" He rubbed his forehead, stared out the window, and then sat down beside me. Soon he was telling me a long, sad story, but I'll tell it the short way.

⁂

When he was young, he married Rosalind, a girl he'd known since he was a kid. They lived in a pretty little cottage, all fixed up cozy with hollyhocks and snapdragons outside the front door. They had a baby girl named Lilly. Every day he played with Lilly, read stories, and pushed her on a rope swing. He told me lots of things about Lilly and how sweet and good she was. When she was seven, like me, she got scarlet fever and died. Rosalind came down with the same thing and passed on a few days later. He stayed locked up in his room and couldn't even talk to anybody for a whole year. He had a hard time telling that part. His face got red, and he had to stop and blow his nose, but then he told about his folks, and that part almost made him jolly.

His folks had titles like Duke, Earl, Duchess, and Lady this and that. I asked if he was a lord and he didn't say yes or no, just laughed. Years later, when his parents died, their money and land went to his brother, Edmund. "That's how they do things in England," he said. "The oldest son gets the whole thing." He'd planned on going to America anyhow, so that was fine with him.

He borrowed some money from Edmund and sailed across the sea. It was a hard journey, but he made it to New York and from there found his way to Iowa. He'd heard that if you could get across all the rivers, even the Mississippi, Iowa farmland cost just a dollar and twenty-five cents an acre. So, he crossed rivers on rafts, rode horses, hitched rides on wagons, and helped watch out for Indians. Some of the Indians they met were scary, but most seemed friendly enough. Some even gave him food to eat, and he'd give them trinkets he'd brought along.

Part way he rode a stagecoach and sat on top with the driver, always watching for robbers and unfriendly Indians. He crossed little streams and finally the Mississippi River on rafts. When he reached Iowa, he found a land office, bought all the acres he could afford, and for the first few months lived in a tent.

Other folks started coming and buying land. He made friends, helped them out, and they helped him. Together, they built log cabins and broke sod. At first he pushed his own plow, but that took too long, so he bought an ox, trapped animals, skinned them, and sold the furs. With money he earned from trading and selling furs, he paid Edmund what he'd borrowed. Then he saved up and bought more land, some from neighbors who found the life too hard. He had more work to do than time, so he hired men to run his farm.

Little by little a town grew up. He owned a big part of it. He said working all the time was just what he needed. It helped him stop brooding about Rosalind and Lilly.

So he set up a general store. It did so well, he started another one, and then a button factory, a tanning mill, and a flour mill. He sold some of those and went into the banking business. There came a day when he knew he was rich enough to live well, so he chose the best spot in town, high on a hill looking out over all his land, and built the fine house he still calls High Point. After word came that Edmund died, he sailed back to England to pay his respects and settle business affairs. The law said all the family property and money belonged to Papa now, but he gave it to his brother's wife, Amanda. He didn't care about England or family money anymore. He had made a new life and had everything he needed in America.

This is where Venetia, Amanda's friend and neighbor, came into the story. She showed up every day for a visit. She said it was to cheer up poor, dear Amanda. Amanda was very polite and always asked her to stay for supper. Then Venetia would take a seat next to Papa. He couldn't remember what they talked about, but he did notice she was really pretty.

Once she just happened to bump into Papa when he was out walking. He offered his arm. He's such a gentleman. They meandered down the garden path and through the woods. He didn't remember what they talked about that time either, but it must have been good, because they got married soon after.

He really missed Rosalind and Lilly, so his idea was that if he took a young wife, he'd get another child. It wouldn't be the same as Lilly, but it might help him forget how sad he'd been. He made it clear to Venetia, before she said she'd marry him, that Iowa wasn't as civilized as England. She said that would be fine if they would have adventures like those he told about. But once she got here, she cried and scolded and seemed to hate everything about the place.

He gave her all the nice things he could think of: a fine house, servants, fancy clothes—whatever she wanted. Still, nothing pleased her. She said she knew he was letting Amanda stay on in the mansion where she'd lived with Edmund, even though it now belonged to Papa, but she didn't realize that he'd given away the whole estate and the fortune that went with it. She said she never heard of such a thing. She only found out after they got to Iowa when a letter came from Amanda, all full of thanks and gratefulness. If she'd known, she would have objected with all the nasty words she could muster, and if that didn't work, she sure wouldn't have come all this way for nothing. That's what she said. There was another man in England that wanted her. Maybe she should just go back and find him.

He thought she'd get over it if she had a baby, but she complained that children get dirty, make noise, and break things. She knew she could get what she wanted. After all, she was a beautiful woman. Why should she have to put up with unpleasant things?

After he told me his story, he stood at the window looking out over the town. "Now, my dear Rosie," he said, "tell me your story. I hope it is happier than mine."

"There's not much to tell," I said. "Flora's dead, and I can't be with Iris."

"You have me," he said, squeezing my hand.

"I want Iris." That was mean. I was sorry after I said it, but if he didn't want Iris, I didn't want to be his little girl.

The next morning, when Agnes brought my breakfast tray, she charged in, breathing like a steam engine. She just couldn't wait to start blabbering.

"Clarence told me something, and now I'm going to pass it on. He took Mr. and Mrs. Hartfield to the train depot early this morning. What do you think of that?"

The sun was barely up. I wanted to cry, but I wouldn't let myself. I'd been mean, and now he was gone.

But Agnes had more to say. "Clarence watched the whole thing. Mr. Hartfield helped her get on the train, but then he jumped off and when the train began to move, he waved his handkerchief 'til she was out of sight. He's arranged things so that when she gets to New York she'll board the finest steamship in the port. Mr. Hartfield doesn't do things on the cheap. From New York to London will take about ten days." Agnes lifted her chin and sniffed, like she was proud to have so much firsthand information.

"Mr. Hartfield told Clarence to pass the message to me, and I was to tell you. He's gone to his office downtown, but he'll be back before lunch. So, now that you know, here's your breakfast, Miss. He ordered it special, just for you: biscuits with fresh raspberry jam, new churned butter, crispy bacon, poached eggs on toast, a fresh cinnamon roll and, if that does not meet with your approval, Miss Rose, I've been told to return everything to the kitchen and bring something that does."

I giggled, and then, trying to act like Venetia, I sniffed and said, "Thank you, Agnes, this will do quite nicely." Was that ever fun!

Agnes' eyes squeezed up like little pig eyes as she left the room. Once she'd gone I told Effie, "Things turned around the minute Venetia left. Papa's a swell fellow!" I buttered a biscuit and topped it off with raspberry jam, then tasted a bite of each thing on my tray. Well, I couldn't begin to eat all of it, but it was a delicious breakfast!

I tried to figure out what was going on. What did it mean? Sure, Venetia would be back, and I didn't fool myself. She wouldn't like me any better than the first time. But Papa liked me, and now I knew why. He wanted a little girl like Lilly. If he met Iris, he'd like her even better than me. How could he help it?

———

But when he didn't show up for lunch, I thought Clarence must have told it wrong. Maybe Papa really did go along to England. Then I'd be stuck here with just Agnes, Miss Henderson, and no way to find Iris. And if I did find her, where could we go? Singing girls on Hartfield's Main Street couldn't earn enough to buy breakfast. We'd get sent right back to the orphanage. Even "Poor Drooping Maiden" wouldn't soften up mean old Mr. Jackson or his kind.

Late in the afternoon, as I followed Homer in the garden, Papa's beautiful horses came prancing up the circle drive, pulling his carriage to the main entrance, just like they did on that first day. He jumped down, walked quickly up the path, and squeezed his big, strong arms around me.

He told Homer to hang a rope swing on a big old oak tree. Papa pushed and kept me flying so high in the air, I could see out over the whole town. Later, we sat under the tree and took turns reading to each other from *The Adventures of Tom Sawyer*. He smiled and gave me lots of praise for my good reading.

That same afternoon, we walked downtown. In the stores he let me choose what I wanted. I got yard goods, buttons, and lace for a new dress. He even bought me another pretty porcelain headed doll. Papa wanted me to throw out the broken one, but I told him I couldn't part with Effie, so now she has a sister. You don't throw away your kid, just because she's got a cracked head.

We stopped at Hattie's dressmaker shop where he told Hattie to stitch up matching dresses for me, Effie, and the new doll. The new one's name will be Matilda when we get her baptized.

"I wish we could do this every day," he said, "but there is always pressing business. All the same, I shall reserve at least one day a week for you alone. We shall take walks in the woods, boat rides on the lake, attend plays and musical events at the opera house."

That magic feeling came back for a little while, until I thought about Iris. Where could she be? Was she all right? If only she was here with me. Homer's words came back to worry me. "Albert and Minnie Knudtsen? You got the better deal."

We sat under the tree and took turns reading to each other from
The Adventures of Tom Sawyer.

CHAPTER 13

RUNAWAY
PETE

My eyes popped open. This was the day. My bunkmates' snoring woke me up from a toss-and-turn kind of night, except I couldn't really toss and turn. Squeezed in our tight bed, it was hard to even wiggle a finger or toe. I tried stuffing my ears, covering them with the ragged old quilt to shut out the noise. The thing that had played cat and mouse with my dreams was first on my mind. Escape! My heart pounded hard against my chest. Another thought piled on top of that first one. Hold back. Calm down. Joe's sharp toenails would stab me if I moved too fast. I started inching slowly, quietly. I had to go easy to keep from waking the other boys.

Butch and Joe's heads stuck out the top. I was squeezed in, pencil thin, stiff as a board, wedged between them, my feet on top and my head at the bottom, up against their smelly feet. We'd been sleeping that way so we'd fit. The trick was to get out without rousing them.

And now I felt pressure on my bladder. I was pretty sure Butch and Joe, with the same problem, would step on my face, but I wouldn't sink to that level, especially today when my whole future depended on a silent, snail's paced getaway. Three boys running away at the same time would be much easier to catch than one.

They kept up the snoring, short piggish grunts, followed by long, buzz sawing groans. Carefully and gradually I sat up. Four middle-sized feet stuck out in the damp morning air. I covered them up. The noisy breathing continued. I lifted one leg over the iron rail. I was short for my age, so it barely cleared the hurdle. The bedsprings squeaked. My other leg gave the boost I needed to rise on one knee and straddle the rail. But now my foot was snagged inside the rag of a nightshirt I'd found stuffed under the bed. I didn't have one of my own. Don't forget, Olson stole the few decent clothes I brought from the city. I clenched my teeth as my nightshirt ripped, making noise like popping firecrackers. At least that's how it sounded to me. I was so dad-blamed nervous.

I froze, but the other boys didn't stir. I bit my lip, then slowly, carefully freed the foot, stretched one leg down, touched the floor, and jerked back as a mouse raced like a shot over my foot. I reached for a shoe, then gave up on it. A fight with the little beastie would wake up the boys and ruin everything. Already, I could tell by their sluggish movements and toned down snores they might wake up any minute. I had to hurry.

I tiptoed, one small step at a time, inching towards the shelf, then pulled on socks, underwear, patched overalls, ragged shirt, worn-out shoes, all courtesy of Old Man Olson.

A rooster crowed. Again I froze. When I was sure it hadn't bothered the boys, I tiptoed out, silently closing the door behind me. I peed in the bushes, and stealthily, quietly inched my way towards the road, eyes scanning left and right in case those infernal dogs showed up, but they didn't. Instead, I heard sweet morning bird calls, a squealing pig, but not a bark or a snarl.

I stretched, breathed in deep gulps of fresh morning air, took a long look at the rising sun, and in the pink dawn of that Iowa summer morning, squared my shoulders and set off for the dirt road that led to town. Once there, I'd find the folks in charge, tell them just what was going on at the Olson farm, and demand freedom for Butch, Joe, and especially me. Then I'd rescue Iris and Rosie.

<hr/>

The next thing happened quicker than you could say "scat." It struck like lightning, or a rattlesnake's bite but without sight or sound. In an instant, I was locked in a vice, so tight, I could barely breathe. I couldn't figure out what was happening. I just felt the racing beat of my heart, the hot blood in my head.

Then, "Pow!" With a hard slam, I hit the ground, tossed like a burst from a cannon. I smashed into the dirt, and the cracking started in. Snap, snap, crack, crack, and something stung like snakebite. I tasted blood, stared at the swirling razor strap above me and beyond that into the crazy eyes of a thing, a shadow, something that looked a little like Old Man Olson, but a bad copy, changed somehow, from man into a raging beast.

<hr/>

Humming sounds buzzed in my ears, nightmares tormented me with monsters, fiends, and cannibals, armed with sticks, ropes, and bullwhips. The whole monstrous gang was chasing me through zigzag paths, tangled vines, and brambles. At every turn, a new blockade flew up, and the evil ones wouldn't stop. They were hot on my trail. I flailed my arms and opened my mouth wide, trying to scream, "Help! Police! Murder!" but no sound came out. I felt like a bug getting stomped on by a heavy boot.

⁂

"Wake up, boy," a squeaky voice poked into this maze of nightmares. Something cool and wet soothed my forehead. A hard, wrinkled hand pressed against mine.

I slowly opened my eyes, then closed them, then opened them once more, blinking with surprise. "Don't! Please! No more! No more!" I cried. "Let me out of this loony bin!"

"Pipe down," Mabel hissed. "I shouldn't ought to be here. I come to make sure you ain't dead."

"Where's Butch and Joe?" I was bewildered.

"Out stacking hay. It ain't but a couple more days and the threshing ring shows up. You'd best get to work right soon, or ain't no telling what he'll do to you."

"You're as bad as he is," I cried, pulling my hand away from hers. "What's the matter with you people? You ain't even human. You're monsters."

"Some things you don't need to know," she said. "Now, I brung you some soup and a hunk of bread. Eat up. Then pull yourself out of that bed and act like nothing happened. You hear?"

"Well, by Jimminy, something did happen," I shouted. "Something pretty close to murder."

"Hush," Mabel said. "He don't recollect nothing. Hashing over old goings on always brings on another spell worse than the last one."

"He's a nut case," I muttered, trying to rise. "Stark raving mad."

"Don't never let me hear you say that again," Mabel said, aiming a hand like she was going to slug me.

"Get away from me, you old she-devil," I yelled.

"Just you hush," she muttered, "I come to make sure you wasn't a gonner. If you turn hothead, well, then it's your own funeral." She turned around and disappeared from the barn.

After a while, I dragged myself out of bed, washed up, cleaned my wounds, and reported to the cow barn. When I came in, Butch and Joe stared at me. I didn't have to say what had happened. They knew all too well.

A few days later, when the shock had worn off, but with wounds still far from healed, my morning sleep was broken up by a poke in the ribs, a shake of the shoulders. "Hey, little buddy, wake up," Joe said. "If we don't get to breakfast before the crew shows up, we're in for it. Rub them sand piles out of your eyes and get a move on!"

Butch and Joe were jabbing me from both sides until I kicked them away. "Cut it out! My back smarts something fierce. Feels like a hundred bee-stings! Besides, it's pitch dark outside."

"We daren't wait for the rooster," Joe said. "We got to eat fast, gulp it down before the old man gets up. He'll check to make sure we're doing our chores.

"Wait 'til you lay eyes on them two up-to-date beauties in the field out yonder," Butch said. "We got us a steam engine and a real live threshing machine. I bet you never did see the like."

"It's the big day. The one we've been talking about." Joe straightened his shoulders and puffed out his chest. "I'll be in charge of the technical work, alongside a couple other highly skilled fellers. Thing is, to undertake a big time job like mine, a fella's got to have experience."

"He thinks he's hot stuff." Butch said with a sniff.

"Takes genuine know-how," Joe kept it up, "because if I don't toss them in right, I'll gum up the whole works, and the steam engineer will blow his stack."

"There'll be this big explosion." Butch gave out a loud laugh.

"Don't you get it?" Joe said. "If the worst happens he's got to shut down the whole doggone pipeline to get the innards unclogged. I know firsthand. Last year I done it a couple times. For sure it won't happen this time."

Butch made gestures to indicate Joe was showing off.

"You got to understand," Joe said. "To do my job I got to know the ropes forwards and backwards. They count on me to do things right, and I ain't never going to let Goodman down." He raised his chin the way folks do when they're so proud of themselves they're about to pop.

"He's showing off," Butch said, "First we got to wolf down our breakfast, milk the cows, and do our chores."

"You're right," Joe said, "When we get all that done, the threshing ring shows up, and everybody hustles like a hive of bees." Both of them were so excited, their words bumped into each other.

"It's all kind of fun when you get right down to it," Butch said.

"Old Man Olson don't act half bad when there's other folks around," Joe said.

"You'd swear he's half-human."

"Are you guys going soft in the head?" I asked. "Ain't this our best chance to let folks know what we're up against? What a crazy devil he is? All we've got to do is show the stripes on our backs. Well, if these folks ain't as low down as Old Man Olson, they'll tell the sheriff, and if he's any kind of a lawman, he'll haul the crazy old coot off to the bughouse."

"Don't even dream about it," Joe said, suddenly gone pale and twitchy.

"They're in cahoots—him and the sheriff." Butch lowered his eyes.

"I'm telling you," Joe said. "The man's got eyes in back of his head, like a schoolmarm, and he's got ways of finding out the least little thing we say or do. Even now, when we think it's safe to open up and spit out the truth, just between the three of us, like as not, he's got ears in the walls."

I laughed, putting on like it would take more than Old Man Olson to throw a scare into me. I rubbed my hand across the wall. "Can't find no ears."

"You ain't had lesson enough?" Butch asked.

"Some folks got to learn the hard way," said Joe.

"Promise you won't spill the beans?"

"Okay, okay—but that just holds for today. I don't aim to be dog meat, and I ain't spending my life getting kicked around either. Most of all, I swear to God, I'll never again meet up with Elvira. I'd bash the old geezer's brains in first."

As the three of us came walking up to the house, the first rays of sun lit up the road. A man wearing a straw hat, dark trousers, and suspenders came along, driving a wagon pulled by a team of strong horses. Beside him sat a plump, buxom lady in a long, calico dress covered by an ample apron, and behind her on a bench sat two skinny boys, dressed in smaller versions of the man's outfit.

"Holy Methuselah!" I whistled, my eyes fixed on those horses. "I'll just bet they're the same handsome chestnuts I spied riding out that first day with Old Man Olson and Mabel. I held my breath and crossed my fingers, passing that fine farm, hoping like the very devil that was where I was headed, but, just my luck, I wound up in this dump."

"That's Neighbor Goodman's place," Joe said. "His farmstead's the showplace of the county. He's the steam engineer for our threshing ring, smart as a whip and up-to-date on all the best newfangled farm rigs."

"Too bad you didn't get picked by him," Butch said.

"He wasn't there. I'd remember that one."

"He don't need a boy," Joe said. "He's a hard worker."

"He's already got two boys of his own," Butch said, "but they're too little to be much good."

"Old Man Olson has us under his thumb," Joe said. "Well, of course, we ain't little, and we ain't his own flesh and blood, thank the Good Lord. He took us in, because he don't want to work hard his own self, and he sticks to the old ways of doing. He ain't about to change, so he'll keep on needing strapping young fellers, and unless we get chopped to bits, those just happen to be us."

"How'd this Goodman get in good with the old timers?" I asked. "Where'd his fancy notions come from, and how'd he talk his neighbors into throwing in with him?"

"The man's a whiz," Joe said, "and a right decent feller. Folks say there were letters flying back and forth from him to the ag school in Ames. That's where all the up-to-date notions come from.

"I expect that's how Goodman came up with the threshing ring idea. He got a bunch of farmers to throw in with him. Olson was the toughest fish to catch, but Goodman reeled him in. The whole thing added up to one swell deal for the lot of them. Nobody, except for Goodman, could've swung it by his own self. He ain't tight-fisted. Not like Olson.

"The factory where them monster machines came from wouldn't send them out 'til they got cash on the barrelhead, so Goodman threw in the lion's share."

"But he let them others in anyhow," Butch said. "Each farmer forked over what he could spare. In Olson's case, a drop in the bucket. He's a tightwad, but Goodman's name says it all. Well, the way it always goes, when somebody stands out from the crowd, the old green-eyed monster gets the best of some. The dumb ones call him Moneybags—behind his back, of course."

"He keeps all the gear at his place, when it ain't in use," Joe said. "In that big humdinger of a barn he's got. His gear's in out of the rain, lousy weather and all, so it don't go rusty and fall to pieces."

"He's the only one in the crew knows how to start her up," said Butch.

"Howdy, Boys," called out Farmer Goodman, jumping down and tying up his horses. His small boys jumped after him and helped the lady out. She was carrying a huge basket of food.

"Go on in, Ma," said the older boy. "Tom and me'll haul in the rest." For such little kids, they sure were ambitious.

Joe threw an arm over my shoulder. "Ouch!" I yelled.

"Oops! Forgot!" Joe aimed his next comments at Mr. Goodman. "Pete here's got a bad case of sunburn." He winked at me. "Mr. Goodman's the steam engineer. He'll set up that contraption you see out yonder. It's a whiz bang of a monster that needs oiling, fitting parts together, cranking up the steam engine, and all that."

"I aim to be a steam engineer when I grow up," Butch said with a grin.

"You ain't cut out for it," Joe said, poking him in the ribs. "Mr. Goodman's got more brains in his little finger than you've got in that whole jackass head of yours."

"Don't sell the little feller short," said Mr. Goodman. "A few years of hard work, sticking to business, trying out every job we got, trouble spots and all, he'll show you what he's made of."

"Well, you set more store by him than I do," Joe said. "He ain't showed a whole lot of horse sense yet."

"Who's your friend?" Farmer Goodman nodded at me.

"That's Pete," Joe said, forgetting again and throwing his arm over my shoulder.

"Watch it," I whispered.

"You one of them orphans?"

"Sort of," I said.

"How can you be sort of?" said the younger Goodman boy. "Either you are one or you ain't."

"Half," Joe said.

"He's half," Butch said. "Ma's dead; Pa's a bum."

That didn't have a good ring to it, but I let it go.

Farmer Goodman and his boys walked on toward the house. As they climbed the front steps, Mabel opened the kitchen door, letting in a whole slew of buzzing flies. Farmer Goodman hurried in, batting with his hat. The boys followed.

"Well, set yourselves down," Farmer Olson said in a friendly tone. My eyes popped wide open in surprise. This was the first time I'd met up with the old buzzard since he just about beat the stuffing out of me, and I'd never heard him talk nice like that.

I think old Mabel was doing her level best to keep us apart, so another major attack wouldn't happen. She knew, just like we did, somebody was going to die—most likely me.

"My three boys got to milk and chore before they set out for the field," Olson said. "And you, Goodman, got your work cut out for you."

It was downright spooky how reasonable the man sounded when outsiders were there.

Mrs. Goodman did the cooking. She brought our breakfast to the table: fried eggs, bacon, cornbread, and hotcakes steaming with butter and maple syrup. Mable stoked the fire in the cook-stove with dried corncobs. We all gobbled our food as fast as Mrs. Goodman brought it.

"Well Sir?" Olson said. "Are you ready for a blistering hot, hard slogging day?"

"It ain't like old times," said Farmer Goodman. "I expect by now you're glad you throwed in with us."

"Cost me an arm and a leg," growled Olson. "If you wasn't such a slick talker, I'd never have gone along with it."

"You'll get your small investment back in spades, not to speak of the backbreaking labor you're saving."

Goodman always answered in a pleasant way, acting like he didn't even hear the old fool's bellyaching.

Old Man Olson kept his face close to his plate, tossing in food like his fork was a shovel.

"Nice day," Farmer Goodman said.

"Gonna be a hot one," said Olson.

"Well, it's August. Good corn's got to have a hot August. Brings on nice tassels."

"Brings on heart failure," said Olson.

Farmer Goodman rose when his last bite was swallowed. "Can't stay to pass the time of day. Got to oil up them machines and get them going before the crew shows up. You, Dick, and you, Harvey," he addressed his boys. "Linger over your breakfast all you need to, but come on out to lend a hand when you've had your fill. I might could use a couple errand boys."

More horses and buggies began to arrive with women carrying large kettles, plates, and baskets of food.

"Mabel ain't up to taking this on by her own self, but neighbor ladies come in right handy on a day like this," mumbled Olson as if talking to himself.

"All right, you rapscallions, before them biddies fill up every nook and cranny—skedaddle." Now that Goodman was gone, Olson, knocked Joe on the head. "You know what you got to do. Get to it and make sure them boys keep their noses to the grindstone. Hear?"

He must've forgot Dick and Harvey were still there. Their eyes widened, big as goose eggs, but Olson didn't seem to notice.

I'd finally got the knack of milking. As we finished up our morning chores, more horses and wagons began to arrive, and the Goodman boys stuck their heads in the barn to see what we were up to.

"What's all the racket?" I shouted, as a noisy clang rang out from the field and a whistle started tooting.

"It's the steam engine that powers the threshing machine," young Dick said. "You'll hear plenty more of that before the day's over."

"Tonight's full moon," Harvey said. "Pa says he'll be slaving away running that machine 'til the wee hours."

I felt the excitement rise as everyone raced to the field, and Mr. Goodman jumped up on top of the wagon to make an announcement.

"Okay, folks, looks like we're all here. Everybody does the same as last time, only now we got us one more kid on the straw pile. This boy, Pete, is from the big city. Show him how it's done, but go easy on him. It's his first time out, and he'll more than likely find the going a bit rougher than he's used to."

Steam belched from the chimney. The belt began to move. Joe stood on top of a wagon drawn by a team of Belgian horses and top-heavy with neatly stacked bundles of oats, grain parts in, butt ends out. The wagon driver pulled his load to the side of the threshing machine. Then Joe and another young man began pitching bundles into the hopper. Men in another wagon, farther out in the field, were loading up bundles, making ready to take over, when Joe and his partner had emptied their load.

Harvey pushed me into place beside the threshing machine where the straw blew out. "Dick and me will be doing the same job as you," he said. I felt kind of dumb doing what those little kids did, but they measured up lots bigger than they looked. They were hard workers.

"Just rake it up, and pile it high," added Dick.

Joe wasn't kidding. The straw and the chaff blew into my eyes and settled under my shirt. Before long the heat of the day, alongside all the raw spots from Elvira, left me feeling the miseries, sweaty, dirty, and thirsty.

Being all caught up in my job, I didn't see him come up on me 'til I felt a strong hand on my shoulder. I was hot as a sun-baked rat and steamed up furious at Joe. Seemed like that fool never could learn a thing. A touch like that made my fresh wounds smart like the dickens. I looked up from the rake, the dust, and the flying straw, with a feisty look on my face, ready to light into him. There I stood, staring into the kind and gentle eyes of Farmer Goodman.

"Son," he shouted, over the noise of the clanking machines, "don't let yourself go dry. When you need a drink, give young Butch the high sign. Don't matter how often. That's what he's here for. I already gave my own kids a break. They're pretty young for this kind of work."

Myself, I hadn't even noticed they'd gone. I'd just kept on pitching away.

"A hot day like this one will be extra tough on a city kid that ain't used to farm work," he said. "From what I've seen, you're a decent, hard working young one, and I don't want to see you sick or passing out."

I gulped. Words froze in my throat. I sure wasn't used to easy treatment and couldn't think of a single word to let him know how I felt. A few embarrassing tears got loose. I mopped them away with my sleeve. I sure as heck hoped Goodman would mistake those stupid leaks for sweat.

He gave me another friendly pat. Somehow, pain like that was fine. It felt kind of good. Then Farmer Goodman climbed back aboard the hissing steam engine, replacing the farmer who'd taken over in his absence, and tended to the controls once more.

Butch rode his horse right up next to me. "Now there's a stunner! What did the man say? I never saw him leave his machine in the middle of a job—ever."

"He said to drink lots of water," I said in as gruff a voice as I could conjure up. I reached for the canteen, took a good swig, then grabbed my rake and tore into that straw pile. I was feeling no pain and didn't give a hoot how much sweat poured out of me. I was a man.

<hr />

Midmorning, two ladies rode out to the field in a small, horse-drawn wagon. They brought coffee, a sweet fruit drink they called nectar, sandwiches, and cookies.

"Hits the spot!" Goodman said, and hats were tossed in the air with hilarious whoops.

"Man!" Joe said, "I didn't think I could hold out much longer. Them ladies do show up in the nick of time."

Butch and I nodded while slurping our drinks.

For two more hours we worked our tails off as the sun grew brighter and hotter, and at noon, when the whistle blew and the machines stopped, we hallooed and threw ourselves into the big haystack. The men sauntered off towards the house and started scrubbing up in pans of water that were set out on the porch. They splashed, head to foot, cleaning up after all the heat and sweat. I expect they felt like they'd hit paradise after that hot morning's hustle.

Mabel didn't have room in the house for such a crowd. Besides, it was pretty much a mess in there, so tables made from boards and sawhorses were set up under the trees. The ladies came running with huge platters of fried chicken, mashed potatoes, gravy, roasting ears, and all that served up with fresh homemade bread and butter. I couldn't believe my good luck. I'd never in my life tasted such good eats and piles of it. All you could eat and then some.

"Hey! Threshing day ain't so bad after all," I said, poking Joe.

"Told you so, but of course I knew you wouldn't believe 'til you tasted the real thing."

"Enjoy it while you can," Butch said. "There's five more farms to go before the ring breaks up for the season. After that we won't eat nothing worth spit 'til next year."

"You ought to come along to a church supper," said Harvey.

"Them church ladies do their durndest to out-cook each other," Dick said, "so we let them know we appreciate their efforts. We stuff ourselves 'til we almost spill over. Of course, we go home with bellyaches, but it's worth the effort. Why not make them ladies proud?" He rubbed his stomach.

Next, the ladies brought out big slabs of apple and cherry pie with home churned ice cream on the side.

When our plates were licked clean, Farmer Goodman approached. "I'd like to give you kids a longer rest," he said, "but the sooner we get back to work, the quicker we can knock off for the night."

The afternoon went just about like the morning, except everybody worked a little slower, the sun was hotter, and our clothes sweatier. We drudged on without bellyaching. Butch came by regular to wet our whistles. Man! It took big gulps and long swigs from Butch's canteen to do the job. The ladies came back in mid-afternoon and again at suppertime with more sandwiches, coffee, nectar, and big, scrumptious hunks of cake.

Everybody worked a little slower, the sun was hotter, and our clothes sweatier.

After supper, Goodman made Dick and Harvey go inside to help their Ma. They raised objections, but being the right kind of boys, they minded their pa.

By nightfall, the full moon and stars lit up the black sky. That made it so the team could keep at it 'til the final shock was pitched and the last bit of chaff was raked into the pile. "Phew!" Butch groaned. "I'm all pooped out."

The whistle blew, and Mr. Goodman turned off the steam engine. He climbed on top of the empty wagon to announce, "Good work, men and boys! We'll take tomorrow off to catch up on things that need doing out home. Come Wednesday, we'll meet at Paulsens' and play this game all over again."

"Some game," I grumbled. "I'm frazzled."

Old Man Olson heard that. "You got chores to do," he growled.

Joe snapped to attention. "We'll get right to them," he said.

Old Man Olson strolled over to talk with Farmer Goodman, and us boys started running towards the barn. "The old bird's loony!" I said. "Why ain't he locked up?"

"Hush," Joe said. "You don't know who's listening and what gets back to him."

I could hear Old Man Olson's growl over by Goodman. He sounded weird, like a ghost from down under, but I was too dog-tired to even think about what that sound meant.

"Let's get at them chores," Joe said.

I groaned.

"Tell you what," Joe said, "Butch and me will take care of the girls. You go feed the hogs and chickens."

"I won't put up with no bellyaching!" Old Man Olson growled, sneaking up from behind. "And don't come crying to me about your headaches and sore backs. I've heard all that before. I don't put up with idlers. Get on with your chores right smart a bit, and come morning you rise and shine before the rooster crows. Got that?"

"Yes Sir!" we yelled like we had just one voice.

⁕

After we finally got done, we dropped in our bed, worn out like overworked horses, but cramped together like usual. We hadn't been resting long when a soft woman's voice cut through the quiet of the place. "Come and get it!" she said, just loud enough for us to hear, but not a speck louder. It was Mabel. She had her hair pulled back in a bun with strays sticking out every which way. She wore a long, homespun housedress with a dirty apron on top. Under one arm she hugged a loaf of bread, while she held onto one of those cast-iron pots with a lid and a round handle on top.

"I figured you might could use a little extra tonight. Hurry up now and gulp it down quick before he finds out." She plunked down the pot, so a bit of soup sloshed onto the crude floorboards. Then she turned and ran out.

"Well, don't that beat all!" Joe said.

"She's as spooked by the old buzzard as we are," I said.

"I don't trust her." Butch said. "She's a parrot. Repeats every stupid word the old man spits out. Either the woman's addlebrained, or it's her own dopey way to stay on his good side. Trouble is, he ain't got a good side."

"Truer words was never spoke. But maybe that's how come she's lasted so long," Joe said. "She don't aim to wind up down by the river—in little pieces."

"I'm too worn out to eat," I said.

Butch and Joe crawled out of bed, filled their tin cups in the near darkness. There was just a sliver of light from the crescent moon. They dunked their bread and slurped their soup fast as it would go down.

I pinched my nose, trying to shut out the barnyard stink, but I had to breathe. I moved my eyes to the crumpled catalog pictures stuck to the wall, the rusty bed frame, the miserable little room we lived in.

There's got to be a way out of this! I felt like saying that but didn't. Butch and Joe dropped back into bed, fitting themselves in on the sides. I got to thinking about Goodman. Now there was the kind of feller I'd work my heart out for, but here I was, stuck with Old Man Olson. I was worn out, but couldn't seem to drop off. I stayed awake, far into the night, thinking.

CHAPTER 14

AGNES SHOWS UP

IRIS

"I can't see no sense to this schooling business," Albert said to Minnie. It was September and country school was about to begin a new term. She nodded, to show she thought so too, but then added something interesting. "You got the right slant on it, Albert, but the thing is, if you'll recollect, they made us sign a paper that day at the opera house. I expect there ain't no way around that."

I hadn't seen the paper, but I kept thinking back to what Reverend Brace said, just before all us kids boarded the train. "Every child will attend public school until finishing eighth grade or beyond if the state requires. No exceptions." He was stern and stiff, but he said what he meant straight out, didn't fudge, and wasn't the sort to pull the wool over anybody's eyes. Remembering that helped keep my hopes up. I wanted to go to school in the worst way. I missed being with other kids, especially Rosie. "I will go to school!" I made myself a promise, fingers crossed, hoping.

Albert and Minnie exchanged funny looks. "I know what you mean," Albert grumbled. "We signed them dad-blamed papers."

That first day of school, I put on a dress from the Children's Aid Society, one of the three they sent with me on the train. I brushed my hair and made myself look as good as I could, considering my wild hair and big feet. Rosie used to say I was pretty, but there was good reason for her to think that. When you really love somebody it doesn't matter much how they look. You just love them, and that's all there is to it. Downstairs, I made breakfast as usual, covering up with an apron to keep my dress fresh and clean for school.

I tried to leave the kitchen clean, neat, and tidy. I wasn't going to give Albert and Minnie one thing to complain about. Then I ran out the back door and set out on the long walk, my heart beating wildly with joy.

School! I'd never been to one, but Flora taught me plenty. Even though it was just play, she was a very good teacher. She was smart, and she'd learned a lot at the mission in Five Points. When she was real little, she was turned loose on the streets while her Ma and Pa worked, but a missionary lady found her lollygagging around one day and took her inside for Sunday School. That same lady taught her to read, write, and cipher. Flora passed along what she knew, years later, to me, and I was able to help teach Rosie. Thank goodness for that!

Would I fit in? Would I know enough to keep up with the others? Would the other kids like me?

Meadowlarks sang from the fence posts; the sun was bright in the blue sky. It seemed the day was made to bring happiness. I knew the way. Albert and Minnie told me exactly where to turn, and all the things I'd see along the way. It was a long walk, but I enjoyed every minute of it. Each step brought me closer to school.

It was a small, white, wooden building with a bell tower on top and several steps up. Some kids were playing a game city kids don't play. A few days later, I learned it was called Annie Over. How happy they looked. What fun!

But when I got there, everybody stopped playing, stood in the grass, arms crossed, just staring at me. My face felt hot as sun-baked brick, my fingers clammy. What had I done wrong? Was it my dress? My hair? My big feet? I did feel hot and sweaty after my long walk, but those kids didn't look fresh from a bandbox either.

I said "Hello," as if nothing unusual was going on. "I'm Iris O'Leary, and I've come to be a student."

After more awkward stares, a boy finally broke the silence. "So you're one of them," he said.

"Them?" I think my voice sounded kind of shaky.

"One of them orphans from the train." I won't say what name he called me.

"Maynard!" one girl said to him, "Ma said you wasn't never to say that. It's a bad word."

"Don't matter if I say it or don't," Maynard said. "She is one, no matter how you shilly-shally round about."

I turned and walked slowly towards the stairs, trying to act like nothing, but I was shaking with rage.

I opened the door to the schoolroom, scared half out of my wits, wondering what horrible thing would happen next. A pretty young woman sat at a desk up on a platform in front. Children's desks of three different sizes were lined up in neat rows down below. The platform made me think of Miss Harkin in the orphanage, and my legs went weak and wobbly.

The woman glanced up from her book and flashed a lovely smile. "Well, hello there, young lady. I'll just bet you are Iris O'Leary. I'm Lucinda Bloom, and I've been expecting you."

Suddenly, as if fanned by a pleasant breeze, I felt cool and happy. "I'm so glad to meet you, Miss Bloom. If you'll just give me a chance, I'll show you, I'm not what they think. I can be a good student. I'll try so hard." The words fairly flew out of me.

"I'm quite sure you will be," replied Miss Bloom. "Now, before that rowdy bunch comes in, let's go through a few exercises. We'll start with reading and arithmetic, just to give us both an idea where to begin. How does that sound?"

"Wonderful," I said.

Miss Bloom handed me a book to read aloud. After that she asked questions.

"Good comprehension," she said. She gave me a slate and wrote arithmetic problems on it. First addition, then subtraction, multiplication, and division. I got them all right.

"You're a bit older than the others, but we'll place you in sixth grade for now," Miss Bloom said, "If you do as well as I think you'll do, you'll soon skip to a higher grade. There are four others at the sixth grade level. This school only goes to eighth. Now it's time to ring the bell. The children will come in, and we will begin our school day. Do you have any questions?"

"What happens after eighth grade?"

Miss Bloom stepped down from her platform, took my hand and gave it a little squeeze. "I'll make sure this is not the end of the road for you," she said.

I followed her as she rang the school bell. The children stopped playing their game and raced to the steps. Once inside, the horseplay stopped. They filed into the schoolroom in orderly fashion and took their places as Miss Bloom directed.

Miss Bloom said a short prayer and then asked me to stand and face the class. My legs felt like rubber, as I stood there facing Maynard and the kids I'd met in the schoolyard.

"This is our new pupil, Iris O'Leary, who will begin as a sixth grader. She will be in your group, Velma, Mabel, Tillie, and Maynard. Please stand and welcome her."

The three girls and the boy I'd met outside stood and stared at me with blank faces.

"Of course, you will treat Iris with courtesy and kindness," Miss Bloom said. "It is very difficult to be a new student. Put yourselves in her shoes, and act accordingly. Now, with that said, you may all take your seats." She told our group to begin reading about the Louisiana Purchase while she heard the first and second graders read aloud. Third, fourth, and fifth graders were to read from their McGuffeys and write up questions to ask each other about their lesson. The little kids marched forward, single file, and sat in tiny chairs up front, with Miss Bloom seated in the middle.

As I read about the Louisiana Purchase, I tried my very best to remember all the facts, in case I'd be tested, but I was soon distracted. A slate was being passed among the four other kids in my group. Miss Bloom was too busy with the little kids to notice. Tillie was the last of the four to read what it said. She let out a snicker and passed it on to me.

Hot blood flooded my face. There before me, in bold letters, was the word Maynard had used on the playground. Bastard! If only I could have talked this insult over with Flora. She would know exactly what to do, but I was almost grown up now. I must

She told our group to begin reading about the Louisiana Purchase while she heard the first and second graders read aloud.

learn to take care of myself. I just hoped that Rosie didn't have to go through anything like this. I didn't tell on them. That would have made things even worse. I would never be their friend, but they stopped using the word. I guess it was no fun when they couldn't make me cry.

I continued making the long walk to school every day and home again in the afternoon. I used the time to memorize my lessons and to daydream about rescuing Rosie.

My routine with Albert and Minnie never changed. One dreary day followed another. Time dragged slowly and wearily by, until the first autumn leaves turned golden and some began to fall. The air was still and dry and filled with dust. When Albert raked, the smell of burning leaves filtered into the kitchen. That rather pleasant smell almost, but not quite, covered up the horrid stink of the pigs.

I knew by this time that in Albert and Minnie's eyes I was not quite up to snuff. Not the bang-up hired girl they hoped they were getting. Minnie kept spouting long lists of things I did wrong, so I didn't dare ask for favors. Since that nasty day, learning how to kill chickens, my skill as a butcher had not improved. But at least my cooking had. It wasn't first-rate, but good enough to get by.

One day, as Albert came hobbling in, just before dinner, he piped up, "Sakes alive! Something sure smells good. By Johnny, it sets my mouth to watering like the creek bubbling up in springtime."

"It's roast beef and apple pudding," I said, feeling pride in my voice.

"Did you mix up the sugar and salt again?" We both laughed.

I pretended his tired old joke was fresh and funny. Albert slapped his knee with delight. I was still just learning to cook. Alongside the stringy beef, I served lumpy mashed potatoes and greasy gravy, but both Albert and Minnie smacked their lips and grinned with pleasure.

The time had arrived. I was scared to death. I'm sure my voice was weak and shaky. "I have something to say."

"How's that?" Minnie cupped her ear.

I gulped and hesitated. "I hope you liked the apple pudding."

"Not too bad," Albert said, licking his lips.

"You're doing some better," Minnie said, smacking hers.

We talked about every dish on the supper table and the good and bad points about each one. Albert hardly had time to say a word. He could win a prize as the world's fastest eater, but Minnie managed to throw out a few complaints.

Albert polished off his last bite, tossed down fork and spoon and was about to spring from his seat. It was now or never. I got up, bit my lip, cleared my throat and started my little speech.

"Before you leave for the barn, Albert—," I stood, twisting my hankie. My face felt like sparks were shooting out of it. I couldn't seem to get the words out.

"Speak up!" Albert commanded.

"It's my little sister—Rosie!" I shouted, "I just have to find her!" I stood rigid, steamy, and trembling. "She means more to me than anything else in the world! You can make things happen in this crazy place, and I can't! Help me! Oh, please help me!" There, I'd said it. I could hardly believe I'd had the nerve. My knees were shaking so hard, I clamped my hands on them, trying to make it stop.

"Mercy me," Minnie snapped. "They told us down to the opera house they was against putting you sisters together. Don't ask me hows come, but them's the rules."

Albert scratched his nose. "Besides, she belongs to the Hartfields now."

"Don't nobody mess with them Hartfields," Minnie said.

"Hartfield's a great man in these parts," Albert added, almost like he was talking about the preacher.

"Hartfield—you see, he's the banker—big feller—and he built the town up from scratch, paid for the opera house, park, bandstand. You name it."

Minnie nodded vigorously with each word of praise. "Half the town either works for Hartfield or borrows from his bank. He's fair and honest as they come, and the man pays right good wages." She scratched her head for a minute, then frowned. "But you can't approach the missus. See, they was high-toned folks back in England! Way above the likes of us!"

"Only the high muck-a-mucks ever get inside High Point," Albert said.

"If we dared stick a foot in the back door, they'd pitch us out like scraps for the junk pile."

"Are you telling me to forget about Rosie? My little sister?" I cried. "That we can't ever be together? Is that what you're saying?" My cheeks were burning. I'm sure I was a sorry sight.

"Well? " Minnie held her head between both hands. Both Albert and I waited for something big. Minnie screwed up her mouth and aimed a piercing gaze at me. "I might just have a card up my sleeve."

Albert grinned and slapped his knee. "There's my woman!" he crowed. I took a deep breath.

"We just might have some pull with their parlor maid." Minnie giggled. "Parlor maid." she giggled so much she had to wipe her eyes, as if she'd never heard of anything so silly. "Did you ever hear the like? Well, they might as well have one. They got everything else. Agnes is the girl's name, and she ain't just any old Agnes. It so happens, we've known this one since she was not much bigger than a thimble. Well, you ought to see her now."

"That's a fact," Albert shouted, grinning as he flipped his straw hat. "Her ma and pa farm just down the road and round the bend. We've known Agnes since she was—not much bigger than a thimble, and if you got a good look at her now, it's a sure thing you wouldn't miss out on Minnie's joke." He slapped his knee again and gave out a big old horselaugh.

"I'm thinking they might could use some extra kitchen help up to High Point, scrubbing pots and pans and such." Minnie winked. You'd have to keep the secret, of course, you being sisters and all, but for right now, the main thing is—"she shook a warning finger at me. "—Don't count your chickens before they're hatched."

Then Albert started in. "Trouble is, since Agnes got that job at High Point, she's taken on airs like she was Queen of Sheba."

"He's got a point there," Minnie said, "That girl acts so uppity, I'd scarce dare even pass the time of day with her."

"Way too high up for the likes of us," said Albert, "and it ain't just her. It's hard to figure just how far this thing goes, like weeds sprouting up all over the garden. Her ma and pa was once plain old dirt farmers like the rest of us. Well, since Agnes has got so high and mighty, they act just like her, noses stuck way up in the air, a-reaching for the stars."

"It ain't a pretty picture," Minnie said, "but give me a minute. I'll slap on my thinking cap and hatch up some kind of scheme. Should be able to pull something out of my bag of tricks. The thing is, if you get in good with them Hartfields, well, maybe Albert and me can get in good too. No telling how far this thing could go."

Albert grinned. "Minnie looks like a barn cat, all set and ready to pounce."

⁕

Several weeks passed. The leaves had gone beyond their gorgeous red stage and now were crispy brown and blowing in the lane. It seemed clear as glass, Minnie had either forgotten or had no intention of helping me out. As she liked to say about other folks, she was "all blow and no go." It seemed even harder than that first time to gather up my courage and demand my rights. Remembering that day, when Minnie's big talk had filled me with hope, made me more miserable than ever.

I kept up my work but didn't move so fast as before. Housework was such an effort. I'd so much rather be studying. School was the one bright light in my life. Without Miss Bloom, I'd have turned sour as a lemon.

⁕

One Saturday morning in October, Albert and Minnie rode off with their horse and buggy and came back with news that important visitors were coming for afternoon coffee. "Stir up another apple pudding." Minnie snapped out orders. "A bowl of that'll crack the hardest nut that's dropped from the tree."

"Nuts? Cracking nuts? What are you talking about?" I asked.

Albert grinned. "Minnie's up to something," he said. "You tell it, Dearie. Just look at her," he pointed to Minnie, whose face had a funny look I hadn't seen before. "Don't she just look like the cat that swallowed the canary?"

Minnie's thin lips widened into a great big grin. "I done it," she said, snapping her finger. "Remember that Agnes I told you about? Well, I've been sleuthing around, found out her day off's Saturday, and she'll be coming home to see her ma and pa. So what did I do? Just threw on my best dress and took out after Albert. It ain't easy to get him cleaned up, but here he is—clean shirt, pants, even a clean handkerchief sticking out his pocket. Well, I can tell you, they stood up and took notice. We told them we had ourselves a parlor maid too, and they should just come on over and see for their own selves. I expect we come up some in their estimation."

"But you just said this Agnes is a hard nut to crack." I said.

"It's all how you look at it," Albert said, scratching his head.

"She used to be more like common folk," Minnie said. "I wouldn't go so far as to say she was salt of the earth, cream of the crop, peachy keen. None of that. You might say she don't even pass muster, but way back when, you could sit down with her and chew the fat. She'd give out tips on cleaning chicken houses, how to keep canned goods from going bad, ways to keep bugs from taking over the flour barrel. Things like that. We all got to find our way in the world one way or another. Well, that's all out the window now. She's picked up a thing or two from that snooty Mrs. Hartfield." Minnie turned up her nose, curled her little finger and strutted about mocking Agnes and Mrs. Hartfield.

"This new Agnes is uppity and tight-lipped as a vinegar bottle," Albert said.

"Oh, she's got tales to tell," Minnie said. "The whole town's on edge, dying to get an insider's look at what goes on in that fancy showplace up on the hill," She was just getting started. "Folks want to know what kind of furniture, do-dads and all the foofaraw and frippery they got in the place—what they eat for supper and what they do after. Agnes has the low-down—secrets galore—but the woman's lips are sealed. Tighter'n a drum."

"Maybe them Hartfields are scared folks'll find out where the gold and silver's buried." Albert laughed, slapping his thigh the way he always did when he thought he'd told a good one. "But the worst fly in the ointment is that dad-blamed rule. That might could squeeze us out, you know. Sisters can't be placed out together. Them bigwigs call the tune, but it's the dumbest tune I've heard yet."

"Iris?" Minnie looked me in the eye. "Can you keep a secret?"

"Of course," I said. "You know I can."

"Well then, you got your marching orders."

"We'll put you to the test," Albert said. "Go stir up some apple pudding. After the eating's over and done with, they'll go home, and you can bet your boots, they'll still be picking their teeth to grab hold of another scrum-delicious crumb. After that, Agnes is sure to put in a good word for you. Remember, though, when they've cleared out, you still got to serve up a larruping good supper for Minnie and me."

"Oh yes, I will! I'll do anything!" I called that out as I hurried to stir up some apple pudding, and prepare the coffeepot. I scrubbed the kitchen until it looked bright and shiny, at least the best I knew how to do. Then I set the table and raced upstairs, taking two at a time, hurrying to tackle my messy hair.

I brushed until my scalp tingled, but the effect was not what I had hoped. I stared at myself in the cracked mirror hanging from a wire in Albert and Minnie's room. I sure didn't look like a stuck-up parlor maid. At first I frowned, then pasted on a smile, which did seem to improve things—a little bit. I donned a clean apron and returned to the bright, shiny kitchen, hoping I'd done enough to impress the fine ladies.

I licked the spoon, tasting my apple pudding. Its sweetness filled the house with its yummy cinnamon smell. I listened. The kitchen clock seemed to tick much louder than usual, and its hands barely turned. It seemed as if two o'clock would never come, and when it finally did, I hurried outside to watch for the Jensen buggy. After ten minutes of scanning the prairie round about, it still had not shown up, so I ran all the way on the long, bumpy lane. Shielding my eyes, I stared down the dirt road. The trees, having lost many leaves, allowed me to see a long way off. When finally a cloud of dust flew up, I ran back to the kitchen, smoothed back my hair, and straightened my apron.

The dust flew across the rutted lane as the horse and buggy neared the barn. Two women, one young and stout, one thin and old, got out, tied up their horse, and walked slowly towards the house. The old woman wore a long black dress and black bonnet. She was slightly bent and held onto the younger one's elbow as she hobbled along. As they got closer to the door, I noticed the young one was dressed much finer than most farm women. Her dress was of pale blue dimity with lace edgings.

They came to the front door. It was the first time we'd used it since I'd been there. Minnie opened the screen door, shooing the flies away as the ladies entered. "Well, if it ain't our favorite neighbors," she crowed, laughing as she wrung her hands. It looked to me as if Minnie didn't know what else to do with them. "Come on in and make yourselves to home." She took them in the parlor where nobody ever sat, but that was just for show. Soon she dragged them to the kitchen.

"Iris, you come on in here and take Mrs. Jensen's shawl, and hang it up there on the hall tree. There's a good girl." I did as I was told and then remained in the hall so they couldn't see me. I was so nervous. "Now, just you ladies set yourselves down here at the kitchen table, and we'll have us a nice big helping of Iris' famous apple pudding and some coffee. Oh, don't that egg coffee smell good? Our girl Iris made it. She's our parlor maid, you know. That girl does know how to make a good cup of coffee. Iris—oh Iris!" Minnie called out to me like she was Queen Victoria. She just had to ring the servant's bell, and her every wish would be granted.

I came back from the hallway, my knees shaking, hands trembling. I couldn't afford to make a mistake since everything, my future and Rosie's, depended on this meeting. I had, over the weeks and months, grown used to these shabby surroundings, but now, with these distinguished guests, I felt at a great disadvantage. I couldn't make the kind of show I'd hoped for. The peeling wallpaper, the pig stink, the worn out oilcloth and cracked linoleum made the whole place seem a mess, even if I had scrubbed it pretty clean.

I knew, although I had not been introduced, that the big lady in blue was Agnes, but I felt a lump in my throat and a skipped heartbeat when that woman looked me over, head to toe. Her eyes seemed to drill right through me, and she said not one word. The old lady cocked her head and squinted like one of the old hens in the chicken yard. "Well?" She crowed. "What have we here? Is this that orphan girl you spoke of or what?"

"You're looking at her," Minnie said with a grin. She pointed at me. "I've been singing your praises, Pun'kin, so flash them a smile." I did my best.

Minnie turned her attention back to the visiting ladies. "Maybe she don't look like much to you folks, and, well, you know, I recollect feeling kind of that way my own self first off, but she's turned out a mighty good hired girl." Minnie's hand flew to her lips. "Oops, I got that wrong. She's our parlor maid. And she takes orders real good, once you get her broke in. She's got the makings all right. Albert and me think that girl's a jim-dandy." I almost had to laugh. This was all news to me.

Agnes' critical eyes once again swept me up and down, head to toe. "If she's such a whiz, how come you and Albert don't hold on to her? Seems to me you're mighty anxious to get her off your hands."

"Oh, you got that all wrong," Minnie said. "I'll make no bones about it. We've been pleased as Punch to have her. She's a perfect little lady, and I reckon it'll bring on the miseries to let her go, but we don't aim to be selfish neither. Fact is, we're feeling right to home with the girl, but the thing is, we got to think of what's best for her, and even if it might just break our poor old hearts to let her go, it's the right and decent thing to do. Could be the very thing to lift the girl's spirits."

"What's wrong with her spirits?" snapped Agnes.

"Oh, it ain't that she goes grumping around, mind you, but I recollect Pastor Fineman put out a sermon or two, maybe three— four—maybe more. He's a great sermonizer, you know. If you'd show up in church once in a while you'd be up on all this. He's one to pound the pulpit. Half the time harping on Christian duty, taking in down-and-outers, widows, orphans, and such."

"Get to the point," snapped Mrs. Jensen.

"Well, you know, Albert and me aim to stand up for Jesus just as good as anybody. So with that in mind, thinking it ain't all that long 'til she'll be full grown, we got to thinking it might be the best thing for her to come work at High Point—do like Agnes here— take lessons on what's what. She'd get a few pointers on fancy doings, cooking and housekeeping tricks, such as them you've taken up. Might even soak up a feel for how to act around high-toned folks. We ain't so much that kind, you know. Not yet, anyhow, but who knows what could come of all this."

"It's altogether wrong to teach these orphans to put on airs," Agnes said.

"What good is all such frippery to such a one as this?" said Mrs. Jensen, peering through her glasses at me.

Minnie tilted back in her chair. "Well, you know, it won't be more than a couple years and the girl's about to turn into a woman." She looked at the doubtful expression on old Mrs. Jensen's face and clucked like she was inclined to do when she didn't know what to say next.

"I know," Minnie said. "I can see inside your head. You don't have to tell me. The girl's just fourteen, but you can't start too soon thinking about such things. Albert and me figure a couple years down the pike, she might need a boost. We'd like to see her come up in the world, and us along with her, of course. At High Point that ain't out of the question. Might be a pipe dream, but it could just happen."

Mrs. Jensen's face lit up with a little smirk.

"Well? It ain't out of the question," Minnie said. "The girl don't stand much chance out here with just Albert and me and the chickens."

"If you think I'll help the lot of you climb the social ladder, you can think again," Agnes said.

"What my girl is trying to say," interrupted old Mrs. Jensen, casting a stern eye at Agnes, "is that the Hartfields might could offer a job as scullery maid, washing dishes, scrubbing pots and pans, mopping up floors and such. It might could get her some pocket money and a bed to lie down on, but scullery maid ain't parlor maid, if you get my meaning, and the sad part is, even Agnes' high position ain't brought her no prospects."

"Wait just a minute!" Agnes started up, her face glowing red. "My situation in the Hartfield household can't be compared to a scullery maid's." She showed her teeth like a big cat ready to strike. "And I could've had plenty prospects, if I had a mind to, but I got no time for it. I'm busy keeping my eyes peeled on that orphan brat. It's my job to make sure she don't run away."

I popped up in my chair like a firecracker had gone off. Minnie shot me a warning glance and spoke real fast, making sure she got the jump on me. "How come the child wants to run away?"

Agnes shrugged her shoulders. "I get so provoked. She's an ungrateful little minx that just needs a good licking, but Mr. Hartfield's a pushover. Now, with the missus it's a different story. She don't like children and makes no bones about it. Strange thing is, he's nuts over this one. Couldn't dote on her more if she was his own flesh and blood. She's got him wrapped around her little finger, and still the imp ain't satisfied. Whoever got the bright idea

181

to send that pack of brats our way must've had a screw loose." Agnes glared at me, as she spoke.

I felt hot blood rush to my face. It could ruin everything if I showed my feelings, so I struggled and managed to keep my mouth shut.

"All the same," Mrs. Jensen said, "my girl has a high position in that fine house, and it's done her good. See how good she talks and how swell she dresses? We're right proud of our girl, and one of these days some rich farmer, storekeeper or such high-up feller will sit up and take notice, settle on our Agnes. Whoever he be, the man couldn't do no better no place, nowhere."

Agnes listened to all that and didn't say "boo," just smiled like it was all true.

I served my apple pudding and poured hot cups of coffee laced with plenty of sugar and fresh cream. The ladies ate and gossiped without mentioning one word about how good the food tasted, but I didn't take my eyes off them. They scraped their plates clean and drank every drop. When I came by, offering seconds, they heaped up their plates and kept on talking with their mouths full. They paid me no mind at all, except to nod that of course I should fill up their coffee cups and give them a napkin and anything else their precious little hearts could take a notion to want.

It was a fearsome thought, now that I'd got a little taste of what she was like, knowing Agnes had Rosie in her clutches. It made me try even harder to put my best foot forward—to convince that shrew and her battle-axe mother that I certainly was up to the Hartfields' high standards. By the way those women gobbled up the treats, there wasn't much doubt, they took a liking to my apple pudding and egg coffee too, even if they didn't say a word about either one.

They didn't seem to know Rosie and I were sisters. I was just sure that if Albert and Minnie didn't spill the beans, Agnes would give me a recommendation. I'd be a happy scullery maid. I'd go even lower if that's what it took to get close to Rosie. I'd slop the hogs if need be. The thing was—I had to get to Rosie before she ran away! When that girl wants something, she goes after it. I know her that well.

The thought of it kept me awake nights. If she ran off, Mr. Jackson, the one who got us in this fix to begin with, would be sure to catch her. He was the sort that didn't give up. He'd send her back to the orphanage. The man had a stone for a heart, and he'd play to win, so his precious rules didn't get broken. I wanted in the worst way to be with Rosie, but I could just as well wish for the moon. I wouldn't do any better.

CHAPTER 15
A WINTER SNOWSTORM
IRIS

I stood by the door and stared out at the road for signs of a buggy, for someone to come and tell me I had a job with the Hartfields, but day followed day with no word at all. Saturdays were especially miserable. I wasn't in school, and my expectations were greater than ever. It was hard, even on school days, thinking some news might come while I was away, but the word I yearned for didn't come.

The one comforting thing was that now I knew there was a connection between Minnie, Albert, and Agnes, Rosie's keeper. Minnie promised, crossed her heart and hoped to die she'd let me know if she got even a scrap of news, good or bad. She kept reassuring me there wasn't a chance in a million Rosie would run away with Agnes on the job. Rosie was clever, but Agnes was ruthless. So, waiting, hoping, and praying, precious time got away—not just days, not just weeks, but months.

School helped to make the long, tedious days pass. Life on the farm was far from pleasant, and I was required to do my chores before I left for school. But once I reached that sweet little building, my mood changed, even though, when out of Miss Bloom's sight and hearing, the other kids continued to torment me.

I didn't care anymore. I didn't need their approval. I got pleasure from my lessons and the praise I received from Miss Bloom. I never missed a day. Albert could always find excuses to keep me home, but I could handle him. He didn't think much of education, but rough and gruff as he talked, he didn't scare me anymore.

One cold February morning before sunrise, I stepped from the house into frozen pitch-dark. I pulled open the squeaky henhouse door, fed and watered the chickens, and gathered eggs into an old straw hat, while one cranky hen pecked at my finger, drawing blood. I pressed the wound, stopped the flow, licked it clean, and hurried back to the kitchen to help Minnie fix oatmeal, pancakes, hash browns, fried eggs, toast, ham, and bacon for Albert, who gobbled all of it down, patted his stomach, and cried out, "Mighty good eatin.'"

When the dishes were washed, dried, and stacked on shelves, I put on my outdoor winter clothes, preparing for the daily walk to country school, exactly one mile down the dirt road. I had been up late working out arithmetic problems and memorizing "The Village Blacksmith." I always studied by candlelight after Albert and Minnie went to bed. Miss Bloom's praise and assurance that one day, after eighth grade, some means would be found to send me to high school, kept me plugging away, constantly working towards that important goal.

More than once Albert grumbled, "Schooling ain't worth a straw. This highfalutin thing called 'edication' won't put food on the table or a nickel in the pocket. No Sir!" At breakfast, he poked his head out of his plate, while mopping up runny egg yolk, and, through a mouthful, commanded, "Today, Miss Iris, you'll stay to home and help Minnie. Big blizzard's a-coming."

"I'll cut across fields," I said. "If I leave now, I can beat the storm."

Not waiting for an argument I threw on my wraps, ran outside, climbed the barbed wire fence, and made my way through corn stubble into the field. The sun peeked through clouds for one brief moment, causing tiny diamonds to sparkle in the field of new fallen snow. I shielded my eyes, gazing across the fields, and saw nothing but white so far as my eyes could see, snowy earth snuggled tightly with snow-white, endless sky.

Spring will come. That thought brought a feeling of hope that I might soon be with Rosie. From other schoolchildren, I had received cheering news of her grand new life. I trudged through the snow, listening to the crunch crunch of my boots, the little squeak that comes when rubber scrapes against something very cold.

A scattering of sparrows hopped about, pecking for grain. How cheery they seemed, and what sweet little creatures they were. The few cows still outside were huddled in a ring, the small furnaces of their bodies keeping each other warm. It was fine how animals knew to help each other when times were hard. A vision of dear little Rosie flashed before my eyes.

As I gazed upwards, the sky darkened. Stringy clouds, like long clumps of hair, began to swirl, twirling, spiraling, churning as ocean waves would do, until it seemed a long black cloth had been unfurled, pulsating with the passion of some strange devil shrouding the Heavens, struggling to form an abyss. That's a word I learned in school. It's a deep hole you can't get out of.

A gust of wind lifted the hat from my head. I ran after it, but every time I reached to grab, the wind blew it farther across the field, tumbling like a top, spinning on its side. The wind swirled it round and round, beckoning, teasing, mocking, then lifted it up, swirled it high in the air and across the fields, tumbling like autumn leaves, until the hat became a small dot, so far away, it would never be my hat again.

Now, my scarf began to whip against my face, my coat flapping, as dishtowels do on a clothesline. Albert had warned that a change was coming, but I had not believed, wouldn't believe, couldn't, I so longed for spring. But I had lost any sense of direction. School must still be far off, and little spits of sleet were striking my cheeks like needles of ice.

To think that only yesterday I had picked the first precious snowdrops. No flowers today, only drifts of snow, growing higher and higher, until my boots would sink in, and I'd be stuck fast.

I struggled to get my bearings, for now the snow was falling even faster and blinding my eyes. School couldn't be far away. If only I had tied my hat more securely. My ears ached each time a blast of wind whistled by.

No birds pecked the earth now; no animal tracks appeared. Strange that even tiny animals knew how to find shelter, a cave, a hollow tree, a hole in the ground, while I could only trudge on, senselessly exposed, helpless. I clamped my mittened hands over my frozen ears, but my arms soon tired.

Had the groundhog seen his shadow? Was this winter's last gasp, or was there still more to endure? I thought of leaves on trees and robins searching for worms and meadowlarks warbling on fence posts.

I had gloried in the season's first snowfall, when the trees were covered with fresh, clean snow. Smoke curled from chimneys, and in the schoolroom Miss Bloom read out loud from Whittier's "Snowbound." I felt safe and cozy then.

How pleasant it must be at this very moment, students toasting their hands and feet by the potbellied stove, sipping Miss Bloom's delicious cocoa. My feet felt numb. It was tempting to lie down and snooze in a snowdrift, but I resisted and trudged on.

I had no idea where I was, or in what direction I was headed, so dense was the whiteness wrapping itself around me. If only I had taken the road, the deep ditches would have saved me. If my right foot sank, I would know there was the ditch, and the same would happen on the other side. Taking the cross-country route had been a poor choice, but it was useless to dwell on it now. I was in the open field, blinded by fast-falling snow.

I might be walking in circles. It happened to people all the time. Keep on, keep on, one foot in front of the other. I had been at it so long. School must be nearby. I tried reciting "The Village Blacksmith" but couldn't remember a single line. The multiplication tables too seemed a mystery. And "The Daffodils," was too sad. By spring my frozen bones would be found, bleached white, flesh gnawed away by animals, and poor, dear Rosie would be alone in the world forever.

Was that a mirage up ahead, or did I see the outlines of the country school? Before death people saw strange things. Dimly, as in a faded sketch, I made out the little white schoolhouse with its shiny bell perched on top, but I could not hear it ring or feel that I still had ears. Had they snapped off like chips of ice? The outlines grew larger, more distinct. I dragged on. Were those steps? A door? Could I climb? I could not, but could only sink and fall into deep, dreamless sleep.

CHAPTER 16
CHANGES AT HIGH POINT
ROSIE

After Mrs. Hartfield left, everything changed at High Point. Agnes wasn't nearly so cross. I didn't have to stay in my room. Papa spent time with me, and we didn't have to worry that Venetia would barge in and spoil everything.

I thought about Iris a lot, but I'd changed my mind about running away. I wanted her with me in the worst way. I'd already talked to Papa about it. He listened and said he understood, but that we'd better not go too fast. We had to wait 'til his wife came back. I was suspicious when he said that, but he looked so sad when he said her name, I stopped begging and let it slide.

In late summer, Papa and I went sailing on the lake and later walking in the woods. He pointed out birds and flowers and trees and taught me their names—all the interesting and wonderful things Miss Henderson didn't care about. He told me stories from when he was a boy in England, and we read books and painted pictures.

Once in a while a letter came from London. Then his face would get serious. He'd wrap his long fingers around the envelope, hurry off to his study and stay there for a long time. When he came out, he was like the bear in my new picture book, just waking up from a long winter's sleep. His face looked old, tired, and puffy. I didn't want to heap troubles on top of those he already had, so I made up my mind, hard as it was, to wait just a little bit longer.

Summer ended. Fall passed by. Soon the first snowflakes came drifting down. Papa brought home a little sled, outdoor winter clothes, and a beautiful furry muff. He made me feel like a princess. One snowy day in February we made a big fat snowman with a stovepipe hat, coal for eyes, and a carrot for a nose. Homer shoveled all the paths so we could run around and play without getting stuck.

Papa attached a rope to the little sled and pulled me around the track. After that, we threw snowballs at a fence, seeing who could make the biggest poof. I was jumping, clapping, and laughing, until I thought about Iris and spoiled everything. It kept happening. Some little thing would set off a memory of her, and I couldn't help it. I'd cover up my face and cry so hard I couldn't stop.

His strong arms held me tight. "I'm sorry, Papa." My voice was muffled by sobs. "I love being with you—but, I can't forget Iris. She's my sister; I miss her."

"My dear Rosie. I know you don't understand, but things are not yet settled with—" He stopped before saying her name. I knew who he meant. After a few quiet moments, he continued. "Well, we'll not wait any longer. Tomorrow I shall make an inquiry. I hoped it would work out, but—," He seemed unable to say more. "I feared—" He stopped again. "I won't burden you with my problems." I felt better when he added the word, "Tomorrow."

The next morning began cold and clear, but before he came downstairs, clouds showed up again, and snow began to fall. This time it wasn't the gentle kind we'd played in the day before. I stood by the window and watched as snowflakes blew down like flour from Cook's sifter. They were falling so fast, we couldn't even make out our snowman. We couldn't see houses or trees, just solid white. It snowed hard like that all day.

We sat by the fire with blankets tucked around us while Papa read "The Snow Queen." In the story, the snow queen kidnapped a young boy. His best friend, Gerda, finally managed to get him back, but it was an awful struggle. All kinds of obstacles got in her way. She never would have rescued him, except that she wouldn't give up. Even more important, she was good and kind and brave. It gave me something to think about, since I'm not any of those, not like Gerda, but at least I won't give up.

It got dark long before suppertime, and finally, I worked up my courage to tell Papa about the strange feeling I had. "Iris needs me," I said. "I know she does."

"I'm sorry, but you must continue to wait just a little longer," he said. "I had planned to work on it this very day, but it's much too dangerous to venture out. When the blizzard is over and the roads are cleared, we'll take action. I promise."

I trusted him. He'd been kinder than I deserved, but I felt all jumpy inside. I just had to find Iris. We'd waited so long, and now, suddenly, another day seemed more than I could stand. I wished I was like Gerda, but I wasn't, so I bit my tongue and tried really hard to think of ways to be good and kind and brave. Of course, being me, Rosie, I was sure to mess up.

CHAPTER 17

A VALENTINE

PETE

I've got to admit, I didn't have the guts to stand up to Old Man Olson. I knuckled under for way too long. It's tough to fess up to it, but I was scared half out of my wits. Even so, I'd made up my mind to fly the coop. Back in The Tombs, my jail-mate, the safe-cracker, used to spout off all the time about breaking out, but he was a windbag. I guess I was one too.

Every time I got myself set to clear out, Butch and Joe talked me out of it. "Wait a little longer," they'd say. "Leave now, you'll end up chopped to smithereens."

So we finished the season, working the rest of the farms with the threshing ring and then harvesting corn for Old Man Olson. We put in long days, getting up in the dark and flopping into bed like dead men long after the sun went down.

Winter came, and the field work was over, but there were still the cows and the other critters to take care of, and when it snowed, we spent our days shoveling. When it didn't snow, we were sent to mend fences, make tools, and clean the barn.

I ain't lazy like Pop. I'd never bellyache about any of it. The three of us weren't just field hands. We were slaves.

One miserable day followed another. I was getting more and more fed up. Once, after Old Man Olson caught Butch and Joe sitting on their haunches, just taking a breather between chores, he yanked out Elvira and whipped them 'til they were bloody as butchered pigs. Lucky me, I was in the outhouse at the time. I swore, if I got half a chance, I wouldn't keep my mouth shut this time. But then I thought it over. That would turn me into dog meat. He'd whacked them hard, but not as bad as the near murder he'd done on me.

They took their licks and went back to work. I was itching to make my getaway. I planned an elaborate escape for the three of us, but Butch and Joe were more scared of me and my fool notions than of Olson and Elvira. I'd about talked my head off before I decided I'd just have to look out for myself. From here on in, I'd keep my plans quiet. I hadn't yet figured out how to do it, but the candle inside my head was lit.

In the half-dark, just before the rooster's crow, I squished myself in best I could, like a spider waiting for a fly, wide-awake in that narrow bed, in between Butch and Joe. It was February, six months since we'd roared out of New York on that train loaded up with orphans.

Hard to believe it had been that long since I'd seen Iris and Rosie. I couldn't get those girls out of my head. I kept seeing cute little Rosie clinging to Iris, and Iris acting like the kind of Ma every kid wants but won't ever get, talking soft sweetness and giving out gentle little love pats.

I thought about my first few years in that stinking tenement, the street below filled with drunks, killers, and thieves. I didn't have much of a life, even when Ma was there. She slaved in a sweatshop and brought home just enough potatoes and oats to keep us alive. I don't know how she got everything done, but she managed to teach me to read and write. Pa couldn't do it, even if he wanted to.

Pa wasn't much to speak of, but I had a soft spot for Ma. Maybe that's why I got so taken up with those girls, watching Iris do all that mothering. I had a notion I could save them both. I know it sounds downright swell-headed, but I really did see myself saving those nice girls from turning into street rats like me.

One long winter night, before sleep came, Butch and Joe mentioned something about a country schoolhouse down the road, around the bend, and up the hill. Like usual, I got to shooting off my mouth. I recollect telling how I wanted more than anything to grow up and be somebody. I blabbered on and on about how I just had to find a way to go to school. The way things were going, none of us would ever amount to a hill of beans.

"School's for sissies," Butch said.

"It's the one and only decent thing about Old Man Olson," Joe said. "He don't hold with book learning."

All squished in there, with Joe's words rattling around in my head, a new thought popped up. Maybe Iris went to that country school. If I could ditch the farm, reach that little white schoolhouse on the hilltop, I might find her. If not, at least I could leave something for her. A letter?

Long ago, on a street in Five Points, I'd seen a pile of cards, all dolled up, with sentimental verses. "Valentines for your sweetheart," a peddler had shouted, and I thumbed through and snorted. "Sappy." That's what I thought then, but now, thinking of Iris,

I wished I could remember even a single verse. If I could lay hands on a piece of paper and a pencil, I'd make one up.

I racked my brain, and a thought popped into my head, like striking light to a candle. Tonight, when the Olsons were in bed, I'd sneak into the house. I'd head for Old Man Olson's desk. I knew exactly where it was. I'd seen it through the window lots of times, a big mess with paper scraps, pencil stubs, and office things scattered higgledy-piggledy. I wouldn't take anything he'd miss— just what I needed, a scrap of paper, pencil, and a little dab of glue. Then I'd beat it, and he'd be none the wiser.

As I scrunched in there, between Butch and Joe, the whole caper grew in my head, and I could hardly wait for my chance. "By gum, I'll do it!" I almost said it out loud, before I remembered not to wake Butch and Joe. They kept snoring. On the sly I'd have to pull myself out from between the two of them. I'd be gone before they woke up, so they wouldn't talk me out of it.

In my head I made up a verse for Iris. She'd be the only one to read this. Tonight, in the moonlight, when I had what I needed, had written out my verse and sealed it up, I'd clear out of this dump. I'd tramp along the country roads until I reached the schoolhouse, and there I'd plant this valentine at the front door. What came next I'd figure out when the time was right, but for sure, Old Man Olson would never find out. I'd bamboozled plenty of crooks in Five Points. He outsmarted me the last time I lit out, but I'd learned a thing or two since then. I'd ditch crazy Old Man Olson and his Elvira. They'd almost done me in once. It would not happen again.

I'd draw a great big heart for Iris, and inside I'd write:

To Iris, My Valentine

Please leave me a note,
One that you wrote,
Under the schoolhouse steps.
Just say where you are,
No matter how far,
I'll find you.

You're sweet as apple pie
Oh, Iris, please reply,
And then give me a clue,
About your little sister too.
I'll run off with both of you.

Don't be afraid.
A swell plan is all made.
Sure as winter winds blow,
Far from this pesthole we'll go.

I thought about signing it with love, but my head felt all hot
and funny. I'd sign it—Pete. It was enough.

CHAPTER 18
REST, RECOVERY, READING
IRIS

I felt my eyelashes flutter; my eyelids close; my eyes open wide. The strange scene danced like an enchanting fairy tale: proper furnishings, harmony, loveliness. The scene expanded, then contracted. I peeked through one eye, then the other. A dream? Oh, let it last forever, this deliverance from crumbling farmhouse, corn shuck mattress, sleepless nights.

My hands stroked the bedding. No lumps, no bumps, but soft, smooth new ironed sheets and eiderdown on top. Sleep on the farm had come only when I was so tired nothing else mattered. Morning bruises appeared and little welts from bedbug bites, but in my new surroundings, sleep was natural, deep, satisfying.

I pinched my ears, remembering the ache of the winter wind's angry bite. They were still there; still in place. Scarcely any pain remained. I was afraid if I touched them, my ears would shatter like glass, but they were firm, and yet, they could be bent. They worked. I stretched my legs. Even the numbed toes felt whole and comfortably warm.

The sound of soft voices filtered through my sleep-muddled ears, gentle conversation, two people speaking, one kind of shaky, like an old lady, another, a sweet voice I recognized.

"Miss Bloom?"

"She's awake, Auntie." Soft lips brushed my forehead. "The danger is past. She's cool to the touch." Miss Bloom wore a white Gibson girl blouse and a long skirt with a slim waist. Her hair was neatly done-up in the latest fashion, a style I had seen and admired in Montgomery Ward's Catalog. Miss Bloom was even prettier than the model. How did she get her hair to go that way? Would I ever get up nerve to ask? And how had I come to this place? Was it Miss Bloom's home? Why didn't they take me to Albert and Minnie's? Miss Bloom didn't answer these questions, because I didn't ask. She started our conversation as if I'd asked something else.

"Yes, I did go to school today," she said, "but Auntie took good care of you."

I turned to the other side of the bed where someone called Auntie stood smiling. I smiled back, then turned again to Miss Bloom.

"What about the other kids? Was anybody else caught in the blizzard?"

"You were the only one to stray from the road. By some miracle all the others got through safely. I must tell you, Tillie Nielsen wanted to pitch in and take care of you, but I told her she must go to school. Auntie was able to see to your needs while I was working."

"Tillie wanted to help me?"

"Yes, indeed. I'm sure she hasn't said so, nor have the others, but several have opened up with their true feelings about you. They gave you a very rough start, but they've come to admire you, your intelligence, your leadership qualities."

"Me? They meant me?" Tears came to my eyes.

Miss Bloom told how she had found me, unconscious, on the school's front steps. "The children were terribly worried about you," she said. "You suffered fits of fever, followed by violent chills. Velma and Mabel tucked their warm woolen coats around you, and then, when the fever took over, all the children took turns bringing cool wet cloths to place on your burning forehead."

"Why would they bother? They hate me," I said.

"Quite the contrary." She changed the subject. "Luckily, just the day before the storm, Maynard Petersen's father piled a fresh supply of wood and coal inside the vestibule. Maynard kept the pot-bellied stove stoked up and belching out heat. Now I must say, all of the children were concerned about you, but Maynard suffered the most, though, of course, he tried not to show it."

"But he can't stand me," I said.

"You are all wrong about that." She continued her story. "So it snowed all day and all night, making it impossible to leave the building. The children curled up on the floor, huddled close to the stove. We shared bits of food left over in people's lunch buckets and used a pail in the vestibule for a necessary. Of course, we couldn't get to the outhouse. The children covered up with their outdoor clothes. I read stories and made up a game to see who remembered their history lessons, complete with dates, people, and places. Later, each child recited a poem they had learned in school.

"Willard recited 'The Tiger,' by William Blake. Then came 'The Chambered Nautilus,' by Oliver Wendell Holmes. Little Holgar, having kicked off his shoes, stood and recited 'The Barefoot Boy,' by John Greenleaf Whittier. We heard 'The Children's Hour' and 'Paul Revere's Ride,' 'Crossing the Bar,' and many more. Some knew every word. Some struggled and had help from others. One by one children dropped off to sleep. Even though I felt my responsibilities, I could not hold out and finally, even I fell asleep."

"Well, how did you get out?"

"When the blizzard finally eased up, late the next morning, farmers got to work with their shovels. It took all afternoon, but they cleared a narrow path, just wide enough for horses to get through. Parents came for their children, mostly by horse and bobsled. Bells jingled as they flew along the road. Albert and Minnie arrived last of all with their swaybacked horse pulling that old bobsled."

"I can't understand why I'm here. Why didn't they make me go with them?"

"I put my foot down," Miss Bloom said in her schoolteacher voice. "I told Albert in no uncertain terms that neither he nor Minnie were strong enough to provide the nursing care you required. Albert could hardly refute that, but he growled about it anyway. He was convinced I could not care for you and teach school at the same time. Well, I assured him that Aunt Jenny, who is spry and able, lives next door. While I taught school, she looked after you, and now that we have the weekend, I take great pleasure in doing so myself."

Miss Bloom smiled. "You should be well enough for school by Monday. This is Saturday, and we have two precious days with nothing we must do."

She cradled my back and helped me get up. "Sit quietly until you feel your strength return." I followed instructions, then gradually slipped my feet to the floor. Miss Bloom let me borrow a robe and slippers and helped me into the front room where a cozy sight greeted my already spellbound eyes.

A coal-fired stove stood in the middle of the room. Through the red isinglass panes on the stove's front, I watched flames leaping from the glowing coals. Miss Bloom said it wasn't really isinglass but thin, transparent mica, just one more new and interesting fact I learned from the world's best teacher.

There was a coziness and warmth in that room that just filled me up with happiness. On each wide windowsill sat a terra cotta pot of bright red geraniums. I didn't know about terra cotta either, but I do now. Miss Bloom told me that the Greeks and Romans had it. Behind the steamy windowpanes loomed piled high drifts of sparkling snow. Then I saw the painting. It took my eye like nothing I'd seen before—a whole field of daffodils, like the Wordsworth poem we'd memorized in school.

"That's Lucinda's work," said Auntie, nodding at Miss Bloom. I'd forgotten, Miss Bloom's name was Lucinda. "She's an excellent artist." Right then and there I decided I'd name my first child Lucinda. Well, of course, only if she's a girl.

I kept looking at all the beautiful things in the room, the sparkling windows, the red geraniums, the white ruffled curtains. "Lucinda has a green thumb too," said Auntie, "and she stitched up the curtains, braided the rugs, tatted the lace around my collar. Lucinda can do most anything."

Miss Bloom blushed. "I have a small library that might interest you," she said, seeming eager to change the subject.

My eyes settled on bookshelves overflowing with titles I recognized from lessons learned in school. *The Complete Works of Shakespeare; Paradise Lost; Collected Works of Keats, Shelley, and Byron; Middlemarch; Silas Marner; A Tale of Two Cities; Great Expectations; The Collected Works of Henry Wadsworth Longfellow; Uncle Tom's Cabin.*

I'd read some and had heard about others. Many more spilled over the shelves. I had never before seen a house with entire shelves of books and wondered how Miss Bloom could afford them. I'd heard teachers weren't paid very much. Many homes I'd heard about had a Bible only. They were the lucky ones. Others had no books at all.

"Most of my books were gifts from Auntie," she said, as if she'd read my mind. "Uncle George, her husband, was a very successful businessman. I bought a few myself, but a schoolteacher's salary could not buy all of these."

Miss Bloom stood at the window where children were sledding and throwing snowballs. "You're not ready to go outside yet," she said, "so let us spend our time wisely. I read to you, then you to me."

What a nice idea! After browsing through the books, I chose *Middlemarch*, eased myself into a wing-backed easy chair, and read aloud. We took turns, and everything seemed perfect until I thought about Rosie and wondered if she was faring as well as I. When we stopped for a little rest, I screwed up my courage and said, "Miss Bloom, Dorothea in *Middlemarch* had a younger sister, and so do I. Her name is Rosie. Mr. Jackson insisted we could not be placed out in the same home. Now I can't for the life of me think why he'd make up such a rule, but he did, and he sticks to it. She's only seven, and I'm all she has. No, I forgot. She's had her birthday and now she's eight. I'm a year older too. Sometimes I think I just can't stand it anymore, not knowing if she's all right. If she were here with us, oh, Miss Bloom, this would be the most wonderful day of my life."

There, I'd tried again. Nothing came of it when I made my case to Albert and Minnie, but that was Agnes' fault. Miss Bloom was different. Her kind face gave me a little bit of hope.

CHAPTER 19

STUCK
PETE

Maybe I should have hit the road after the valentine caper, but I'd heard tales of folks lost in blizzards, found stiff and frozen in the snow. Some bodies didn't show up 'til spring thaws. I thought long and hard about making tracks, getting as far from Old Man Olson as I could. I'd pick up some kind of work in a place where folks treated kids like humans; but February in Iowa is risky business. It's smart to stay put 'til the ice breaks up and you've got half a chance.

Butch and Joe didn't know what I'd been up to that February night. When I wrote the valentine, I thought I'd go back a few days later to see if Iris answered back, but I never made it. The noose was getting tighter.

Olson didn't miss his things. From that mess on his desk, what I'd made off with didn't make a dent. All the same, I could tell right off, he knew I was up to something. The old coot was always on the prowl, sniffing out the least sign of mutiny. If he thought he wouldn't get caught, he'd have had us in leg irons, turning us loose just long enough to work 'til we dropped.

When things warmed up, he'd have a considerable sight more to do. Maybe his watch dogging would slack off. I figured my chances would be better if I'd just wait it out, so I did, but in the meantime, I paid close attention to what he said at meals.

Finally, warm weather came, and one morning at breakfast Olson and Mabel started blabbing about that new hired girl over at Albert and Minnie's. They sure wished they could get hold of one like that. The more they talked, the more I was sure that hired girl was Iris.

Then one day in June I heard him tell Mable he was off to Knudtsens' with a load of hay. So I wolfed down some mush and cut out even before Butch and Joe finished theirs. When Olson came out, I was buried deep in the pile of hay he planned on carting off to Knudtsens.

I'd been burning up with rage towards Olson. I could have made a run for it, but I had to keep my head, take my time, and figure out how to rescue Iris. My chances were better if I took one step at a time. I wiggled close to the edge and poked a big hole through the hay so I could see out. That way I'd learn the way to Iris' farm. Once we got there, Olson went inside to fetch Albert. I wiggled out, jumped from the wagon, and tore out to hide behind the barn.

When I was well hidden, I shook off bits of hay and chaff, peeking out every few seconds to see what came next. They must have done a heap of talking inside. It seemed like forever 'til they came out. Finally, they got to work, but those two were no great shakes at pitching hay. Before they got a good start, Butch, Joe, and me would have had the job over and done with.

But finally, Olson rode off with his empty wagon, none the wiser, and I followed on foot, headed for purgatory, staying well behind so he'd never know what I'd been up to. Butch and Joe were real put out when I wouldn't say where I'd been, but I couldn't afford to let them in on it. They wouldn't mean to, but sure as thunder comes on the heels of lightning, they'd louse things up. I was feeling cocky as Olson's roosters with a map inside my head and directions for exactly where to go.

I'd developed some skill as a fair to middling pickpocket in Five Points, but I'd hoped to mend my ways in Iowa. Those girls sure did make a guy want to do right. But on the other hand, a fella's got to do what he's got to do. I'm sorry to say, after that run in with Elvira, I did some serious backsliding, took up my old light fingered tricks, fitting myself up for the day I'd bust out. I'd got the taste for it that night swiping things for Iris' valentine. So this time I snuck in a good while after the candles were snuffed.

First thing I did was filch some bread and meat for the road. I calculated hard times were coming. It's dog eat dog out there. Too bad, after those girls got me almost civilized, I was sinking back into my evil ways. It did bother that little man inside my head. I tried telling him Olson never paid me one red cent for all the work and sweat I'd put in, free for nothing. I said Olson owed me plenty, and so thieving was the only way to make it right. But the little guy still insisted it was wrong.

I did what I needed to anyhow, making ready for the big day. First off, I made up to the dogs, fed them up so good the night before, they slept like they'd downed a couple Mickey Finns.

That morning, as happened time and time again, the other boys' snoring woke me up from a crazy, mixed-up dream. Something in the air felt like that day of disaster when I'd tried this same caper. I thought about how Old Man Olson laid crouched outside, like a snake in the grass, nabbed me good and proper, and pretty near did me in. I got my nerve back though, at least some of it, when I recollected what I'd managed to pull off in February, delivering Iris' valentine. Sneaking around in the sticks is a whole different game than prowling back streets in New York.

Well, I dressed without making a peep, keeping watch all the time as Butch and Joe snored their heads off. As the rooster crowed, I tiptoed from the barn, peeking left and right to make sure the dogs weren't out. I held my breath, watching and waiting for Olson and Elvira to spring on me, but the coast was clear. With my knapsack slung over one shoulder, I rounded the corner, hid behind a shed, and crept from one tree to another.

I was feeling a little bit easier, so I played some tricks on myself to keep up my nerve. First I was an Indian. I'd been tied up by white settlers but had busted through the ropes and was running from one hiding place to another. When I got tired of that, I turned into a soldier separated from his unit, searching high and low for the rest of the company. I raised dust with every step, as I marched, left, right, left, right down that long dirt road.

When I'd cleared the hill, reached a valley, and was sure nobody on Old Man Olson's place could see me, I took in a deep swallow of fresh air. The sun was just rising, and bright, glowing colors spread over the horizon. I tried to spot the Knudtsen place but couldn't see it. I was okay with that, since I knew just where to go.

I ran for a while, then stopped, rummaged through my pocket, wiped sweat off my forehead with a shirtsleeve. I wiggled my other hand around in my pocket and calmed down some when my fingers closed around the few bucks I'd filched from Old Man Olson. What was running down my face should have been just sweat. Too bad, but some tears did get mixed in. Oh boy was I glad nobody was there to see.

The sun was barely up. My stomach was growling like a famished pup. Time to milk the cows. Butch and Joe would have extra work, and I felt pretty bad about that too, but I'd make it up to them someday—when I got rich and all that.

I hadn't dared give a hint of what I was going to do. Butch and Joe wouldn't mean to, but for sure they'd spill the beans, especially if Old Man Olson raised an arm or pointed a finger at Elvira. They'd squeal like stuck pigs. Why couldn't they wise up? They'd lived through Five Points same as me. I took my know-how from street fights, crooks, and dodging cops. Butch and Joe somehow missed out on that fine education.

After swiping the bread and meat, I'd also filched a few bucks from Olson's desk. He had big bags of dough stashed away. I was pretty sure he wouldn't miss the little bit I took.

But then I got to thinking, maybe I'd need more food. I wasn't just providing for me. I'd be responsible for Iris and Rosie too. Thieving didn't seem quite so bad if I did it for them. I tiptoed back to the kitchen and was scrounging around for more things to eat when I heard Mabel's footsteps and skedaddled quicker than a mouse runs from a cat.

If we ran out of grub, I'd steal eggs from henhouses and melons from fields. I wouldn't tell those girls how I got the things. I'd get them all settled, fine and cozy, under a weeping willow tree in some nice woods where nobody would find them, and then I'd sneak off and do my evil deeds.

As I went hiking down the road, a meadowlark warbled from a fence post. A south wind whistled through the cornfields, and the sun was spreading out a swell show behind me. Flaming shades of red and orange bounced from the sunrise like a mirror across the entire sky. A train whistling in the distance got me thinking about our long journey from half a continent away—me and those girls. I'd soon find Iris and get her sprung. Then we'd go for Rosie.

I could feel the train's rhythm like a heartbeat as it clickety-clacked across the miles. Rows of half grown corn stretched out in great big fields, and the dazzling sky spread out forever over farmhouses, windmills, and corncribs. I sat down next to a rippling stream that splashed into a creek. I cupped my hands and took a deep swallow, then spit it out. It tasted like mud.

I'd been putting in long, hard days with Olson and had no time to think about all the good things there were to see around the area, but now I really looked things over. The land hereabouts made me feel swell, just to look at it. I watched the grass waving in the ditch, sniffed at the wild roses, whistled as the red-winged blackbirds scolded and the meadowlarks warbled.

This is the life! I said to myself. *It was worth it to get out of that filthy city.* And now I was quit of the stinking farm as well. I skipped a few rocks the long way down the creek, picked up some more, studied them, thought about how old they must be, and

A south wind whistled through the cornfields, and the sun was
spreading out a swell show behind me.

wondered who else had picked them up long before my time. I found one shaped like an evergreen tree. *An arrowhead maybe?*

Butch and Joe once told me there were Indian burial grounds nearby.

Maybe an Indian boy used to play in this creek. I bet he even tasted the muddy water and spit it out. I wanted in the worst way to hunt up a deep spot and take a swim.

I heard the clip-clop of horse's hooves, so I ducked into the ditch and hid behind some cattails. After the horse and buggy passed, I breathed easier, but it was clear that taking a dip would have to wait 'til after I'd rescued Iris. Maybe that wouldn't work either. I couldn't take off my clothes with a girl around. But then, swimming was less important than rescuing Iris.

Walking on, more careful now, I came to the long, rutted lane. I remembered the place from the day I hid in Olson's hay wagon. So I followed the lane, but crouched down, creeping through the tall weeds towards the barn. I couldn't let them see me up at the house. That barn looked like it could bite the dust any minute. If I owned a farm, I wouldn't let things fall apart like that.

I stared at the house. Iris was a prisoner in there. The thought made my muscles tighten, my teeth clench, and my skin kind of prickle up. I hid in the weeds behind the barn, watched, and waited. Soon she'd come out to feed the chickens or weed the garden, and when I laid eyes on her, I'd whistle the tune I'd done on the train to entertain the girls. I'd whistle so soft and low nobody else would hear, but she'd remember and know it was me. She'd edge up slow, like she was just looking at a robin or a dandelion. That way nobody in the house would catch on. Then, for a split second, I'd stick out my head so she'd know, and I'd signal to keep still.

I'd already spilled the beans in the valentine note, so she'd be expecting me, and she wouldn't be scared like most girls. Iris had guts. She'd come to me behind the barn, where nobody else would see, and first off I'd give her a great big bear hug. Then I'd lift her up, like it's done in books. She'd twine her arms around my neck, or maybe I'd toss her over one shoulder. I'd be gentle, though, like Robin Hood or Sir Lancelot. Once we'd compared notes and figured out where to go, we'd make a beeline to rescue Rosie.

I was cranked up, ready for action. I'd already hid in the ditch from the buggy that passed me by. But now, faintly, the other way from what I'd heard before, there came the sound of horse's hooves. The wheels had the same squeaky sound. The horses' clip-clop kept getting louder and louder, 'til they sounded way too close. Pretty soon I heard stones bouncing on the lane. The pigs were squealing; the cows bellering; and the dog, who hadn't noticed me crawling in, got all worked up and barked like Jesse James and his robber band were coming.

The wheels stopped squeaking; the stones stopped bouncing. I pressed myself flat against the dirt. Scary thoughts went popping through my brain. *It could be the buggy that passed me on the road. Somebody must have seen me. Were they coming back to get me? What if it was Old Man Olson?*

"Whoa!" I heard that loud and clear. My body turned hot as a stove-lid. Then I froze, clutched the Barlow knife I'd lifted from Olson, and peered through the weeds. I got just a glimpse of something huge and black moving towards me. *Too big for a dog. Did Olson steal a circus bear? He'd pull every trick in the book to get his hands on me.*

I pressed my face against the dirt. In that position, I couldn't see a thing, only listen, as whatever it was came closer and closer and closer. The grass went rhythmically swish, swish, swish, and then, all at once, that stopped; and everything got still as a graveyard at midnight. A warm grip clamped down hard on my neck. I dropped the knife and felt the shock a wild creature must feel when a trap springs on him. He can struggle 'til he's blue in the face, and all the strength pours out of him, but he's caught. Well, I've been through the mill a time or two. I'm not some ignorant wild thing, so I knew in my bones, I'd be better off dead.

CHAPTER 20

SHAME
PETE

I was sure the monster clamping down on my neck was a big black bear, but it was a giant, a real live one with a black, bushy beard, all slicked up in a black suit, black shoes, and wide-brimmed black hat. But from where I was hiding, with my face in the dirt and eyes barely able to see, he did look like a big black bear.

The giant got right to it and hauled me in the buggy to his office, which was in a large, white house across the road from the country church. I put two and two together and figured he was the preacher. What I remember most is the two of us, the giant and me, staring each other down, like two fighters in a boxing ring just before a match.

The room was almost as scary as he was. The walls were lined with bookshelves, full to bursting with fat volumes in matched sets, kept behind glass doors, like they were too good to be touched. The bearded giant sat in his leather armchair, behind a huge wooden desk, all stacked up with papers, pens, and blotting paper. His enormous hands, with fingers laced, were slapped in front of him on top of a fat black Bible.

For what seemed like ages, he didn't say one word, just sat there with his eyes drilling holes through me. It put me in mind of the owl that used to hoot outside the barn. I always felt that bird was fixing to eat me for breakfast.

The giant had shoved me into a low chair, while he sat on a platform, so I had to look up at him. That was okay. I was used to being a low-down nobody. My face felt hot. Sweat ran out of me like the creek I'd just played in.

If he hadn't showed up, things would have turned out different. I'd have rescued Iris. She'd have gone all mushy and called me her hero. But no sense thinking of that. My grand scheme was over and done with.

"You have a lot of explaining to do," the giant finally said in a voice like thunder. I kept thinking about bugs—the advantage they'd have in a situation like this. When a man goes after a bug, the little wiggler can slither through a crack in the floor, and it's over and done with.

"Early this morning Eli Olson's barn burned to the ground." The giant said this like he was preaching a sermon. "What remains is an ash heap; but, of course, this is not news to you."

"Huh?" I felt the blood drain from my face. I couldn't get the words out. How could that be? There wasn't even a candle burning when I left. Butch and Joe were sound asleep.

"And that's not all," he growled. "Arson is a crime. A felony. The punishment will not be pleasant. Eli Olson has reported the three boys he so generously took into his home are missing. What do you have to say about that?"

I couldn't get a word out. I could barely breathe. What happened to Butch and Joe?. Were they all right?

"When I spotted you in the ditch, I had my suspicions. Turning back, as you know, I found you sneaking up to the Knudtsen home, clearly with nefarious intentions. I knew then, with certainty, you were one of those boys. So I am asking you to make your confession. You are in deep trouble, young man. If you are truthful, things might go a little easier for you. Now tell me. Where are the other boys? We know there were three of you. Three arsonists. Start talking!" He raised his voice and smashed down a fist. "Now!"

I jumped from my chair.

"Easy does it. You must tell the truth."

"I am telling the truth. I haven't got the least notion about a fire." I was shaking all over. "I left early this morning before Butch and Joe woke up. See, I finally got up the nerve to run away, and it was high time. For almost a year I took that old geezer's guff. All of us kids were told, before we got on that trickster train, that everybody would be sent to school, at least 'til we finished eighth grade, and even longer, if we wanted to go. That preacher said there were laws about it. He even said we might be put to work, but we'd be treated like family. Some joke! Old Man Olson used us like slaves."

"Lies!" the preacher shouted with a horrible frown on his face. "Olson assured me he did what he could to turn you boys around. It was his aim to help you live a decent life. Obviously, you don't know right from wrong, so he had to be firm. He says that you were incorrigible."

I stared at the floor. If I told what really went on with Old Man Olson and Elvira, I'd be a dead man. If what I said got back to Olson, he'd take it out on Butch and Joe, and if he ever got his hands on me, I'd be skinned alive.

"Butch and Joe didn't do it," I said with my fingers crossed behind me. "They wouldn't do a thing like that. They're good boys." What a liar I was. I knew they did it. Why wouldn't they? I hate telling falsehoods, even when they're meant to help my pals. I felt rotten. Maybe the giant was right. Seemed I just couldn't do right.

"Where are those boys?" he thundered. "How do you explain their disappearance? You, my boy, will be charged with a felony." Then he lowered his voice. "But if you cooperate, perhaps your sentence will be lighter than theirs."

I couldn't see the point of answering, since he already had me tried and convicted. I just sat there staring at the floor until he changed his tactics. He came down from his platform, walked around to me, laid one big old hand on my arm, lifted my chin, and looked me in the eye, almost friendly-like. "Now son," he said, "tell me everything that you remember. If you cooperate, you have nothing to fear."

Nothing to fear? I couldn't believe he'd said that. A man of the cloth. Preachers weren't supposed to tell lies, even little white ones. If he'd do that, what could he expect from me? I wanted in the worst way to come out with it, to say, "That lunatic beats us with his razor strap. He'd as soon slice us in half as look at us. He was fixed to murder us and cut our bodies up in little pieces." But I held my tongue. It's hard to admit, but in a tight spot, when I think I'm not long for this world, a yellow streak runs straight down my scarred up back.

CHAPTER 21

AT LAST

IRIS

What a sweet surprise! In mid-February, just before the big snow-storm, Pete sent me a valentine with some very pretty verses. He made them up himself. He said he planned to come and rescue Rosie and me, but he didn't show up. I'm sure he meant well. I left a note for him under the schoolhouse steps, just as he asked, but he never came to pick it up. I think he still liked us, Rosie and me, at least I hoped he did.

When I recovered, after the snowstorm, an arrangement was worked out so that I could live with Miss Bloom during the week. Then I'd go back to the farm to help out on weekends. When I came back, even after one day off, Minnie's kitchen was always a mess, and it took some time to get it neat and clean again. When school let out for summer vacation, I had to stay on the farm. Summer is busy out there; and they needed me, but I hated leaving Miss Bloom. She promised, come fall, she'd work on Albert and Minnie. If we were lucky, maybe they would let me live most of the time with her.

My real problem was that I'd worked too hard on my lessons. It may sound strange to other kids, but I loved homework. I always did more than the assignment. That meant staying up late to work by lamplight. I was promoted to seventh grade, then eighth, and finally I finished up all the eighth grade requirements, which meant I was finished with country school. Miss Bloom promised she'd keep it a secret so I could stay. She let me help with the little kids and brought lots of books for me to read. Anyway, the new high school wasn't built yet, so I had plenty of time to read, study, and prepare myself for a new challenge.

Albert and Minnie were not always nice, but they weren't evil. All the same, I didn't want to stay there longer than necessary. Would anyone choose to be an unpaid servant on a run-down farm with two old grumps?

Now, I'm going to repeat something Miss Bloom told me. I found it pretty interesting. One morning she hitched her horse to the buggy and headed on down the road towards the country church, just outside of town on the south end. There's a cemetery surrounding the church and a parsonage across the road. That's where Pastor and Mrs. Fineman live.

Mrs. Fineman came to the door and flashed one of those fake smiles, the kind most anyone knows for what it's worth. Miss Bloom said she wished to see the pastor. Mrs. Fineman said he was busy; but if the teacher had time for a cup of coffee, they could pass the time together 'til his conference was over.

So Miss Bloom sat down at the kitchen table. Mrs. Fineman brought coffee and cookies and then, in a low voice, said that the Pastor was interviewing a criminal. "It's one of those orphans that came last summer on the train," she almost whispered. "Those New York folks send their problem children out here and expect us to straighten them out. We never had such troubles before they showed up."

She moved a bit closer to Miss Bloom. "Have you heard the latest?"

Something about Mrs. Fineman made Miss Bloom want to leave, but she tried to be polite.

The other woman licked her lips. "I heard it from Mrs. Rush, our neighbor from down the road. She ran right over here early this morning to let me in on the news. Eli Olson's barn has burned to the ground. Not a stick remains." She clucked and shook her head.

"That's a fact!" She must have thought Miss Bloom didn't believe her. "Well, the Olsons were kind enough to take those boys under their wings, three young devils who needed a firm hand. And that's the thanks they get." She listed all the dreadful things she'd heard about each boy, especially Pete.

"Those rascals should have been locked up months ago. The Olsons have been much too generous. That's what makes it so sad. Just to save those children from reform school, Eli took in the first two when nobody else would have a thing to do with them. The third one acted up from the time he got here—a real New York hooligan."

"Why haven't I seen those boys in school?" Miss Bloom asked. "I must say, my very best student came to Hartfield on that train." It sounds like bragging to repeat what Miss Bloom said about me, but it has to be told. It's part of the story. It really is.

It seemed like Mrs. Fineman didn't want to hear anything good about orphans. She just kept on babbling. "Luckily, my husband apprehended the worst scoundrel—caught red-handed, just as he was about to set another blaze. That young firebug was hiding behind the Knudtsens' barn. There is no doubt what he was up to. Pastor is in his office this very minute questioning the little fiend."

Miss Bloom stood up to go, but Mrs. Fineman popped out of her chair and gestured to stay put while she ran across the hall. Miss Bloom heard a knock on the study door and the woman calling, "Matthew!" That's Pastor Fineman's first name. "Miss Bloom is here, but she'll leave if you don't take a moment."

"Send her in," he replied, through the closed door.

<hr>

This part's by Pete:

I heard a knock on the door. After the giant and his missus shot a few words back and forth, a pretty lady came in. I jumped up and tried to make a gentlemanly bow, but as usual, I messed up. Man, do I hate it when my efforts turn out awkward and clumsy. I sat back down feeling kind of miserable.

"My dear lady," said the giant. "It is such a pleasure to receive you. I hear such fine things about your work at the country school." Boy, did I sit up and take notice at that. If this was Iris' teacher, I was in luck. The preacher spread it on, smooth as butter and sweet as apple pie. You'd never know it was the same grizzly bear that just gave me the third degree. "I do hope you will not leave, Miss Bloom, before announcing the purpose of your visit." He flashed a smile, like half a ripe tomato, not a pretty sight.

After sitting down next to me, Miss Bloom said she was sorry to bother such a busy, important man and all such truck, the way ladies carry on. She didn't stare me down the way the Reverend did. She looked me over pretty good, though, but in a friendly way that made me feel like I might stand a chance with her around. The giant hauled the chair away from his throne, positioned it carefully on the other side of Miss Bloom, and sat himself down.

"I understand there has been a fire," she said to the preacher.

"There has indeed." His glare just about burned a hole right through me.

"Is it true that you came to Hartfield last summer?" She was asking me.

"Yes Ma'am."

"On the train from New York?" She'd left out the part about me being an orphan, and a bad one.

The pastor swallowed his smile and answered for me. "Your understanding is correct, Miss Bloom. I hope it is possible for us to discuss your mission in his presence. I dare not let the ruffian out of my sight."

"Are you Peter Freeman?" she asked, looking right at me.

"How'd you know my name? Let me guess." I said it nice and polite as I knew how. "You must've found the valentine."

"Indeed I did," said Miss Bloom. "I did not read it. After all, it was addressed to Iris. She told me all about you, explaining that you are an honest, forthright boy, so I'll ask the appropriate question. Did you start the fire? Perhaps by accident?"

"I did not!" I felt my insides churning, so I stood up, with arms at my sides, fists clenched. "I wasn't anywhere near the place when that fire started. I'd been gone since the crack of dawn. I didn't take leave. I'll confess to that. I hightailed it out of there for good reason. I figured on rescuing Iris, biding my time out behind the barn. I hoped she'd come out, but just my luck. The Reverend caught me like some miserable rat in a trap."

"Sit down, boy!" the giant growled. "Arson is a reprehensible crime." His eyes squinted like a pig's would, and he rolled that big word around in his mouth. "You have much to gain if we believe you. On the other hand, you have everything to lose if we do not. I am personally certain that you are guilty. However, we intend to be fair and to give you a chance to prove your innocence, if by some miracle that might be the case."

"This is America," Miss Bloom piped up with a schoolteacher snap in her voice. "We are all innocent until proven guilty."

I let out a deep breath. She had such an earnest look on her face. I felt like she might give me a break, maybe even take my part, if she heard the whole story.

"Miss Bloom," the pastor spoke up again with an exasperated edge to his voice. "Did you know about the fire before my wife informed you?"

"No, I did not."

"Then tell me, why did you come here today of all days?"

"To discuss another of the orphans—Iris O'Leary." I almost fell off my chair. And then that pretty schoolteacher told the giant all she knew about what had been happening with those girls. Man, was I relieved to hear they were both safe.

She wound up saying, "At present Iris is once again living with and working for the Knudtsens, just until school resumes in the fall. She is not legally bound to do so, but she feels a moral obligation. That should give you an indication of the girl's character and integrity."

Wow! Miss Bloom sure could talk the King's English. Man! She made me sit up and take notice.

"What you have said speaks highly for the girl and for you, Miss Bloom," said the preacher. "But there must be more to the story, or you would not have come to see me at this time."

"That is true," said Miss Bloom. "Here is my problem. I understand that Iris' younger sister, Rosie, was placed in the home of Mr. and Mrs. Jefferson Hartfield. Upon arrival, the girls begged to be placed together. Now, I have been told there is an inflexible policy stating that siblings cannot be placed in the same home. I have not met Rosie, but I am certain she must be as devastated by this separation, as is Iris. Being orphaned at an early age is dreadful enough, without losing one's only sibling as well. The policy is not only ridiculous but cruel."

"That's the God's own truth!" I piped up. Then I stopped dead and thought about what I'd just said. See, Miss Harkin made us memorize the ten commandments. If we missed one, she'd whack our knuckles. We said them about a million times a day, so I guess I couldn't forget a single one. Now I thought I might have gone and broke number two in front of a preacher. The giant gave me an evil look, but I was wound up like a top and couldn't seem to stop.

"Those girls stuck up for me when I didn't have a friend in the world. They're swell kids who deserve better, and I'm going to do something about it."

The preacher didn't say it, but I knew what he was thinking. If I didn't keep my mouth shut, he'd shut it for me.

Miss Bloom said she wanted to talk to the Hartfields, but from what she'd heard about the missus, she didn't dare to show up at the mansion without an invitation.

Her voice changed from how she sounded before. She shilly-shallied around, looked at her shoes, and then, kind of sheepish like, asked the giant if he'd be her go-between. She didn't want to start out on the wrong foot."

"Now that you mention it," the giant said, "there is something I'd almost forgotten. Hartfield contacted me some time ago with a request, and I've let it go for far too long. Managing my flock keeps me constantly occupied, I must confess. The fact is, you have misjudged the man. It is true, his wife is a bit distant, but he is decent, honorable, and not one to frighten anyone, certainly not a fine, respectable woman such as you. I told him I would give his request prayerful consideration, and now it seems the answer has come. As we all know, the Lord works in mysterious ways."

I was ready to jump up and holler, "Hooray!" but then he threw in the kicker. After clearing his throat, he looked me over like I was a lowdown skunk, and growled, "This boy is a ruffian and a criminal, wanted by the Sheriff. I have no choice but to deliver him to the authorities. Do not try to persuade me otherwise. My decision is firm as the rock of Gibraltar."

"I won't try to argue with you," Miss Bloom said sweetly, "but please, could you wait just a little longer?"

At that moment we heard another knock at the door. Mrs. Fineman was telling somebody to come in. "Oh, do honor us with your presence." She sure could lay it on thick.

Before we could guess who it was, a gray-haired gentleman, dressed like a Wall Street banker, stepped in. I'd seen the type in the city, but not in Hartfield.

The giant wore preacher's clothes, and I ain't saying folks downtown don't fix up for church and such, but I've been stuck at Old Man Olson's place so long, the look of this one made me sit up and take notice.

The giant pasted on that half tomato smile again and jumped up from his chair. He looked about a thousand feet tall. "Welcome, my dear Mr. Hartfield! We are delighted to have you join us!" He poked out a paw, and shook the man's hand like he really was a big old grizzly bear. His face turned all red, and it took him a while to figure out what to do next. When he finally got hold of himself, he made a big, swooping gesture. "May I present Miss Bloom?" That sure did tickle my funny bone, but I kept a poker face and didn't let on.

Hartfield gave a gentleman's bow, a first-rate lesson in tony ways of doing. I knew I'd try that one out on Iris if I ever did get the chance.

Mrs. Fineman came tripping in with a soft chair for this distinguished guest. Before Mr. Hartfield sat down, he shot me a friendly smile. "Young man, I have not had the pleasure." He even walked over to shake my hand. Boy, was I was bowled over.

The giant cleared his throat and then frowned. I knew he wanted to tell Mr. Hartfield all the dirt on me, but Miss Bloom spoke up first. "May I present Peter Freeman from New York City." Boy oh boy, she had a sweet voice. I'd never been introduced like that, and it sure did lift my spirits.

Pastor Fineman showed he was none too pleased, but he let it go. "How convenient you happened by while Miss Bloom is here," he said. "I had just promised to arrange a meeting for the two of you and your lovely wife. Miss Bloom wishes to discuss one of her students, a girl named Iris O'Leary."

Mr. Hartfield perked right up. "My young ward has told me all about Iris. The two are sisters. Poor, sweet Rosie has been waiting for far too long, and so, finally, this is indeed a splendid opportunity to reunite those dear girls."

Miss Bloom smiled at me, and oh man, did I ever smile back.

"It is my understanding that Iris lives and works at the home of Mr. and Mrs. Knudtsen. I am not acquainted with the couple, but I shall rely upon you to arrange something, so that Iris may be released from her contract, if such a thing exists. It is of the utmost importance that these children be reunited. I am prepared to provide a home for both of them."

Miss Bloom looked like she wanted to jump up and give Mr. Hartfield a big hug, if she wasn't such a fine lady. Her happy face showed how she felt. "Your offer is generous and most kind," she said looking straight at Mr. Hartfield. "If such an arrangement can be made, I shall be overjoyed. Now, we must do everything possible to convince the Knudtsens. They are not easy people to deal with, but I feel if anyone can succeed, it will be you, Mr. Hartfield." She flashed him a great big smile, and he sent one right back.

Pastor Fineman popped up from his seat. "I must convey my apologies. I have been remiss in neglecting this situation. I do realize it has been far too long since you first approached me with this problem, Mr. Hartfield. You must understand, my flock is large, my duties great, attending the sick, the infirm, those weak in faith. But now, let me attempt to make amends. Let us settle the matter quickly. All of us together shall make a pilgrimage to the Knudtsen farm. Let us do it at once."

Both Hartfield and Miss Bloom stood up. The giant fastened his eyes on me and frowned. I expect right then he wished he wasn't a man of the cloth so he could say a few choice cuss words. Maybe he was thinking, if these fine folks hadn't showed up, he'd be rid of me. He'd have turned me in a while ago. I'd be under lock and key and out of his hair.

"It seems our only option is to bring this young arsonist along," he said, glowering at me. "The rascal must remain under surveillance until justice can be done."

When we got outside, Mr. Hartfield hurried to Miss Bloom's side and whispered something in her ear before offering his arm. She hooked in, climbed into his fancy buggy, and off they went. The giant shoved me into his old rattletrap and slammed me onto a seat. We followed in the dust of the happy couple, a caravan of determined folks headed straight for Knudtsen's farm. I had my fingers crossed.

CHAPTER 22

THE MEETING
PETE

By the time we reached Knudtsen's farm, my heart was pounding like a bass drum. I didn't get to rescue Iris, but I'd see her soon. That made getting caught almost worth it. A mangy old dog just about yapped his head off when we rode up, and right away a farmer in bib overalls poked his head from the barn door, dropped his pitchfork and came limping out. The old geezer put me in mind of a jackrabbit. He hopped towards the dog and tied him up. After that, he stood stock-still, eyes fixed on those high-toned visitors in the front buggy.

A woman in a plain housedress and stained apron stuck her head out the back door and screened her eyes, like she was trying hard to see who was coming without so much as an invite.

Mr. Hartfield waited 'til the dog was tied up, then jumped down to help Miss Bloom from the carriage. A real gentleman, that Hartfield. I watched his every move, so I wouldn't forget how to do it. Once again he made a handle of his arm, and she hooked hers in. I couldn't wait to try it on Iris.

Pastor Fineman gave me a nudge and yelled, "Get out," so I jumped, and he stepped down. His legs were so long, it was no problem for him. He grabbed onto the neck of my shirt, like I might make a run for it, but he didn't need to bother. This close to Iris, I wouldn't leave her behind. I really didn't give a hoot what happened to me right then if those girls could have a decent life. I looked around for Iris but didn't see her. I kept my eyes fixed on the door, eagle-eyed.

I ain't proud of this next part, what I was thinking, but I've got to tell it anyhow. After folks got settled in the parlor, the preacher grabbed me by the collar and shoved me down beside him. "Sit there, and don't move a muscle." he growled.

I could have made a run for it. If Iris didn't show, I'd already picked out a slick path from the kitchen door. The dog would yip his head off, but he was tied up, and I've run from cops about a million times. I'm a born outlaw and can't help thinking like one.

A real street rat would lam out of there without thinking twice, but I was different now. I could jump a boxcar to Frisco, stow away on a freighter to Outer Mongolia, and live a brand new life without all this aggravation. But the little man inside my head wouldn't let me, not before I'd proved myself to Iris and Rosie. I've done plenty I ain't proud of, but I ain't a firebug.

The giant introduced folks that didn't know each other and then told them all to sit down. There weren't enough chairs, so the preacher slammed me down on the floor in front of him. Miss Bloom sat close by. She gave me a friendly little pat, so I stretched up and whispered, "Where's Iris?"

"She's with Aunt Jenny at my house."

I nodded, trying to hide my disappointment.

The preacher focused on Albert and then on Minnie. He smiled and tried to look like a fair-minded fellow, but I was onto him. "We have come on an important mission," he said, "to discuss the future of two orphan girls, one of whom you Knudtsens know very well." He spoke in that deep, preacher voice that scares the dickens out of folks.

"First on the agenda I shall ask Mr. Hartfield to state his case, then Miss Bloom, and finally, Mr. and Mrs. Knudtsen. I trust that arrangement is agreeable to everyone."

Miss Bloom and Hartfield nodded, but it took a long time to get anything out of Albert. Minnie kept her mouth shut, but she kept jabbing Albert in the stomach 'til he finally piped up. "I guess you can start out that way, but that don't guarantee how this thing will end up."

"Mr. Hartfield has the floor," snapped the preacher.

There was a long, quiet spell. Then Hartfield spoke up. His voice wasn't scary like the preacher's. It was kind and friendly, and it was plain as day, even if he hadn't been all duded up, the guy was a first class gentleman.

"It has been my privilege during the past year to share my home with little Rosie O'Leary," Hartfield said. "I have come to think of this child as my own precious daughter, so, naturally, I wish to adopt her, give her my name and all the accompanying advantages. A personal problem has caused some difficulty in this regard, but it is my hope that the difficulty will soon be resolved.

"Rosie is happy at High Point, except for the absence of someone who is dear to her." He stopped and paused a long time, like he was thinking. "Of course I am referring to the absence of her older sister, Iris. The child is terribly distressed over this separation. She walks in her sleep and cries out for her sister. I have consulted with Dr. Hargrave, who assures me the symptoms will disappear, if we are able to reunite the girls. The solution will be simple, since I am more than willing to adopt them both. I shall provide whatever is necessary to give them a good life and, thankfully, I can give them advantages others cannot."

Albert threw him a dirty look, but Hartfield kept on talking. "Unfortunately, a situation exists in my home that requires a change. I am referring to Rosie's governess, Miss Henderson. For some time I have intended to replace the woman, but have not found a suitable candidate. I am, however, determined to resolve the situation."

"Seems to me you think you can buy anything you want," Albert butted in. "I guess you don't know me. I ain't one to take a bribe, if that's what you're aiming for."

"Hold your horses, Albert" the preacher broke in. "You agreed to speak after Miss Bloom. Mind your manners and give the others a chance."

Miss Bloom spoke up in her schoolteacher voice. "As you know, I have become well acquainted with Iris. She is a bright girl, an exceptional student, intelligent and hard working, and has earned the respect of her classmates. I just can't say enough good things about her."

She turned to Albert and Minnie. "Iris has worked on your farm since August of last year, doing so at some sacrifice to herself and her own interests. Legally, she was not bound to do so."

"What do you mean, legally?" Albert fired off. "We signed them papers. They wouldn't let us have her if we didn't sign, so we sent her to your dad-blamed school, but I was against it all the way.

Book learning's the ruination of farm kids. That girl's head got stuffed with such high falutin' ideas, if it went on much longer, she wouldn't want to work no more. Minnie and me tried our level best to train her up, turn her into a first-rate hired girl. Shaw! We was even ready to let her go that one time."

Minnie piped up. "We aimed to get her trained up in the house-keeping trade. Of course, she'd have to learn the fine points from Agnes, or she wouldn't measure up. Trouble was, Agnes turned out no help at all."

Albert nodded fiercely. "That bossy old maid acted like a job might be coming through any day now, but it never did. Her fault. Not ours."

"Maybe she thought Iris would outshine her, take over the top job her own self," Minnie squeaked. "It's high time Mr. Hartfield hears firsthand what that high-toned parlor maid of his is really like."

Mr. Hartfield said nothing, just let them talk.

"We never aimed to hold the girl back," Albert said. "Fact is, we was told in no uncertain terms about the rule. No putting sisters together. Well, we thought it was a blockheaded rule, so we tried to set things straight by playing a harmless little trick."

"Yup! We did stretch the truth a mite," Minnie added, "but if Iris could put on like they wasn't sisters, she might could work at High Point and put in a good word for us while she was at it. Folks never know when they might need a helping hand. The other thing was, Albert and me figured when she'd reach the age where such things matter, she'd meet up with the quality, get a chance to come up in the world. And if she got a good provider, a fine house, and all that, well, we'd move right in with her. Won't be long before we'll be getting up in years, you know."

"Jackson made up that rule," the preacher said. "As you may recall, he took over for me when I was laid up. Perhaps he wasn't the best substitute, but he offered, and sick as I was, I didn't have time or inclination to look any further. Well Sir, he did what he did for your sake, Mr. Hartfield, since you asked for just one seven year old girl. Jackson told me, when he first set eyes on that little one, and checked out her age, he allowed as how she was just the ticket, but, of course, to get your order right, he had to find a way to get rid of the sister." He scratched his head and looked at the floor, like he was sorry he'd put it quite that way. "I just mean," he wiped his forehead with a handkerchief and then went on, "Jackson had to find a good home for both of those nice girls, and so he gave the older one to the Knudtsens. What else could he do?"

Mr. Hartfield closed his eyes, slapped one hand on his forehead, and breathed deeply, like he could barely believe what a mess had come from his simple request.

"Well, all that's water under the bridge now," the preacher said, kind of fast, so he could get over that rough spot as quick as possible, "and the thing is, I have enough influence to change the rule, if that's the way you want it."

"Wait just a doggone minute," Albert growled. "You better not forget about Minnie and me. Iris is our hired girl. We've got used to her, and Minnie ain't up to running a big house, garden, and chickens all by her own self."

Minnie started to pipe up, but Albert shushed her.

"Your wife just said you wanted the girls to be together, even played tricks to make it happen," said the preacher.

"That was then," Albert said. "I hadn't thought the thing through. How will Minnie get along without Iris? I tell you, that's what has me on the anxious seat. Iris worked like a plow horse—for nothing a-tall." Maybe Albert didn't know it, but he was stepping right into his own trap.

"What was the length of the contract?" Mr. Hartfield asked.

"You got me there," Albert said with a sigh, "but a deal's a deal. That girl's ours."

The arguing became more intense. Albert and Minnie became more and more stuck on their own demands, and the preacher kept shouting back until the whole thing seemed hopeless.

Albert finally got so mad he threw an old tin can across the room and told us all to clear out. He'd had enough. Iris was their hired girl, and that was that.

Now I got hot under the collar. I knew I was supposed to keep my trap shut, but I'd come up with a humdinger of an idea and couldn't hold it in. "Mr. Hartfield, Sir." I had to work up my nerve to speak to the great man. "You know everybody in these parts. Folks look up to you. I bet you could find a new hired girl for Albert and Minnie."

"Young man," growled the giant, "you are getting way above your station. You are not to say one word. Do you hear me? You have nothing to do with this."

"Let the boy speak," said Miss Bloom. "He makes more sense than you do."

The preacher hung his head, kind of like he'd been slapped.

So I pumped up my nerve and went on talking to Mr. Hartfield. "You said you needed a new governess. Well, why not hire Miss

Bloom? If she came to your house instead of going to the country school, you could get rid of that one you don't like."

Miss Bloom stared at the floor. Then, in a soft, rather sad voice, she murmured, "I have already signed next year's contract. Oh, how I would have loved—"

"The president of your school board has an outstanding loan at my bank." Hartfield interrupted. "I have no doubt we can come to terms."

"But the other children. I cannot leave them without a teacher."

"Miss Bloom," I said. "Leave it to Mr. Hartfield. With his connections, he'll find someone to take your place."

Minnie spoke up. "Well, I won't let go of my hired girl. So there!"

"Oh yes you will," I said all bold and brassy. She'd got my dander up now. "Mr. Hartfield can fix everything. He'll find you a hired girl, dirt cheap if that's all you care about. So there too!"

The preacher tried to shush me up, but he was too late. Minnie was still jabbering away until she stopped to think about what I'd said.

"Dirt cheap?"

"Oh, no you don't," Albert punched Minnie. "Nothing doing. We ain't letting that girl go. No sir!"

"You said you couldn't be bribed," I said. I'd met up with enough crooks and panhandlers to figure out where this was going.

Albert chewed on his lip.

"Albert and me, we've got to have a talk," Minnie said as she yanked his arm. He got up and followed her from the room.

They were gone a long time, but they finally came back, Albert looking kind of sheepish. "You got yourself a deal!" Minnie shouted, aiming her words at me. Albert didn't say a word.

Everybody started talking at once. I could have turned cartwheels. I was so keyed up and tickled over how things were turning out. I sat back in my chair, grinning, twiddling my thumbs, trying like the very deuce to make them think I was a fine, upstanding boy.

But once the fancy folks drove off, the preacher tipped his hat to Albert and Minnie and shoved me in his buggy. Off we rode to meet the sheriff and those "evil outlaws." Sure as birds fly and rabbits hop, a peck of trouble was waiting for the three of us, Butch, Joe, and me—three street rats, caught in a trap, with a spring so tight, we'd never be able to wiggle out of it.

CHAPTER 23

DEEP TROUBLE

PETE

Butch and Joe sat slumped in their chairs, heads down, like convicted crooks waiting for the hangman. When I parked myself next to Butch, he cupped a hand over his mouth and in a low voice said, "We ran like lightning to get shut of that dad-blamed fire, but then we got picked up on the road, only a mile or so past Olsons'. Dad gum it! I didn't mean to do it. If I wasn't such a clumsy cuss, the lantern wouldn't have tipped. It's true, I'm an ignorant clodhopper, but I ain't no firebug. It's a crying shame you and Joe got caught up in this mess. Looks like we're all three going to swing."

I stared at him and then at Joe, a couple of fool headed pranksters. How did it come to this? Seemed like Butch was telling the truth. Boy, did I ever hope so. An accident could be tolerated, but not arson. The giant stood in the doorway, filling it up, top to bottom and side to side. He came on in, followed by the sheriff.

"You didn't get very far did you boys?" Sheriff McCarthy said, his strong hands on his hips. "I'm feeling pretty doggoned let down. We gave you fellows a second chance, and you botched it."

"Seems the law's after us, no matter what we do," Joe said.

"This ain't the first time you boys let us down," the Sheriff put in. "Let me remind you what we discussed last time we had our little talk. When was it? A couple years ago?"

"We'll take the blame for that one," Joe said. "But this time it just happened. Cross my heart and hope to die. We ain't to blame."

"Seems we're just plain jinxed," Butch chimed in. His voice was all choked up, but he went on with it. "Something got into me. I don't know what. I got up, lit the lantern and then crawled back in bed. Joe and me was half-awake, knowing it was time to go a-chorin', but we was all tuckered out, fighting sleep, knowing we had to get up. I'd hauled in a bunch of hay a couple nights before, thinking it would make the floor a little nicer to walk on, not so dad-blamed filthy. Well, I accidentally knocked the lantern over, the dry straw on the floor caught fire, crackled, sparked, and blazed. The flame burst into one great huge sheet of fire that zipped across the floor and up the walls. The place went up in smoke before we could smother it.

"We got the animals out, then ran to the pump for water, but it was too late. The fire was out of control, so we made a run for it. We kept looking back, and pretty soon we watched Old Man Olson and Mabel come running out of the house, him in his nightshirt, his nightcap still on, her in an old rag of a gown, her hair an unholy mess. They both yelled blue murder, but we just kept on running. Pete wasn't there, and Joe had nothing to do with it, so if you got to blame somebody, you'd best take it out on me."

"Now I'm going to tell you something," Joe said. "Butch didn't tell the whole story. We was dead tired, knowing we had to put in one more backbreaking day with Olson lording it over us. Every day, seven days a week, we worked our tails off. That slave driver

240

had us scared spitless. I'll tell you straight-out. Pete here was long gone. The rooster hadn't crowed yet. Butch and me was trying to wake up, knowing we had chores to do before the boss came snooping. If he found us snoozing, well, you don't even want to know what he'd do to us."

The sheriff sighed. "After Olson offered to take you in, I recall telling you boys it was your last chance. You swore you'd turn over a new leaf. So now I got to say, I'm real put out with you kids. You dropped that chance like a chewed up chicken bone."

"Sheriff McCarthy," From the other side of the door we heard a loud voice.

"Yes, Deputy Smith."

"There's a man here named Goodman. Says he wants a word with you."

"Send him in," said Sheriff McCarthy.

Farmer Goodman entered, took off his farm cap, plopped it on the sheriff's desk, looked each of us boys in the eye, serious and slow, then turned to the sheriff. "The word is out. It's spreading like wildfire through the whole county that you got these boys under arrest," he said. "Now I know these boys, Sheriff. They were part of my threshing crew; two the summer of '79, three in '80. They're good, trustworthy, hard-working lads. In fact, I could hardly make them quit when the day's work was done." He was pushing it when he said that last part, but we sure did appreciate his words.

The Sheriff frowned. "We can just as well get on with the booking," he said. "Follow the usual procedure, Deputy."

"Wait just a doggoned minute," said Butch. "Here's something that might could make a difference." He signaled for Joe and me to line up with him, the three of us with our backs to the sheriff. "All right boys, pull up your shirts."

We yanked them up all at once.

"Jumping Jehoshaphat!" yelled the Sheriff. "What in the devil's been going on in that barn?"

"I heard a thing or two from my boys that made me wonder," said Goodman, "but what we see here is the work of a fiend. Speak up boys, and tell the unvarnished truth."

And so our story came tumbling out. Each of us spilled the beans as we saw it, the whole, miserable affair. We told about the bad food, no schooling, no pay, taunts, beatings, threats of getting chopped in pieces."

Butch told it so good that before he got done, the men pulled out their handkerchiefs and took a good blow.

It was graveyard quiet while the minute hand on the big wall clock crept around like a slug. "Mr. Goodman, Sir," I said, "You were good to us. I'm just wondering. Could you use three field hands at your place, not just for threshing, but for good and all?" He didn't say a word, and I was sorry I'd put him in a bad spot, but then he scratched his head and spoke up.

"It so happens, I tied up some cash in a new parcel of land, which means I could use some experienced workers. You boys have made your share of mistakes. You ain't Sunday school boys, but I've seen the kind of work you can do when you get treated right.

"I've got two of my own, but they're too young for man's work," he said to Sheriff McCarthy. "Listen here. I'll take these striplings off your hands, that is, if you can patch things up with Olson. You'll have your work cut out for you. He's a mean old polecat, as you can see for yourself by the stripes on their backs."

The sheriff said nothing for a long while. He leaned back in his chair like he was thinking. Finally, he spoke up. "I might just go out on a limb and let you have them, for now. But first we got to hear from Olson. It's his barn that went up in smoke."

He turned to the three of us. "If the man wants blood, I expect we got to give it to him. Now boys, I want you to understand, if he does go for Goodman's proposition, don't forget: mess up one more time, and you're done for. You'll be carted off to Fort Madison, and nobody on God's green Earth will get you out of it. Got that?"

The giant sat quietly and watched, not saying a word.

Joe stuck out his hand, and the sheriff shook it. Butch followed suit, and so did I. "Thanks, Sheriff," Joe said, "If you give us a break, you won't regret it. Not this time. Not ever."

"We'll show you what we're made of," Butch said, teary-eyed.

I couldn't think up anything new to say, so I just said, "Likewise," hoping it didn't sound fresh or smart-alecky. Of course, knowing Old Man Olson, we still didn't expect much. He'd want us drawn and quartered, but at least, now the sheriff and Goodman were on our side.

The sheriff turned to the man who'd let in Mr. Goodman and said, "Deputy, go on out to the Olson place and get the old fellow to come in with you. Let's get the thing settled once and for all."

The sheriff, Goodman, and the boys waited with me. The preacher said, since he didn't find any matches or fire making things on me, he guessed he must have been mistaken.

"Sorry, Son." He patted me on the shoulder, then stood over me for a long minute not saying a thing. Finally, he told us he was all tuckered out and was going on home. He tipped his hat, wished us God's blessings, and went out the door kind of quick-like. The sun was going down when the deputy returned with Old Man Olson in handcuffs.

"Well now, Deputy, I didn't say arrest him, did I?" said the sheriff. "I just thought we ought to talk."

"Well, Sir, it was the goldurndest thing yet. I went out to do just what you told me, Sheriff McCarthy, but Olson was there sitting on the porch steps. The woman sat in the rocking chair, and when I rode up, he yelled to get off his place, or he'd blow my brains out."

"Don't you never mind," the woman said. "He's in one of them spells he gets." So I took a step closer. Quicker than you could skin a rabbit, he raised his rifle and fired. Either he ain't a good shot, or I got lucky. The bullet whizzed right on past my left ear. I twirled out my pistol and aimed to shoot him in the arm. Just skimmed off a little skin, but scared him pretty good, so he dropped his gun, I cuffed him, and here's our prisoner, not much worse for wear. This joker's crazier than a hoot owl."

When Old Man Olson's medical needs had been met, and he was safely locked up in a cell, screaming his head off and rattling his cage, the men sat down to talk.

Butch, Joe, and me sat watching all these goings-on with jolly good cheer. I ain't proud of myself, but after what he'd done to us, it was hard not to feel pretty swell. The old devil had got his comeuppance.

"Good work, Deputy," the sheriff said, clamping a hand on his shoulder. "We'll keep the old coot locked up 'til we can get somebody from Mt. Pleasant to haul him to the loony bin." He sat down and scratched his head. "What about the woman? How'd all that go down with her?"

"There's the peculiar part. She seemed pleased as Punch to get rid of the old coot. That's how she acted anyhow. It was the golldurndest thing. I told her what we had in mind for the boys, and she was all for it. Said she wouldn't press charges if we'd build her a new barn.

"We'll do it!" I said. "We'll work and slave 'til Mabel's new barn's up."

"It's a deal!" said Farmer Goodman, slamming one fist into the other. "These boys will do their share, and I'll round up the neighbors. With all the manpower we can muster, we'll throw her up in no time flat. I'll furnish the lumber myself."

"I guess we earned our keep today," the sheriff said to the deputy. "Let's go on over to the pool hall and tip a few." Goodman loaded Joe, Butch, and me in his wagon, and off we rode to that modern, up-to-date farm of his, laughing and singing the Ioway song all the way.

CHAPTER 24
I GET THE NEWS
IRIS

One summer day, after I'd worked really hard weeding Minnie's garden, I got permission to visit Miss Bloom. I walked all the way to see her. When my beautiful teacher opened the door, she gave me an extra warm hug. With a twinkle in her eye, she asked me to sit down. "I have very good news for you, Iris!" she said. "My dear girl, you are going to live at High Point with Rosie, and you will not be a scullery maid. No indeed! Mr. Hartfield is delighted to welcome you as Rosie's sister and a cherished part of his family." My jaw must have dropped like a brick.

"Oh! If only Albert and Minnie will let me go." I knew how stubborn they could be.

"Your young friend, Pete, came up with some marvelous ideas," Miss Bloom said. "Going along with his suggestions, Mr. Hartfield worked things out. Albert and Minnie will give you no trouble at all." She patted my arm. Tears came quickly, but they were tears of so much joy, I couldn't hold them back.

We rode together in her buggy. When we got to the house, Miss Bloom helped me pack my things. Nothing felt real. I was sure it was all a dream. I sat down and tried to believe.

"I have accepted Mr. Hartfield's offer." Miss Bloom interrupted my thoughts. "I'm going to be your governess and Rosie's as well."

She waited for me to say something, but I couldn't even talk.

"I shall be with you at High Point every day but Sunday." Suddenly, the oppressive weight of sadness and loss, that had burdened me for so many months, flew away. I popped up and twirled like a whirling dervish, 'round and 'round the room, laughing and crying 'til I had to sit back down and catch my breath.

"Of course, once the new high school is built," Miss Bloom continued, "things will change."

I knew it was too good to be true. My breath stopped for a moment until she said, "I shall continue to teach Rosie, but you will be going on to bigger and better things. The best part is, you can still live with Rosie and Mr. Hartfield, even when you're in high school, since it's only a short walk from High Point."

I was beside myself with joy, but I still had questions. Miss Bloom knew my concerns and reassured me.

"While we watch the new building go up, we'll get you well prepared. I predict you will be the most advanced student at Hartfield High and all ready for college."

"College?" I couldn't believe my ears.

"By the way," she skimmed right past that question and explained the whole day's affairs, "Your friend has been exonerated. The fire happened accidentally, and Peter Freeman had absolutely nothing to do with it."

"How? What? Why?" I was so keyed up, I couldn't think straight.

"What will happen to Pete now? Where will he go?"

"He has a home with a fine family, the Goodmans. He will work for them all summer, and in the fall he will study at country school, working for the Goodmans when he has the time."

"I owe so much to Pete," I said. "Wouldn't it be wonderful if we could see each other once in a while. I've been thinking about all the things that have happened to the three of us."

"We'll make sure you see each other," Miss Bloom said.

I could barely wait to respond. "What do you think of this idea?" I asked. "Mr. Hartfield's driver could bring Pete to High Point every day after school and return him to the Goodmans when we're done. That would give the three of us time to work together on a project I just happen to have in mind."

"Well, Dear, if it is a worthy project, I don't see any reason why not."

If my idea worked out, not only would I be with Rosie, but we'd get to spend lots of time with Pete.

The sun poured in through Miss Bloom's spotless windows, and the sky was the purest blue without a cloud. Nature's beauty matched my spirit. I was sure I was in Heaven!

⸎

The next morning Miss Bloom sat with me in the porch swing. I was ready and waiting when Mr. Hartfield's splendid carriage came for me. I wasn't sad leaving Miss Bloom, because I knew she'd be with me every day at High Point; and now, finally, I'd be with Rosie.

When we reached High Point, my little sister came running, shouting my name. "Iris, Iris, Iris!" It seemed she couldn't stop saying my name. We hugged and laughed and cried and jumped and squealed and couldn't stop. "Oh, Iris, my Iris, I've been praying," she cried "It's so wonderful. The good Lord really does listen, even to kids." She started doing a little happy dance, and I joined her. We danced together, leaping and twirling until we fell down laughing. She'd grown at least an inch in the year since we'd seen each other, but she was still the same sweet, saucy Rosie. Mr. Hartfield stood watching us, hands in his pockets, smiling when he wasn't puffing on his pipe.

An angry lady came stomping out, blustering like the north wind. We almost bumped into her as we ran, hand in hand, through the front door. The woman clomped right on past us, then turned and said, "I'm not one bit sorry to be leaving." She stepped back, looked me straight in the eye, and growled, "The trouble began the minute that little minx arrived." She pointed at Rosie. "It's no wonder the missus went away."

As she stomped off, Rosie clapped her hands, like brushing off dirt. "Good riddance! You just met the world's meanest governess!" Mr. Hartfield tried to conceal a chuckle, and when the woman was out of earshot, he roared with laughter. Then he lifted dear little Rosie and gave her a great big hug. It did my heart good to know my little sister was loved like that.

The mansion was bigger and grander than anything I'd even dreamed about, all done up with fine artwork and furnishings. Best of all, I got to share a room with Rosie. And what a room!

Agnes was stiff but polite. "Oh, well," I said to Rosie. "Maybe she isn't so bad after all."

"Don't let the old grouch fool you," Rosie said with a giggle. "She knows where her bread gets buttered."

My clever little sister had an answer for everything. I'd learned that day at Albert and Minnie's that Agnes was no friend of mine or of Rosie's, but who was I to complain when everything else was turning out swell?

True to her word, Miss Bloom came every day, even all that summer, and our lessons were as interesting as they had been in country school, even better, since now we had her all to ourselves. In time I would go to high school, but I was in no hurry. I was thrilled to have this time with Rosie and Miss Bloom.

And now I could stop worrying about Pete, since his troubles with the law were over. Pete had a good home and would be going to country school come September. I knew how important it was to him. But Rosie could always think up something to worry about. "What if Miss Henderson takes Miss Bloom's old job? Pete would never get along with that cranky cluck. There'd be war!"

Papa told Rosie not to worry. By the way, just like Rosie, I began to call Mr. Hartfield Papa. I loved the sound of it. Papa took a real liking to Pete, and good old Pete kept coming up with more great ideas. He suggested that since Miss Henderson wasn't cut out for school teaching, she might like a job in Papa's button factory. When Papa suggested this to her, she grumbled at the very idea, until he explained that it was the kind of job where she could boss folks around. He didn't put it that way. He would never tell a lie, but he sure did know how to soften things up, and it worked. She took the job. I did pity the poor workers that had her for a boss.

One day when Pete was exploring Main Street, he met a young lady named Miss Sparks. Pete could get most anybody to open up and tell their life story, so he found out she'd just graduated from Normal College and was looking around for a job. Pete told Papa, who told the president of the school board, and she was hired on the spot, like magic. Papa really liked Pete, and when that young man presented a notion to him, if he approved, dear Papa could make it happen. So now it was settled that Pete could go to school, and from what I'd already seen of that boy, I knew he would do very well.

In the fall, every day after school, Clarence drove the barouche, with Pete in it, to High Point. We hadn't seen him in more than a year, so when he first showed up, the three of us, Rosie, Pete, and I, danced around in a ring and laughed and cried and laughed some more, almost the way it was the day I arrived. We were that glad to be together again. I won't say what project I had in mind. It's Pete's job to tell that, but I will brag just a little and admit, I did have a very good idea.

One Sunday night we all went to a picnic supper at the church. Pete came with us and sat at the table alongside Rosie and me. Papa and Miss Bloom sat on the other side, talking like they hadn't seen each other in a hundred years. When we finished eating, they sent us kids to play in the cemetery outside the church while they walked down the road, arm in arm.

Papa started coming into the schoolroom late afternoons, just as Pete was leaving. He'd whisper in Miss Bloom's ear, and we soon figured out he was asking her to stay for supper. It didn't seem to take much coaxing. After the meal they'd go off by themselves.

"We are discussing your education," he said without even a hint of a smile. Rosie and I winked at each other. Who did he think he was kidding?

Papa told us a circus would be coming to town. We were boiling over with excitement. Friday, just before the big day, Miss Bloom left early. She said Aunt Jennie needed help canning apple sauce, so she couldn't stay for supper. The next morning, though, she would come early, and we'd all go to the parade together. Papa hoped we wouldn't be disappointed, since the circus wouldn't have three rings, just one.

"Big shows don't come to small towns," he said. That didn't bother us, since we'd never seen any kind of circus. Agnes said a big tent had gone up, just outside of town, so Papa promised he'd walk with us to the country. But he wasn't quite ready yet. We'd have to wait for him.

So Rosie and I went to our room, trying to stop fidgeting. Waiting was hard. I sat on the bed trying to solve an arithmetic problem. Rosie played with her dolls. Our door was open, so we could hear a lively conversation going on downstairs, but we couldn't make out the words. I figured it was a peddler who'd made the mistake of knocking on the wrong door. Agnes could be snappy with folks who didn't know their place. Rosie tiptoed out to peek, then came racing back, her mouth wide-open.

"What?" The wild look in her eyes scared me.

"It's a ghost!" she whispered. "It's down there with Agnes. Come on!" she tugged at my skirt. "It looks like—well, you just wouldn't believe it." She burst out with it. "It's a ghost! It looks like Flora!"

"No!" I said it as quietly as I could. "Remember, we both saw what happened. Flora is dead, and I don't think she would turn into a ghost."

"Hurry up!" She grabbed my hand and yanked, so I followed her.

We crept part way down the stairs and peeked through the balusters. I saw for myself, it was no ghost. It really was Flora.

I screamed and took off running down the stairs. Rosie came yelling and almost tumbling after me. We tackled our Ma, hugged and kissed her, and cried and laughed until tears were soaking up our hankies.

Of course, Flora was dressed in her finest city clothes. Agnes didn't take her eyes off her. We were so thrilled that our Ma wasn't dead that we forgot everything else, even the circus. Finally, as she always did, Flora took charge.

"No more tears," she said. "I'm here. I'm alive, and so are you. Now, if you tell me your adventures, I'll tell you mine." We followed Agnes into the parlor. It took a while to calm Rosie down, but when she finally stopped jumping all over the place, she curled up on the velvet settee and nuzzled against Flora's shoulder.

We told all about the year we'd spent, absolutely certain our Ma was dead, especially how we sisters had been torn apart and longed to find each other. Flora listened, dry-eyed. She hadn't changed. Plucky as ever!

When we finished, Flora told her story. "Archie, my former gentleman friend, who, if truth be told, was no gentleman, broke down the door, and before I could defend myself, he grabbed me 'round the neck and squeezed 'til I couldn't catch my breath. Everything went black. I passed out.

"The brute must have left, thinking he'd done me in, but the old hag from the room down below heard the commotion. She waited before coming upstairs, making sure the coast was clear, so

It was no ghost. It really was Flora.

he wouldn't do her in like he'd done me. By the time she found me, you girls must have run off.

"I suppose I looked a fright, because once she laid eyes on me, lying there white as a corpse and conked out, the woman screamed and hollered bloody murder 'til everybody in the building came running. That's what they told me. How would I know? I was out cold. So the room filled up with riffraff from upstairs and down. Somebody ran outside to find a cop, and I don't know what happened then.

"I woke up in the hospital, feeling like I'd been turned inside out. After a while a cop came in, so I told him the last I knew, you girls were hiding under the bed. I wasn't thinking straight, not knowing how long I'd been out. I thought you'd still be there. You always waited 'til I told you to come out. I promised him a nice little present, once I got back on my feet, if he'd go get you and take you to Mrs. Fletcher. I even wrote her address on a scrap of paper so he could find her with no trouble at all. She's always glad to take care of you, and she ought to be. I pay her plenty. He said he'd do it right off. That put my mind at ease, so I didn't think any more of it."

Rosie and I stared at each other in that way folks do when they can't believe what they've heard, and then we both glared at Flora.

"Don't look at me like that," she said. "Nobody bothered to tell me you'd disappeared. I could always count on Mrs. Fletcher. Besides, I still had a black eye and too many bruises to be seen in public. Honest, I was all set to come for you, but before they'd let me out of the hospital, I came down with pneumonia and just about croaked. Well, I fought back the grim reaper twice; so, after a few more weeks in that pest house, I finally flew the coop.

"I told the director what happened, and he put me right back on stage. I'm prettier than my understudy, so he'd sure missed me." She smiled like she'd won first prize.

"Once I got my part back, I hurried across town and went straight to Mrs. Fletcher, busted right in without knocking, couldn't wait to see my little darlings. I called out your names and when you didn't come, I yelled top of my lungs. The woman stared at me like I was out of my head, said she didn't have the least notion where you were or what happened to you. Well, I can tell you, I wouldn't believe the woman. I shook her by the shoulders and screamed. I tell you, I almost lost my mind.

"I pestered the cops too. A lot of good that did. Couldn't even find the officer I'd been counting on. He never did get his present. Well, the whole mess took forever, just to get somebody to listen, and when they did, I'd get that look like I must be nuts. So then I knew you'd been kidnapped. Or maybe Archie, that rat, that criminal, that beast, got his filthy hands on you. I looked high and low and tried to find somebody, anybody, to listen, but the best I'd get was a blank stare.

"So finally, many months later, somebody said, 'Try the *Children's Aid Society*,' and there I met up with the meanest female in all New York City, and that's going some."

"Miss Harkin!" Rosie and I shouted at once. We couldn't help laughing.

"Dreadful woman. Well, she'd hardly take the time to listen, but finally, after I'd made a scene that would have done me proud on stage, she said you'd been there a long while back but were gone again. She refused to say where you were, no matter how I yelled, pounded my fists, and screamed blue murder.

"So then I made up to the janitor. As you know, I do have a way with men, and although he was a low sort of fellow, I had little choice. He wanted in the worst way to make up to me. You know how it goes. So I made him take a peek at the record books when the higher-ups weren't looking. The poor fool found papers on both of you. Said the *Children's Aid Society* was shipping orphans by the trainload, and they'd sent you girls to a place called Iowa.

"'What's the town?' I screamed. The dumbell had barely peeked at the record books and got half the information. I was mad enough to spit. I could have torn the place apart, but instead, I kept on playing up to the poor sap. I made him look up the records one more time.

"He was so scared of Miss Harkin, he kept saying, 'No, no, no, she'll eat me alive!'

"But I lifted my skirt, just enough to expose one of my gorgeous ankles. Well, he just about fainted, and it didn't take but a whipstitch before he thumbed through some more papers and whispered, 'Iris and Rose O'Leary—Hartfield, Iowa.'"

We hugged each other and giggled. Flora hadn't changed one bit.

"There's more," she said. "My first night back on the job, that funny looking playboy, the one I met at the Astors' party, came to see the play. My part was small, but that didn't matter. I was all dolled up in a spiffy outfit and, of course, the audience loved me. After the show, he came backstage to look me up. One thing led to another, and as you can see, I'm back in business."

She held out her soft, pretty hand with those bright, red nails, and a huge, sparkling diamond ring. "This one's real!" Her voice rose. "Georgie's filthy rich, and just nuts about me." She stopped long enough to let it all sink in. "He has a fabulous apartment on Fifth Avenue. I told him that before I'd set up housekeeping with him, I was coming to Iowa to bring back my two darling daughters.

"First thing he wanted to know was how old you are. He didn't say much about Rosie, but he did say he guessed she could come along. She'll grow up eventually. Well, as soon as I told him Iris must be fifteen by now, he lit up, saying one of his pals was looking for a pretty girl about that age. All his friends are swells. It's a marvelous opportunity for you, Iris. With your hair done up, powder, paint, and a new grown-up wardrobe, you won't know yourself when you look in the mirror. Glamour comes in a jar, you know." She giggled.

"If his friend is anything like Georgie, you'll be wearing a ring like mine and living the high life. That's why I taught you to read and cipher. I had to make sure you'd fit in. I was aiming for the top, and that's what I've got." She tweaked my cheek. "Always thinking of my girls, you know."

After that she didn't look at me anymore or give me time to say what I thought about it. She just kept on blabbering. "So that brings us to the present." She snapped her fingers. "Go pack your bags, and I'll take you with me. We'll stay at the rooming house and leave on the morning train." Agnes popped from her chair and ran from the room.

"Where's that woman going?" Flora blustered.

"To get Papa," Rosie said.

"Papa?" Flora looked at Rosie like she'd just turned bank robber. She didn't have to wonder long. Papa came running, pale, and breathless, Agnes trailing behind.

"What is going on here?" He pointed an accusing finger at Flora. "Who, Madam, are you?"

Flora rose and with quiet dignity said, "I happen to be these children's mother. That's who."

He stared at Rosie, then at me.

"She's Flora," Rosie said, looking up with her round, innocent eyes. "She used to be dead, but she woke up."

He stared at Rosie with horror, then at me, like we'd played a dirty trick on him. "So, the joke's on me," he said. "I would not believe Venetia. I was certain she was being cruel and suspicious. She called me a fool—said I couldn't smell a swindle that was right in front of my nose." He turned to Flora. "How much do you want?"

"I simply want my children," she said, lifting her chin indignantly. "I'm a decent woman, I am, and a very good mother if I do say so myself."

Agnes glanced nervously from Flora to Papa. It seemed she was scared to speak up, but she finally did. "This ain't what you think, Sir." She looked at Flora. "Please, Ma'am, tell Mr. Hartfield your story, the way you told us. He's a fine man, a good, kind gentleman. He'll listen, and he'll be fair." Out of the corner of one eye I watched her aim a sly little wink at Flora, not visible to Papa, but a signal Flora would understand.

So Papa sat down. Flora told her story all over again, of course, omitting her plans for me, and as her long story got longer, going on and on and on, his face softened up a little bit. She stretched her story out considerably, including all kinds of pitiful details she'd made up, like the accidental death of her dear, departed husband, and omitting the true part about her boy-friend and his pal. Rosie and I exchanged looks. Flora's really good at make-believe. At the end of her story, Papa wiped away a tear. Once he'd composed himself, his handsome smile assured all of us that he wasn't mad anymore.

"Of course we're pleased that you came back to life," he said, looking seriously at Flora. "Your story is almost too strange to be believed, but I do believe you. So now the girls must make a choice. It is really too much to ask of children." He turned solemn eyes on Rosie and then on me. "My dear children, this decision will have a profound effect upon the rest of your lives. Consider carefully.

"I shall understand if you go with your mother. There is a bond between mother and child that I cannot duplicate. However, we three have come to know and love one another. If you wish to stay with me, my offer stands, with Flora's permission, of course.

"I have not yet confided the latest news to you. Venetia will not be coming back. Today we are officially divorced. I want the three of us to be a family. I had planned very soon to arrange legal papers. I sincerely hoped to adopt both of you. If you choose that path, Miss Bloom will continue as your governess, and we will always welcome your mother and your friends into our home, especially Peter Freeman."

Flora sat with folded hands. She said nothing, but the little smile on her face showed she knew we would choose her. From our earliest days, she'd made us obey like trained puppies.

I stood up and moved towards the door, pulling Rosie along. "Let's talk this over," I said.

Papa nodded. I'd never seen him look so sad.

As we left the room, I heard Flora whisper, loud enough so we could hear, "They're good girls. They always do the right thing."

Upstairs, all by ourselves, I put it to Rosie. "I will not go with her. I just won't! But you can, if you want to. Her plans would split us up anyway and make me turn out just like her. I refuse to have any part of that, but she is our mother. So, my sweet sister, what will you choose? Iowa? New York? Papa? Flora?"

Rosie stared at the floor, then at me. She couldn't seem to get the words out.

"Say what you want, Dearie," I said. "Don't worry about my feelings."

"Well," she stood twisting one foot and her hanky at the same time. "The truth is, I'm glad Flora came down from her cloud. I didn't like her watching us morning, noon, and night. It was creepy."

I had a hard time waiting for her answer, but then she whispered, "Don't you know, I would never leave you. I'm staying right here—with you and Papa!"

I threw my arms around her and squeezed ever so tight. Tears flowed from both of us.

"Did I choose right?"

"You goose!" I laughed as I dried my eyes. "I've never been so happy in my whole life! Rosie, dear, you must understand, I had to give you the choice. It's serious business to take a child from her mother, but if you had chosen that path, I would eventually have come to rescue you anyway."

"Can we still to go to the circus?"

We laughed and hugged and laughed some more, but deep inside, we were really scared. How would Flora take the news? We knew she'd kick up an awful row.

We walked slowly into the parlor.

"We've made up our minds," I said.

Flora's face lit up. Papa looked sad.

"We're staying. Both of us. Right here!" Rosie announced this while looking at the ceiling to avoid Flora's eyes.

Flora slumped in her chair. Maybe she wanted us to think she was dead. Again. "Don't do that!" Rosie cried, "You're not dead. We're glad of that! But now you can just go back to your new gentleman friend, 'cause we don't want him or any of his pals either. We're staying with Papa."

"I have my rights," she screamed. "I can make you go with me."

I stared at Flora with angry eyes. "I refuse to turn out like you, and I won't! Papa will give us a decent life. We've come too far to let you spoil everything."

Papa looked at the floor, folded and unfolded his hands and didn't say anything. I could tell that Flora's gentlemen friends and that part of the story were news to him, terrible and disgusting news, but kind man that he was, he felt sorry for Flora.

She stood up and stomped her foot like she might kick a hole in his beautiful oak floorboards. "You have the money," she said, sneering at Papa. "You think you can buy anything you want, but the law is on my side."

"Are you threatening me?"

"You bet your boots I am."

"You intend to take this to court?"

"Just watch me."

"The girls have made their choice. Surely you wouldn't drag them off against their will."

"I don't care! I don't care! They belong with me. I'm their mother." She kept stomping first one foot and then the other.

"Girls," he addressed Rosie and me. "This is not the sort of discussion you should hear. Please, go to your room. I will come for you when this matter has been settled."

I stared at Rosie, and she stared at me. Then I grabbed her hand and we raced upstairs, but we didn't go to our room. Instead, we crouched at the top of the stairs, where we could not be seen, but could hear what was said below.

"Now, Madam, my eyes are opened. I know the kind of life you live, and I think I know what you want. I am prepared to meet your terms. Will you accompany me to my attorney's office? With his assistance, we will draw up legal papers whereby you give up all rights to the children. Then I will legally adopt them."

"What's in it for me?" said Flora.

"Name your price."

She did. It was an awful lot of money, but Papa agreed.

"Oh, there is just one more little thing," Flora said. "Since I can't have the girls, I'm taking Agnes with me. I need a personal maid, and she tells me she'd love to see the big city. What country girl wouldn't?"

Rosie and I winked at each other. "She'll get what she wants, and he'll make the sacrifice," I said.

When Papa and Flora returned from the lawyer's office, both were smiling. Flora stayed the night in one of the finest guest rooms at High Point.

The next morning Miss Bloom arrived early, thinking we'd all go to the parade. But we did not. Instead, Miss Bloom stayed behind with Papa, and Clifford took Rosie and me, along with Flora and Agnes, to the depot. Agnes was all smiles as she lugged two of Flora's heavy bags. A porter, short of breath, followed behind with the rest, more than he could comfortably carry. Agnes tried her best to imitate her new employer. Ever since Flora arrived, Agnes had been watching and trying to mimic her every move.

Rosie and I hid smirks behind our hankies. Flora hugged me first and then Rosie. Parting like that should have made me sad, but I could not pretend. I shuddered, thinking of the plans she'd made. If I'd have gone along with her, Rosie would have met the same fate when she got older. We knew Flora's Irish pluck would see her through, whatever happened, just as it always had. We waved goodbye as the noon train chugged out of sight.

That evening Miss Bloom stayed for supper. Before our lessons the next morning, she told us that she and Papa had spent the evening reading poems to each other. I winked at Rosie, and she winked back.

CHAPTER 25

OUR FUTURE AT HIGH POINT
ROSIE

A few days after Flora left, Papa and Miss Bloom sat down with Iris and me and told us they were getting married. The best news ever! Iris and I squeezed each other and could hardly believe our dear Miss Bloom would soon be our new Mama. She wouldn't put on airs and say we were her sisters. She said she'd be proud to tell folks we were her daughters.

Papa hired a new maid to take Agnes' place. Her name is Hattie, and thank goodness, she isn't one bit like Agnes. Hattie is young and pretty and talks nice and polite to us, like we aren't street rats that don't even deserve to be here.

I told Hattie that Agnes called us little troublemakers. She smiled and said we were more like little angels. I wondered what Agnes would say to that. Papa reads us stories at night before we go to bed. Iris and I are both really good readers, but that time with Papa is our favorite part of the day.

Aunt Jenny is sewing a fancy dress for Miss Bloom and matching ones for Iris and me. The ceremony will be at High Point.

Pastor Fineman will do his part. The guests will be Aunt Jenny; Miss Sparks; Clarence; Homer; Cook; Hattie, the new maid; and last, but not least, Pete. Our dresses will be white cambric with green sashes. Homer promised to make up a splendid bouquet of white lillies for Miss Bloom. She doesn't expect it, but Iris and I have already decided we'll call her Mama. Homer said he will also pick some pretty white flowers for Iris and me, and Iris will weave them into garlands for our hair. I think we will look like fairy princesses.

⁂

After the wedding, Cook will set the dining room table with company dishes, company silver, and big bowls of flowers. Iris and I get to choose the menu. We've decided we will all eat roast beef, mashed potatoes with that yummy brown gravy cook makes, fresh green beans and sweet corn from the garden. We think that will make a perfect Iowa dinner. After that, we will all eat a delicious piece of wedding cake, baked by Cook, of course, and then everybody will live happily ever after.

⁂

Oh, one more thing. I will stand in front of the mirror in Iris' and my bedroom and twirl around and around in my fairy princess dress and think magic thoughts, because everything that happened and keeps on happening is magic. It is just wonderful! And wonder of wonders, I have my Iris back. That is the best of all!

CHAPTER 26

DOWNSIDE UP

PETE

So now you know. The project Iris had in mind was for us three kids to write a book. I knew she'd do her part. She's the smartest person I know, and with Iris setting her words down on paper, Rosie'd do okay too, but I never thought I had the grit to knuckle down and do my bit. I can thank Iris and Miss Bloom, who will soon be Mrs. Hartfield, for making me stick to business. Iris said, since I was first one in, it was fitting for me to throw in the final touch, so here's the wind-up.

After Iris came up with the idea, Miss Bloom said we had a good story to tell, and she'd help us tell it. That lady straightened out most of my wrong spelling and bad grammar, but she left some in, so readers would know I was on the level, not faking it. Once I'd set down those magic words, "The End," I figured I'd shake her hand, and then Iris and Rosie's too. I'd follow it up with a fancy bow, the way Mr. Hartfield always did. That man's, a real gentleman if there ever was one.

Once I was in the clear with the law and boarding with the Goodmans, I spent weekdays at country school alongside Dick and Harvey. In school Butch, Joe, and me got tossed in with the little kids, but we didn't care. We had plenty of catching up to do.

Butch and Joe put on like they weren't keen on book learning, but that's just what they wanted folks to think. We were all wowed by the new teacher, Miss Sparks. She was no Miss Bloom, but still, we called her a crackerjack.

Butch and Joe haven't started any fires lately. Like me, they're breathing easy now that Old Man Olson is under lock and key. Then too, they aim to do right by the Goodmans, so they pretty much stay out of trouble. The first day of school I had to set Maynard Petersen straight with a few well-placed punches, but that settled it, and ever since, he's tried to be my buddy. Iris laughed real hard when I told about that.

New York's a metropolis, but before Flora left, I filled her in on Pa's name, some clues on what he looks like, and a few samples of his nutty doings, just in case she ever runs into him. She said she'd keep an eye out, and when she finds him she'll let him know I'm alive and kicking.

Every day, after school lets out, Clarence stands like a doorman, waiting by the schoolhouse while us kids pile out. He drives me up to High Point in that classy George IV Phaeton. He shows me all the fine features of Mr. Hartfield's barouche. Ain't another one like it west of the Mississippi.

I would like to horse around a bit with the girls. What red-blooded fellow wouldn't? But we haven't had much time for it. Had our hands full putting this book together. Miss Bloom helped us set down on paper what we could recollect about New York, the train ride, and the year we spent in Hartfield. It's been a year that turned our lives upside down and then downside up.

I still hang around with Butch and Joe, since we live together with the Goodmans, a fine, top-notch family. We'll be working hard in the summers, but we're treated decent. Goodman pays right good wages, even to fool kids like us. The food is lip smackin' good, as opposed to Mabel's slops. After school we do a few chores, but Mr. Goodman puts schoolwork first. Who'd ever think we'd get a boss like that?

Old Man Olson's still stuck in the loony bin. Whenever his name comes up, folks shake their heads and mutter, "Hopeless case."

Old Mabel has herself a brand new barn. Us boys finally got the hang of hammering nails in straight, and so we helped Mr. Goodman and the neighbors put it up. That crazy Mabel sure has changed her tune. She runs the place better than the old coot ever did. She got herself a hired man with a wife and a couple kids. That was Hartfield's doing. He put up the money, and the hired man built a new house for his family, not far from old Mabel's.

Mr. Hartfield lets Albert and Minnie come to High Point once in a while so they can take a gander at Iris. They put on an act, like they miss her just awful, but Mr. Hartfield found them another hired girl and gave them a big stack of dollar bills. After that they didn't miss her quite so much. Besides the dough, they wanted a taste of high society. A tall order for those two.

Miss Bloom and Miss Sparks are trying to sand down my rough edges. A new high school is going up just a block from High Point. They say if I study hard, I'll get to go there. Every time I walk by and hear those hammers pound, my heart beats so hard and fast I figure folks will think a brass band has come to town. I'll have to work like the dickens to catch up with Iris in the brains department. But if all goes well, I figure there might come a day when the two of us will be sitting in there side by side.

I sometimes lie down under a tree and dream about what it will be like when we're all grown up. High school seems almost beyond my reach, but still I've started figuring what we'll do after we graduate. I've made up my mind to study hard, save up a pile of dough, and someday go to college with Iris. She thinks that's a swell idea. Hartfield will pay her way, and I don't mind working my tail off for Mr. Goodman. He pays us good wages. Butch and Joe fritter theirs away on stupid things, but I keep a notebook and write down every penny I spend. All I ever buy is a gift for the girls now and then. The rest goes in the bank.

Hartfield's my model. I hope to turn out just like him. I can't expect to get rich, at least not like him, but I aim to be a real gentleman. Iris likes the idea. And I figure when we get done with college, we'll see to it that Rosie gets her chance. I can't write down here how I feel about Iris, but I guess it ain't all that hard to figure out. Just thinking about her kept me going when it seemed like the whole world was sliding down a rathole.

If Iris and her little sister ever have troubles, even little ones, I'll rescue them. I still have to prove I ain't your run-of-the-mill street rat. When I used to play mumbletypeg, I could hit a bull's eye most every time, so I figure as long as there's folks around like Miss Bloom, Miss Sparks, Hartfield, Goodman, and most of all, Iris—and her little sister Rosie, I'll aim steady and hit the mark. I've made a pledge to Iris. I won't say what it is, but you can bet your boots, I won't ever let that fine girl down. I figure a fellow's got to straighten up, work hard, and do right. And that about sums it up.

The End

Afterword: The Orphan Train

The photograph of three ragged boys, asleep beside a trash pile, on a New York City street, surprised and disturbed me. It accompanied "The Orphan Train Comes to Clarion," an article by Verlene McOllough, featured in the *Palimpsest*, Fall, 1988, a publication of the State Historical Society of Iowa. That photograph and the companion article stirred my imagination and spurred me on to further research, resulting in this novel.

Much of the orphan train movement is attributed to Charles Loring Brace, who studied at Union Theological Seminary in New York City, graduating in 1849. He became a minister to poor people on Blackwell's Island (now called Roosevelt Island) and then to the poor at Five Points Mission, located in New York City's most wretched slum. Here he observed children on their own, sleeping in dirty streets and alleys. They sold flowers and newspapers, sang popular songs for pennies, shined shoes, begged, picked pockets, and found other schemes to barely survive.

Shocked at these conditions, Rev. Brace founded The Children's Aid Society, organized training programs, lodging houses, job finding services, and more. Still unsatisfied, certain that the city was an unwholesome place for homeless children, he made provisions to send them by train out of the city to small towns and farms, mostly west of New York where he thought they would have a better chance for a decent life. From 1854 to 1929 more than forty-five states received these children. Some even went to Canada and Mexico. For many it was a wonderful opportunity, but some were exploited, mistreated, as well as physically and mentally abused. This was not what the Reverend Brace intended.

Not all of the children were orphans. Each child had a unique story. Some simply had parents who were too poor to care for them. At least two hundred thousand children, perhaps more, were "placed out." Dealing with vast distances and such large numbers, it was difficult to supervise the movement's operations, and sometimes mistakes were made.

For The Love of Pete presents the stories of three such children, who lived only in my imagination but had much in common with Reverend Brace's "orphans." The town of Hartfield, Iowa, and all of the characters in the book are fictional but based upon real stories and places. Some of the actual orphan train children suffered through experiences similar to those of Pete, Iris, and Rosie. All were hoping for homes with kind foster parents who would provide a decent, loving environment. Like today's children, they simply needed a chance to develop their abilities and talents in order to grow up to live happy and useful lives.

Ethel Kjaer Barker, daughter of a Danish Lutheran pastor, spent a happy childhood in Dwight, Illinois; rural Iowa (between Cedar Falls and Dike); Salinas, California; and Des Moines, Iowa. Her degrees are AA from Grand View College, Des Moines; BA and MAT from The University of Iowa. She taught remedial reading to Junior High students and in so doing recognized the need for books that educate while holding students' interest. At an early age, while the two little girls were happily playing school, her sister taught her to read. Ever since, she has found great delight in books. She currently lives with her husband, a retired high school principal, just outside of Iowa City, Iowa. *For The Love of Pete: An Orphan Train Story* is her first book.

The Ice Cube Press began publishing in 1993 to focus on how to live with the natural world and to better understand how people can best live together in the communities they share and inhabit. Using the literary arts to explore life and experiences in the heartland of the United States we have been recognized by a number of well-known writers including: Gary Snyder, Gene Logsdon, Wes Jackson, Patricia Hampl, Greg Brown, Jim Harrison, Annie Dillard, Ken Burns, Kathleen Norris, Janisse Ray, Alison Deming, Richard Rhodes, Michael Pollan, and Barry Lopez. We've published a number of well-known authors including: Mary Swander, Jim Heynen, Mary Pipher, Bill Holm, Connie Mutel, John T. Price, Carol Bly, Marvin Bell, Debra Marquart, Ted Kooser, Stephanie Mills, Bill McKibben, and Paul Gruchow. We have won several publishing awards over the last nineteen years. Check out our books at our web site, join our facebook group, visit booksellers, museum shops, or any place you can find good books and discover why we continue striving to "hear the other side."

Ice Cube Press, LLC (est. 1993)
205 N. Front Street
North Liberty, Iowa 52317-9302
steve@icecubepress.com
www.icecubepress.com

Riding the rails with two
wonderful passengers
Fenna Marie & Laura Lee